Embracing your [illegible]

Karen,

[illegible]

Lori Hines

The Ancient Ones

Lori Hines

International Standard Book Number
ISBN-13: 978-1519415554
ISBN-10: 1519415559

Printed in the United States of America.

CHAPTER ONE

An abrupt arctic chill permeated the surroundings of the long abandoned assay office at Vulture Mine in Wickenburg, Arizona. Lorelei shivered as she glanced at her temperature probe. It had dropped to twenty-five degrees inside the dilapidated building—a major decrease from the usual forty-five degree night air. But the darkness was the worst. A total, all encompassing mass that emitted shadows from everywhere, yet nowhere. Fear froze her feet to the dusty, rotting wood.

She hadn't wanted it and didn't ask for it. Yet Lorelei Lanier, investigator with the Arizona-Irish Paranormal Research Society, had a way with ghosts. A gift bestowed her the same day her mother died—June 13, 2011—almost a year and a half ago. At 2:13 a.m., the minute after her death, Aimee Lanier had appeared at Lorelei's bedside. Her long, silky brown hair, porcelain skin and welcoming smile made Lorelei ache inside.

"It's all over for me. I love you Lorelei. You've always been very special—more than you realize. I'm leaving you with something important. There will be those that need your help. Don't deny them. And don't deny love." Sitting down on the bed, she gently held Lorelei's hand, kissing her on the cheek. Then her mother morphed into a beautiful pale yellow mist, which rose into the atmosphere, leaving Lorelei alone and confused.

A few days later, she realized what her mom referred to. Out on an early morning hike, Lorelei noticed an elderly man walking with a beagle. As he passed by, he smiled and said hello. She returned the greeting, but something made her turn around and look back. The little dog let out a yip. Then they both suddenly faded into nothing but grayish-white vapor. As they vanished into the warm summer air, she heard the word "lost" as a whisper on the wind.

Running back to the parking lot, Lorelei saw him again, standing ten feet away from her car—the black, white and tan dog in a sitting position beside him. But they had appeared so quickly in front of her she couldn't stop . . . and she ran right through the man. Loneliness, fear and suffering overcame her: the man's incessant thirst in the summer heat without water, the growing queasiness and gnawing hunger, then the frigid nights and his last moments as he lay dying along a narrow trail. She had cried for hours after the experience. It hit her—her mother had somehow passed down her own psychic/medium skills to Lorelei. Being with her mother had never been boring. Lorelei always heard about the spirits that pursued Aimee in an effort to relay messages to loved ones. Or the ghosts that were simply confused and needed help passing over.

Now Lorelei would be looked upon as a nutcase. Someone who saw things that weren't there.

An explosive, indistinguishable yell brought Lorelei out of her reverie. A man's excruciating scream of torture caused her to whip around. The unseen spirit waited—agony and suffering its companion. The sound lasted a few seconds and came from the tree behind the assay office; an old, massive ironwood with a thick trunk and deadwood branches hanging as lifeless as the corpses that once decorated its highest limb.

Though she couldn't see this particular entity, Lorelei felt its terror, as an invisible tight rope wrapped around her neck. She tried to scream for help but couldn't. Her hands threaded around her throat, she struggled to breathe. Looking up, she saw the shadow of a dark-haired man kicking helplessly. His eyes bulged as he struggled in terror, clawing helplessly against the rope around his neck. A few seconds later the apparition vanished from the branches of the tree, releasing her from the grip of the residual haunting.

Gasping for air, shaken and vulnerable, Lorelei heard a faint thump in the corner of the dust-filled room. After what she had just experienced, Lorelei thought she would run but didn't. Thought she might pee her pants, but didn't. Instead, she stood her ground and continued to scan the environment for movement.

Fumbling for her flashlight, she struggled to pull it out of her jacket pocket. Barely managing to switch it on with her shaky right hand, she peered around cautiously.

A dark shape, low to the ground, came stealthily toward her. Gasping, she swerved her light to see what it was.

Damn cat. She sighed in relief, realizing one of three black strays she had seen roaming the property had followed her into the building. It purred and rubbed against her leg. "You scared the crap out of me." She leaned down to scratch its back. The other two cats came out of hiding, all vying for her attention.

An unexpected breeze slipped by and she gasped. Tightening her grip on the flashlight, she held the audio recorder toward the movement. She quickly spun to her left and aimed the beam of light at a floor-to-ceiling chain link fence protecting shelves of dust-coated bottles of chemicals, a brick furnace, and rusty tin cans.

"I know you're here." Her voice trembled as she communicated to the unseen spirits. Frost escaped from her lips like a long trapped ghost. "Were you one of the miners?" She gave the apparition a few seconds to respond, not knowing if she would hear the voice herself, or if he would communicate through the recorder. "Or were you a worker in the assay office?"

How brave would all those investigators on the paranormal reality shows be without the camera crews, she wondered, trying her hardest not to dash out of the creepy structure.

Lorelei whirled toward the sound of footsteps coming down the narrow stairwell. She let out a relieved breath. It was only Shannon Flynn, FBI agent and paranormal investigator.

"How's it going down here?" Shannon asked.

Lorelei's light revealed the six foot tall woman with dark, wavy red hair, wearing a dark green ski jacket, jeans and hiking boots.

"Did you hear that yell a minute ago?" Lorelei asked.

"No, I didn't hear anything from upstairs. It's obviously your gift. There's a spirit trying to communicate with you."

"For a few seconds, I thought I was choking to death. I saw someone hanging from there." Lorelei pointed to the window across the room where the tree still stood proudly behind the building. "His scream sounded so real," she muttered.

"Well of course." Shannon approached Lorelei and inspected her neck. "There's no sign of rope burn. Are you okay now?"

"Yes, I'm fine," she said, rubbing her neck. "It only lasted a few seconds . . . but that poor man. I saw him struggling for his life."

"It's going to seem real to you if you're the one experiencing it. You've been through this before, though you mentioned you've been in denial until recently."

"That medium experience took all three voyances. I saw him hanging to death, which is the clairvoyance, I could hear him yelling which is the clairaudience, and the clairsentience came through with his emotions. It's so damn frustrating, seeing all this pain and suffering in peoples lives. And I never know if others are hearing or feeling what I am."

Shannon looked down at the three felines still circling Lorelei. Lorelei couldn't take a step without tripping over them.

Mom, why did you do this to me? She spotlighted the well-worn wooden planks, rusted antique furniture and tattered gray uniforms that still hung on hooks. *It's bad enough I had to deal with your sudden death, but to pass this ability on to me at the same time?* "Damn it, Mom," she said aloud, without realizing it. Another quick, cool breeze passed by—this one much closer.

"Lore, maybe there's a reason she handed this ability on to you. Your mother knew you were interested in the paranormal. That makes you much more accepting of being a medium than most, therefore more open to helping those who need answers or closure. Every talented medium I've ever met have had to verify whether a spirit is communicating only with them, or with others as well."

Lorelei sighed and glanced at the tiny red light on her recorder. "Maybe I caught something on audio—an electronic voice phenomena that will prove what I've been experiencing."

Lorelei stood silently. Then she pulled out her Mel-Meter, a device monitoring electromagnetic frequency and temperature. "The EMF, or energy reading, indicates it's thirty-five degrees in here—ten degrees cooler than outside. It was down to twenty-five while you were upstairs."

"Brrrr." Shannon drew her jacket in tighter. "That is cold. Let's just talk. Maybe we'll get some responses to backup your readings."

They both watched for signs of movement, continuing their conversation in low tones in order to hear anything.

"It's so hard to believe this picturesque, serene desert was a bustling city with miners and their families," Shannon said. "There were five thousand inhabitants at one time. Unfortunately, many of the buildings have completely disintegrated."

"The caretakers, visitors and investigators have all witnessed stuff all over the property," Lorelei said. "The smell of cakes baking, men standing outside of the bunkhouse, light anomalies at the schoolhouse, the laughter of children, footsteps here in the assay office, and a floating head at the ball mill—those are just a few of the accounts I've heard about."

"I think you're experiencing more than most normally do."

Right after Shannon finished her sentence, a hand grabbed Lorelei's shoulder. A deep, raspy voice came from right beside her. She looked over at Shannon, who casually pulled her long hair back and took a sip from her container. The fiery FBI agent apparently hadn't heard or felt anything.

Not again! Enough is enough. Lorelei got up so quickly she tripped over the cats on her way out of the antiquated structure. Standing right outside the building, with scrub brush and piles of wood and rubble, Lorelei pulled her jacket closer in response to the cold air and ominous atmosphere.

Shannon caught up with her then placed a hand on Lorelei's back. "Are you okay? What happened?"

"What do you think? Something grabbed me, and then a male voice said 'Help me find them.'"

"I didn't see or hear anything. Though I did get a spike in temperature and EMF right before you ran out. Lore, I have to record your response since it was in alignment with my readings in there."

"Thanks, Shannon. You're going to let the whole damn group know I ran out of there like a chicken shit."

"Of course not. But I do need to tell them you reacted to a possible presence right as I got those unusual readings. You're not a chicken shit. Everyone knows that. This is a whole new life for you, and I know it's not easy. But you have to accept your abilities and let us help you."

"What does anyone on the team know about this?" Lorelei asked.

"Hellooooo. I've worked with psychics and mediums in the past and can hook you up with someone. And Ian is Wiccan so he knows about that stuff. Though he claims he doesn't have the ability you do, I'm sure he knows plenty of people with that talent." She nudged Lorelei playfully and winked. "And I know he would love to give you private lessons."

"He's not interested. He's only being nice." *After Patrick's suicide, I'm just not sure I can ever think about getting involved again.*

"Whatever." Shannon rolled her eyes. "Lore, you can stay out here if you want, but I'm going back in until the guys get back from the power mill and the blacksmith's house." She didn't wait for Lorelei's reply, merely turned and walked back into the assay office.

Lorelei heard Shannon interrogating whatever spirits might

be present.

"Come on. There must be somebody here," Shannon said as soon as she stepped back in to the building. "You tried to communicate with my friend. Did your family live here?"

Lorelei glanced down to see all three cats at her feet.

Okay Lore, you can't disappoint the team. If you can't handle your emotions on a regular investigation, then you won't be invited to help with the criminal cases.

She heard Shannon's feet scuffling quickly around on the dust-covered planks.

Taking a few quick strides back into the building, with the cats in tow, Lorelei pulled a towel from her bag and placed it on the ground, then sat down cross-legged.

Shannon came over to sit next to her, and then placed her arm around Lorelei's shoulder. They both laughed as the cats climbed all over their laps.

"You definitely have a way with animals," Shannon said.

"Thanks, Shannon," Lorelei said, grateful for her friend's humor. She pulled her KII EMF meter out of her backpack and turned it on. "Should we see if we can get responses with this?"

"Sure." Shannon took the EMF meter from Lorelei and placed it in between both of them.

"This device on the floor will indicate your presence through your energy." Shannon glanced around the darkened room, seeking any sign of potential spirits.

"We'll ask you some questions and give you time to answer," Lorelei said. "Can you make all of these different colored lights flash once for yes and twice for no?"

There was a brief hesitation. Then the lights on the KII meter lit up once.

Lorelei's jaw dropped and she glanced at Shannon, who sat stiffly in place, eyeing the darkness.

Lorelei took a deep breath, afraid the response would be much more than flashing colored lights. "Someone whispered, 'Help me find them,' a few minutes ago. If you're still here, were you referring to your family?"

The display flashed twice.

"It's working," Shannon said. "And the LEDs lit up all the way to red, indicating a more powerful field." The beam of her flashlight slid along the walls for any movement. "It's pretty intent on communicating."

"The temperature's dropping too." Lorelei rubbed her arms. She leaned over to glance at the Mel-Meter. As they both watched, the EMF reading jumped to 2.8 mG.

Lorelei continued the questioning. "Were you one of the miners?"

The KII meter flashed once.

"I just heard the same raspy male voice say yes," Lorelei said. "Which is in agreement with the ghost's response on the KII meter." She glanced down at the hand-sized device. "The spirit seems to be weakening since the LEDs are only lit up to the middle." She kept an eye on the display.

"Well, I didn't hear anything. But then I never have the same fun you do." Shannon winked at Lorelei and uncrossed her legs to stand up and take pictures. "Flash," she said. Then, "control shot" to verify any anomaly that might be caught in the first photo.

"We did get some great feedback from the KII," Shannon said. "And from our own medium meter."

Lorelei rolled her eyes. "Great. Now I'm being compared to a piece of equipment."

"All kidding aside, Lore. Keep in mind that even though your own internal senses tell you there's something, or someone around, we still need to record and back that up with readings."

Both of them jumped as Shannon's cell phone rang. It was Brandon, the co-founder of the Arizona-Irish Paranormal Research Society. Shannon pushed the speaker function key and his voice rumbled through the handset. "Hey, are you and Lore still in the assay office?"

"Yeah," Shannon said. "We've had quite a bit of excitement. We were getting some responses on the KII and some temperature drops, so I was taking pictures. Lore's had her talents tested as well."

"That's awesome," he said. "You both might get the prize for the most activity. Dale, Ian and I will meet you at the assay office and then we'll divide up to investigate the hanging tree, bunkhouse, cafeteria and schoolhouse. I'll probably send a few people out to the schoolhouse, and the rest of the team can check out the other three areas. They're right next to each other, so shouldn't be too difficult."

"Can't wait. See you in a few." Shannon slipped her cell phone into its holder. "I think I'll leave my audio in here." She set her recorder on an old square, wooden table with peeling mint-colored paint and a slightly broken leg.

Lorelei decided to use the team's handycam to record any potential evidence until the rest of the team arrived.

Well, no other messages from the afterlife, but it's only a matter of time.

Ten minutes later, footsteps crunched on the dirt and gravel. They glanced up through an glassless window surrounded by brick to see Brandon, Ian and Dale approaching.

Lorelei found herself watching the tall man in the middle; Ian Healy—pagan, Wiccan, healer and paranormal investigator. She realized she was holding her breath as the strikingly handsome full-blooded Irishman approached.

She hadn't known she was staring until Shannon cleared her throat. Embarrassed, she turned away. "For God's sake, Shannon. You look like the Cheshire cat grinning like that."

"It's so funny. Ian stares at you like that when you're not looking, and I catch you ogling him. I wonder how long it's going to take to get the two of you together."

The three men entered the assay office.

Brandon pulled out a candy bar from his bag. "Hey ladies, ready to move on?"

"Sure," Lorelei said. "Had more than enough excitement in here." It had become very warm since Ian walked in. She snatched her towel and backpack off the dirty planks and stepped outside.

Her heart jumped a beat when she saw him following her.

"Lore, why don't we head up to the old schoolhouse? I want to see if I can spot some of the mysterious light anomalies."

"Uh, okay." Her heart pounded and her palms started to sweat.

"Good. You can both head on over," Brandon said. "Shannon, Dale and I will split up between the saloon, bunkhouse and hanging tree. Ian, when you're both ready to head back, grab the tripod, camera and voice recorder that I left."

"Will do," Ian said. They both headed out, their beams of light bouncing across the parking lot and peeking down a dirt road that led to another section of the property blocked by a sign reading STAFF ONLY—DO NOT ENTER.

"So, Lore." His low, sensuous voice made her tremble. She pulled her jacket tighter.

"Are you warm enough?" he asked.

"Yeah, I'm fine. Thanks."

"How long have you . . ." they both said at the same time.

Ian chuckled then held his smile.

"Go ahead," she said.

"I was wondering how long you've been interested in the paranormal?"

"That's funny. I was going to ask you the same thing." She kept her eyes on the ground as she walked. "Pretty much my whole life. I had an imaginary playmate when I was five years old. I still remember her brown hair, big brown eyes, and fair skin so clearly. I played with Cara almost every day. Then one afternoon my parents walked in when we were having a tea party. My mother saw her, too."

Ian stopped in his tracks. "You mean she was a ghost?"

"Yeah, though being that young I had no idea. She was someone that kept me company. I was extremely shy and it was hard for me to make friends."

"Wow, that's pretty amazing stuff. I've been touched a few times on my arm during investigations, witnessed some strange things during ceremonies, but to interact on a regular basis with one . . . maybe you've always had that ability with spirits."

"I didn't really develop this ability until after my mother's death. I know spirits are sometimes more attracted to children. Anyway, that was the last time I saw Cara. Once my mom saw her she never returned."

They walked in silence for a minute. "So what about you? You're from Ireland—home of all those amazing castles, folklore and faeries."

"Like you, I've had an interest my whole life. But I suppose it got much stronger with something I witnessed when I was twenty-two, before I moved away from Ireland."

They walked up to the one-room schoolhouse with weathered, warped wooden planks—some of which hung halfway off of the structure, two windows with no glass, and an open doorway in the middle.

Lorelei waited for Ian to continue his story.

She placed her recorder on a windowsill, pulled the video camera from her backpack and started to record footage.

"I saw a banshee," Ian said.

The camcorder came down for a few seconds. "Really? Isn't

that Irish mythology?"

"That's what I thought. A banshee is one of seven types of fairies in Ireland. They're appointed to forewarn the members of ancient Irish families of their time of death. And they can appear in a variety of guises, including a young woman, a stately matron or an old hag."

"So which did you see?"

"A beautiful young woman, thank God."

Lorelei laughed. "Where did you see it?"

"I heard her first. A screeching sound. It sent chills down my spine. I'd say a cross between the wail of a woman in mourning and the moan of an owl. I had been driving down a dark country road late at night with my window down. I didn't expect to see anything, but she suddenly appeared within fifty feet of my car in an open field. I couldn't miss the floating white apparition in the darkness."

"Did you stop to take a closer look?"

"I slammed on the brakes and looked over, not quite sure what I was seeing. I watched her for about thirty seconds. Then she vanished."

Lorelei smiled at him. They stood across from each other. Neither could look away. She turned away and continued to film. For the next ten minutes, Lorelei wandered outside to take video of the playground, then re-entered the old schoolhouse where Ian was investigating. She felt a small hand tug on the hem of her jacket and turned her head quickly. "Ian, do you have your audio recorder on?"

"Yeah, it's in my back pocket."

"Something just grabbed me, and I thought I heard a little boy giggle."

Lorelei stared intently into the shadows. "Can you tell me your name? I felt you tug on my clothes. I know you're here. Please don't be afraid."

Ian came next to her and held out his Tri-Field EMF detector. "It's fluctuating between .5 and 3.5." He whispered so softly she almost didn't hear.

Though she knew she should be concentrating on other things, Lorelei could only imagine him pulling her close to him, leaning down to kiss her with that mouth . . .

Then a gunshot echoed throughout the silence of the desert.

CHAPTER TWO

Dale, Brandon and Shannon entered the dining hall connected to the partially collapsed saloon. The former kitchen contained shelves displaying gallon sized containers of food, Folgers coffee tins, and various cans of vegetables. An antiquated stove and a metal sink leaned precariously to the right, threatening to dump the well-worn pots and pans.

"Did anyone see that?" Dale looked up into the second story of the assay office. "I saw something upstairs next door—looked like a bright white light. I think I'll head back over for a minute."

"Wait. Take this with you." Brandon tossed a walkie-talkie to Dale.

Dale, the other co-founder of the Arizona-Irish, caught the radio in mid-air and ran out of the dining hall. He entered the assay office and ran up the narrow stairway to where he had seen the mysterious light. Cracked, dirt-caked panes of the upstairs window displayed abstract finger drawings and JOHNNY LOVES MARCIA scribbled in big letters.

"Brrrrr." Dale crossed his arms and tried to warm himself. The sudden temperature drop made him reach for his EMF detector. "Crap, it's only thirty degrees in here." The hairs on his arms stood on end. He felt like he was being watched.

He turned around to see a dark presence, over six feet in height, pass in front of him. He gasped as the shadow suddenly collapsed in on itself and transformed into a dense black mist, floating in mid-air. The terrifying entity then bounced off the ceiling, becoming a baseball-sized orb of dark blue light. As Dale watched, the anomaly shot down the narrow stairwell.

His heart pounded as heavy footsteps stomped around on the first floor. "What the fuck?" Dale started back down to follow the sound. There was no banister, so Dale placed his hands on both walls for support. He took another step, then his flashlight flickered and went out. “Shit. I just put new batteries in this thing.” He pounded the flashlight against his palm.

“Who are you?” Dale cautiously continued down the treacherous stairway, feeling for the next step with his foot. “I know you're here because I heard you.”

Did I hear someone's feet scuffling below?

“Brandon, Shannon, is that you?” There was no answer. He pulled his audio recorder from his back pocket like a gunslinger preparing for battle.

“Okay, who's in here with me? Were you the ghost that turned into the ball of light I saw upstairs?”

Dale rammed his left knee into an old metal sewing machine and desk–complete with a pair of ripped tan trousers caught in the needle. “Damn it,” he yelled, jumping around on one leg.

After the pain subsided he started snapping pictures. *There it is again. Another scraping sound.*

Following the repeated noises of what sounded like heavy footsteps, Dale reached a square opening, five feet by five feet, leading ten feet down. He aimed his flashlight at a handwritten sign in black letters: BULLION STORAGE ROOM VAULT UNDERGROUD. GOLD AND SILVER BARS STORED HERE BEFORE BEING SHIPPED OUT.

To hell with it. I want to see what this is about. He used the light from the Mel-Meter to climb down the built-in, risky rungs into the dismal vault. As he placed his recorder on a dirty shelf with rusted containers and empty glass jars, a few eight-legged shadows scurried across and over his hand.

“Jeez!” Dale yanked his hand away and shuddered.

He snapped some pictures of the underground pit to see if he could obtain any evidence of what had made the noises.

He noticed a major temperature drop. The EMF device indicated a gradual decrease from forty-five degrees to thirty-eight, thirty-five and finally stopped at thirty-two.

“If anyone is here, please make your presence known. I heard something down here a minute ago. Was that you? How long did you live here?” A few minutes later, the temperature went back up to forty-five. If anything had been in the area, it had quickly vacated.

I better get back to the team. This isn't safe being in here alone.

As he climbed back out of the bullion room a frigid breeze blew by. He was pushed back down—hard. It wasn't far to fall, but it was far enough. His slightly stocky 5′7 frame fell into the underground vault with such force that it knocked the wind out of him.

He sat up, gasping and choking. A minute later, he climbed out, this time unimpeded. Switching on his flashlight, he was relieved to find that it worked.

Brandon ran into the building and found Dale. "Hey man, what's going on? I tried to get a hold of you by radio. Why didn't you answer?"

"I must have left my walkie-talkie upstairs when I first came in here. I think I put it down when I pulled out my flashlight."

Brandon rolled his eyes. "Dumbass."

"Yeah well, this time you're right. I went down there." Dale pointed to the small pit. "To investigate some sounds I heard and went to climb back out. I was almost to the top of this built-in ladder when a blast of bitter cold air hit. Some force knocked me back down. I could have sworn I saw a dark human shape right before I fell."

Brandon's eyes bulged in surprise. "No way. Well, I'm glad you're okay. I think you should take a few minutes and relax—make sure you haven't injured yourself."

Dale and Brandon both turned to see Lorelei and Ian running toward the assay office.

"What . . ." Lorelei leaned over to catch her breath, ". . . happened. I heard a gunshot."

Dale and Brandon glanced at each other.

"What? Neither of us heard anything," Dale said. "But I did have some excitement in here a minute ago."

"That's about when I heard the shot," Lorelei said. "Ian said he didn't hear anything either. I'm obviously going insane."

"Okay, you may not have heard the sound, but you do smell that, right?" Lorelei inhaled deeply, while sliding her eyes around the dimly lit room. "Gunpowder."

"Sorry, Lore," Brandon said. "All I detect is the same musty smell as when I first walked in here."

"What's going on over here?" Shannon asked, joining the team. She glanced over at Ian and Lorelei. "Hey, I thought you both were supposed to be at the old schoolhouse?"

"We were," Ian said. "But Lore heard a gunshot so we ran back here."

"You're really on fire tonight." Shannon said excitedly, giving Lorelei a gentle punch in the arm. "How were you able to tell what direction the gunshot was coming from?"

"You know, I'm not sure." Lorelei looked around in confusion. "I ran in this direction when I heard it, but I'm not sure why. I'm not sensing anything unusual right now."

"There's nothing anomalous as far as temperature and EMF either." Dale glanced at the Mel-Meter. "Though there was a thirteen degree drop when I was down there." Dale glanced down into the storage pit. "Sounds like I might have been smack in the middle of a residual haunting, according to what Lore experienced."

"I don't know," Brandon said. "Dale, you said something pushed you down, which implies an intelligent haunt. The spirit interacted with you. And it didn't seem to like you being here."

"And Lore had a man speak to her in here. Perhaps it's possible to experience both types of hauntings at once. I mean the fact that spirits are constantly reliving an event is residual, but they can also interact with you while it's happening."

Lorelei shined her flashlight within inches of the wall.

"Lorelei, what are you doing?" Shannon's flashlight beam blinded Lorelei briefly.

Dale, Ian and Brandon walked up behind her while Lorelei slid her two forefingers over a section of wall next to the disintegrated uniforms.

"Look," Ian said. "She found the damn bullet hole."

Dale, Brandon, Ian and Shannon leaned in close.

"Help me find them," Lorelei whispered.

"What?" Ian asked.

"When Shannon and I were in here earlier, a male voice told me, 'Help me find them.'"

"So he was the one that was murdered?" Brandon raised his handycam to record the bullet holes and Lorelei's reactions. "Is he looking for the people that killed him?"

"No," she replied in a trance. "He was the murderer. 'Help me find them' meant he was searching for the other two men that raped and tortured his wife. He wants to finish the job."

"Raped and murdered his wife?" Shannon said. "He told you that?"

"I can sense it," Lorelei whispered.

"How horrible," Ian said. "Wait a minute. Then how did he die?"

"He was hung for avenging her death." Lorelei glanced in the direction of the hanging tree. A single tear rolled down her cheek. "He died out there."

***

An hour later, Shannon's phone vibrated while she stood inside the bunkhouse with Brandon and Dale. She glanced at the text message that stated A CASE FOR YOU. RIGHT UP YOUR ALLEY.

She walked back outside. Lorelei and Ian were at the hanging tree taking pictures, involved in a recording session.

Instead of replying to the text, she called the sender.

"What's up?" she asked Special Agent in Charge, Adam Frasier.

"Didn't expect to hear from you so soon," he said. "You're gonna like this next one."

Not only was Adam direct and to the point, he also had a tendency to refer to cases as if he were recommending a favorite flavor of ice cream. "We've got a case in Dragoon, Arizona. Cochise County Sheriff's Office received a call from the owner of the Texas Canyon Ranch, Melissa Harlow. She came across a male body on her property."

"Did she see anything unusual about the body? And why did you say this was up my alley?" She watched as a two foot rattlesnake slithered out from under a pile of wood ten feet away.

"He was found on Friday, the sixteenth. No markings that the ranch owner remembers."

"What do you mean, 'that she remembers?'"

"She left the area for fifteen minutes to call the sheriff's department. When they arrived, the body was gone."

"What? Is she sure she went back to the right place?"

"Yes." She heard a deep inhale of a cigarette, part of his two pack a day habit.

"Melissa's lived on that property for over five years, claims to know all sixty acres very well. And the sheriff said his deputies scoured her property, as well as the neighbors."

"This could be a practical joke," Shannon said. She looked down to see a plate-sized tarantula crawl stealthily over her tennis shoe. She let out a piercing scream.

Brandon, Ian and Dale came running over. They glanced down to see what her eyes were focused on. "It's not going to hurt you. It's out hunting for food."

She looked up at Brandon. "Yeah, and I could be its next meal!"

"Sorry, Adam," she said. "A giant spider just crawled over my foot. This damn place is alive now. It's a good thing this investigation is ending."

Shannon heard him laughing hysterically on the other end of the line.

"An FBI agent that's more terrified of critters than murderers."

"Okay, okay. Now that you've gotten your jollies. What was I saying? Oh yeah, sounds like it could be a practical joke. How could the body vanish in a matter of minutes? And she didn't get close enough to identify any markings."

"There are other events going on in the area that are adding to this particular mystery."

"Supernatural then," Shannon said. Brandon and Dale had started to pack the equipment. She covered the phone with her hand and said, "Hanging it up?"

"Yeah," Dale replied. "My back's starting to hurt from that fall."

"Wolf-like creature," Adam continued. "She's heard howls late at night. Caught sight of something with reddish eyes and long fur. We've learned that others in the town of Dragoon have had very frightening experiences."

"Are we staying at Melissa's ranch?"

"You got it. We'll need your team out there as soon as possible." After another long, slow exhale he said, "We don't want the community in a panic. I told Melissa you'd all be out there within the next few days."

I take it the Cochise County Sheriff's Department's been notified that our special team is going to be in their jurisdiction?" Shannon bent down and grabbed her backpack.

"Yes. But don't expect a welcoming party. Lorelei, Ian, Dale and Brandon are approved to stay on as consultants. If this works out, we can keep them on as needed."

"Great. We'll be out there Thursday." Shannon ended the call and approached the group as they loaded their equipment into Dale's SUV.

"That was Agent Frasier. We all have our next assignment.

Team, welcome to your first official investigation with the FBI."

"Awesome!" Ian gave Shannon a high five. "Can't wait."

"That is exciting," Lorelei said. "I hope my psychic and medium abilities don't fail me on a real investigation. This one at Vulture Mine was only a case for us to brush up on our investigative skills."

"If you prove half as talented as you've demonstrated here, you'll be a huge help to the team and the FBI."

"What are the details?" Dale asked.

Agent Frasier mentioned the owner of the Texas Canyon Ranch found a male body. But that's not all that's been happening, which is why we're heading out there. Other members in the community have also sighted strange occurrences."

"Wow," Ian said. "Sounds interesting. I assume you mean the Texas Canyon off of I-10 near Benson and Tombstone?"

"That's the one. Short notice, I realize. But I need to get up there and start working with the sheriff's office," Shannon said. "I would like us to be out there Thursday morning."

"Should by okay for me," Lorelei said.

"I do have a project to finish for a client," Ian said. "But I'll do what I can to complete it before then."

"Dale?" Shannon asked.

"I'm good to go. Being out of work leaves a lot of time open for me."

"Brandon, what about you?" she asked.

"No go. Things are pretty hectic right now with my software business. I can't afford to take the time off. But I'm available to help with evidence analysis."

"If everyone can complete as much of their own audio and video as we go along, that will be a great help to Brandon. Copy everyone in the group on what you find regarding this investigation and post to our forum," Shannon said. "Brandon, whatever doesn't get done, don't stress. This case in southeast Arizona will take precedence. Dale can contact you with anything he needs help with."

"Absolutely," Dale said. "There's going to be four of us out there obtaining audio and video, so I'll need all the help I can get."

"I'll see you all real soon at the ranch. Let's plan on meeting out there Thursday morning around 10 a.m." She waved and threw her backpack in her Jeep Cherokee.

A message? She viewed the number on her BlackBerry. *Must have come in when I was on the phone with Adam.* She watched as Lorelei and Dale pulled out from the parking lot. Recognizing the number as her boyfriend, Jeff, she anxiously connected to her voicemail.

After this long evening, it will be good to hear his voice.

"Hi Shannon. It's Jeff. Listen, I hate to do this on the phone, but I think we should give it a rest. It's not you. I just got involved too soon after my separation. I mean, we started dating before I even moved out of her house. Hey, I'm really sorry. But you're a great girl, and I know you'll find someone else. Well, good luck and everything."

The recorded click felt like a fateful stab in her heart. The finality of it all left her hopelessly empty inside.

Why does this keep happening?

On the way to her hotel in Wickenburg, she tried calling Jeff. There was no response. She called eight more times with the same result.

"Listen, Jeff." Shannon left another message on what she vowed would be the last attempt. "I can't believe you broke up over my voice mail. What have I done? I thought things were going so well. You made me believe things had been over for a long time with your wife, and that you were ready for a real relationship. Was that all a lie? Please call me. I really want to work things out."

But she knew he wouldn't.

Another one bites the dust. Isn't there an old song with that title?

Tears rolled down her cheeks as she drove the twelve miles back to town. *For someone who has such great intuition, why the hell can't I tell when I meet a man that's no good for me?*

CHAPTER THREE

Lorelei felt comfortable with the warm tones of Ian's house—similar colors to those in her own Mediterranean home. But that's where the commonalities ended. Ian's house had a stone fireplace with pottery and artifacts and a coffee table that mimicked an Indian drum. Two spectacular paintings of Native Americans were perfectly poised above the black leather couch.

Lorelei had gotten a call from Shannon on Sunday night requesting an evidence analysis of Vulture Mine the next day, in order to be ready for the criminal case.

"Hey guys," Ian said to Lorelei, Shannon, Brandon and Dale. "Finding evidence through a photograph doesn't happen often, but when it does, it can be a good one."

Lorelei stepped over to Ian's computer, and stared at the shadow hanging from the ironwood tree at Vulture Mine. He had managed to capture the image after her experience in the assay office.

"Wow." Dale's mouth opened wide. "Fascinating, but it might not necessarily be the same victim Lorelei encountered. Keep in mind, there were others who met their fate for murder or stealing gold."

"You can see the rope right through the apparition." Brandon indicated a white line around the neck of the dark grey specter.

"Has anyone come across audio of the man Lore communicated with?" Dale asked. "I reviewed evidence from my handycam and recorder, but didn't hear voices or the gunshot."

"Lore and I are going through evidence of our time in the assay office now," Shannon said. "Considering how much activity went on, I hope there's some proof to account for it."

Lorelei stared at the ghost dangling lifelessly and shuddered, remembering the sharp threads that had cut into her own neck as he was dropped callously from the branch twenty feet above.

"I almost forgot," Lorelei said. "I did come across chilling children's laughter from when Ian and I were investigating the inside of the old schoolhouse. I felt something tug on my jacket and started asking questions. That's when I picked up the sound."

"Oh yeah," Brandon said. "You sent me that audio. Lore, it's not just one child. Dale and I heard at least two, a boy and a girl. But you're right. It does sound pretty creepy."

"Ian, how about you finish analyzing video from the old schoolhouse?" Dale asked. "Brandon and I will work on the time spent at the ball mill and powerhouse, and Lore and Shannon can continue with the assay office."

"Good idea," Brandon said. "Give a shout if anyone has a question on what they've found. As we all know, it's so easy for evidence to get tainted, or not be real activity at all. And since we're about to work our first case with the FBI, the Arizona-Irish has to ensure we follow scientific protocol. If there's any question at all, then the audio or video can't be considered paranormal."

Dale sat down in front of his computer. "That means on any case we work. Not just the ones we're hired to help the feds with. Especially considering none of us ever know when we might get solid proof—on a training/skills brush-up mission like Vulture Mine, or the mysteries that Shannon brings us on to assist with."

"Keep in mind," Shannon said. "Any evidence the team finds on an official investigation with the FBI will only be used as support for what Lorelei's psychic/medium skills detect, and for case support. There are way too many unknowns about the spiritual realm to use as final evidence."

Lorelei and Shannon sat back down in front of their laptops and placed their headphones on to continue with the video and recordings.

Fifteen minutes later, Brandon spoke up.

"I can't believe this." Brandon stared intently at his PC. "I think I caught video of the man who was involved in the accident at the mill, where steel balls crushed rubble and ore."

"The guy who was sliced in half?" Lorelei jumped up from Ian's kitchen table and ran over to look at what Brandon had found.

She bumped into Ian on the way. But instead of moving out of the way, he stood there staring at her.

"Oh, s, sorry," he stuttered, blushing. Then he turned toward Brandon.

Lorelei nervously brushed her hair behind her ear. She looked up to see Shannon, Brandon and Dale watching her and Ian.

Lorelei tried to take the focus off of what had just happened. "Brandon, that's great video. You can clearly see his dark hair and black shirt. And there's nothing where his torso and legs should be."

"Wow," Ian said. "He's looking right at you. Or us, rather since we were all together."

"None of you saw anything when Brandon was filming?" Shannon asked.

Ian, Brandon and Dale shook their heads.

"Amazing," Shannon said. "He's floating in mid-air—right by the stairs where others have seen his spirit."

"There's something so gruesome about bottomless apparitions," Lorelei shuddered.

They all returned to analyzing their audio and video. But only a few minutes later, Lorelei caught something on her recorder that backed up what she had heard during the vigil in the assay office.

"Shannon, listen to this."

Shannon placed Lorelei's head phones on. "Great find. Guys, Lore picked up audio of the hanged man saying, "Help me find them. And it's a class A."

Dale and Brandon both listened, their jaws dropping. "That's one of the best EVPs I've heard," Dale said. "It's a whisper, but a very distinct one."

Lorelei took the head phones back from Shannon. "Unfortunately, I haven't heard much else. And I didn't come across anything out of the ordinary in my photos."

"No worries," Ian said. "Finding one piece of evidence is pretty phenomenal. I'm still reviewing video from the old schoolhouse. So far, I haven't discovered anything to back up the laughter you heard. But those temperature drops we both experienced were pretty interesting."

"Ian, wait." Lorelei touched his arm to get his attention.

"Oww," they both said at the same time. A visible spark emanated between them, catching the attention of everyone else.

Again, Shannon, Brandon and Dale stared at both of them. And they were all grinning mischievously.

Lorelei tried to ignore them. "Sorry," she said, blushing. "It's just, I noticed some sort of light anomaly in his video footage."

"Please tell me you're not referring to an orb," Brandon said. "Ninety-nine percent of the time, those things are bugs or dust."

Lorelei rolled her eyes. "No, this wasn't an orb." She watched as Ian rewound the video. "There," she pointed. "See the pulsating blue light in the doorway of the schoolhouse?"

"What the hell?" Ian said. "I looked right past that."

"It's easy to do my friend," Brandon said. "When you've been staring at a computer screen for hours at a time. This is exactly why it's better to do this as a group, so we can help each other catch stuff."

They all gazed at the anomaly, which hung there for a few seconds.

"Ian, it seems to be watching you," Shannon said. "Is there any audio while this is going on?"

Ian increased the volume and played back the video. There was nothing but silence.

"You didn't see that with your own eyes?" Dale asked.

"Hard to believe, but no. Or I would have mentioned while I was filming," Ian said. "I think this happened when Lorelei was out investigating the playground."

They watched as the strange light collapsed in on itself. Then it vanished.

"Okay, that was very weird," Brandon said. "Lore, did you see that during the investigation with Ian?"

"I thought I saw a light, but it was moving. And it wasn't that color."

"This is extraordinary to find all this evidence," Dale said. "And we haven't even finished going through everything."

Lorelei glanced up to see Ian pouring a cup of soda from one of the two liter bottles on his kitchen island. His back to her, she found herself imagining what waited underneath his jeans. *Briefs or boxers*, she wondered. And that's when he turned around and saw her staring. She averted her eyes to her laptop as she felt her face burn with embarrassment.

Unfortunately, Shannon didn't miss the incident. The more Lorelei thought about it, there wasn't much that Shannon did miss.

"Lore, did you want a drink?" Ian asked.

"She wants much more than that," Shannon mumbled.

Lorelei kicked her under the table. "Um, sure. Iced tea is fine."

As he placed the cup next to her, she noticed he trembled slightly, almost spilling a little of the drink.

She noticed Shannon was still smiling.

"Hey, what about the rest of us?" Brandon asked. "We don't rate because we're not hot blondes?"

"That's right," Ian said. "But I won't hold that against Shannon—I plan on getting her a drink as well."

"None of you know what you're missing until you've had a redhead," Shannon said.

"My wife is a redhead." Dale got a bottle of water from the refrigerator.

"So you know the real score," Shannon said, winking at Lorelei. Then the agent's face became serious as she glanced back down at her computer.

Lorelei leaned over and glanced at the image of the saloon and dining hall on Shannon's screen.

Ian, Brandon and Dale watched her scroll through a series of pictures that unveiled a group of four men sitting at a round table playing cards. One man was taking a swig of beer when Shannon snapped the photo.

"Cool!" Brandon said. "A residual haunt. That's wild—those men are in the middle of the collapsed wooden beams and rubble having a good ole time. In their dimension, it's probably still in the early nineteen hundreds."

"Hold on." Brandon ran over to his laptop. "I heard laughter on my recorder while investigating in there. I thought it was Ian since him and Lore were heading over to the schoolhouse at the time." He played the audio out loud for the team.

The sound of deep, raucous laughter surprised Lorelei. "That's definitely not Ian," she said. "We weren't making that much noise—only talking at a normal level."

"Listen carefully," Ian said. "You can hear clinking."

Brandon rewound the section of audio and increased the volume.

"He's right," Dale said. "Sounds like glasses or beer bottles hitting together."

Dale's glanced down at his cell phone. "Crap, I've got to go. My wife texted me. I need to head home. I'll finish what little I have before the ranch investigation."

Lorelei, Shannon, Ian and Brandon continued analyzing evidence for another few hours.

"Let's call it a night," Brandon said. "We've all been at this for a long time and I've got a headache. Thanks for letting us meet at your place, Ian." Brandon shook hands with him. "Hey everyone, send over any questionable evidence as soon as you can. I'd like to try and get this case wrapped up within the next week, since we'll have the Dragoon case."

"See you on Thursday." Shannon waved goodbye, and left quickly with Brandon so that Lorelei and Ian would be alone.

Lorelei packed her laptop up, watching Shannon leave. "This was a productive session. Between finishing up the Vulture Mine case and starting a new official investigation, we're all going to be busy."

Lorelei picked up her empty cup and went to throw it away. But when she turned around, Ian stood right in front of her.

"I'll take that." His soft tone of voice and gentle manner left her breathless.

"Lore, you can stay here if you want. It's getting late and it might be safer."

"I appreciate that, but I'll be fine."

"If you're sure. Call me when you're home." Ian held her hand briefly. A fierce flame sprung up within her.

"You're so sweet." All she could think of was taking him in her arms, kissing his sensuous lips. . . "I better get going."

She could barely walk to her car she trembled so badly.

How come he has this affect on me? I've been in relationships before, and it was never like this.

Lorelei placed her laptop on the passenger side floor. A single red rose lie on the seat. There was no note—only the most perfect flower she had ever seen.

She glanced up to see Ian's curtains drop back in place and his shadow walk away from the window.

CHAPTER FOUR

Lorelei pointed to a monstrous boulder on the side of the highway. A huge malformed rock had a rounded eye-shaped slit at the top, complete with what appeared to be an iris in the middle. The malevolent grin was enhanced with a wide, slightly upturned crack. Three layers of rock fat rested heavily on top of one another.

"Hey guys," Lorelei said. "That boulder looks like Jabba the Hut, doesn't it?"

"Cool." Dale slowed his vehicle. "Did you see its eye? It actually had the same evil, shifty look. Hey, that one there looks like a certain part of the female anatomy." He indicated two similarly shaped round boulders a few feet apart.

"Careful, Dale," Ian said. "We have a woman in the car."

"Leave it to Dale," Lorelei said. "Oh, those are so fake."

They all laughed and Dale picked up speed again.

"This is a cool part of the state," Ian said. "My son and I did a long weekend trip to Tombstone, Bisbee and the Chiricahua Mountains—all of which are fairly close to where this ranch is."

The gleam in his eye, his smile and the lilt in his voice made the love for his son obvious. *Would Ian have room for someone else in his life? Hell Lore, why are you even thinking about that? You don't need that sort of complication.*

"He must have loved Tombstone," Dale said. "We went there as a family a few years ago. My son didn't want to leave. I thought he would be a little bored. But that kid is actually into history. *He* read stuff to *me* about the city. Most twelve year olds only want to watch the gunfights, shows and drain their parent's wallets. This kid stood in front of every damn display, teaching Cindy and me history."

"Aren't there a lot of paranormal groups that go out there?" Lorelei asked. She tried not to stare at Ian as he removed his sweatshirt. She felt her cheeks flush as his shirt lifted up slightly to reveal a well-toned stomach.

"Absolutely," Dale said. "Big Nose Kate's Saloon, Bird Cage Theatre, Boothill Graveyard, and Schieffelin Hall are all well-known for ghostly activity. Tombstone is the most renowned of Arizona's old mining camps. When Ed Schieffelin came to Camp Huachuca with a party of soldiers and left the fort to prospect, his comrades told him that he'd find his tombstone rather than silver. So, in 1877 Schieffelin named his first claim the Tombstone, which is how the town was named. Days of lawlessness and violence nearly had the President declare martial law. The violence climaxed with the infamous Earp-Clanton battle, fought near the rear entrance of the O.K. Corral in eighteen eighty one. So with all that, you would think there would be something."

"That's pretty impressive, Dale," Lorelei said. "I always have trouble remembering a lot of detail."

Ian looked over at Lorelei. "Supposedly, Tombstone is America's best example of our 1880 western heritage, which is well preserved with the original buildings and artifacts featured in numerous museums."

Did he just do that to try and one up Dale's history brief?

But as they turned down the road leading to the Texas Canyon Ranch, her senses screamed so loud that she gripped the car seat in anxiety, the veins in her hand almost bursting from the effort. Lorelei suddenly had a feeling what was going on out here had nothing to do with a simple prank.

"I think that's where we're staying." Dale pointed at two aging, single story buildings with a brick courtyard. Both structures were duplicates of each other—white with slanted dark rose stucco tile roofs and matching doors and window sills.

"Looks like Shannon's here." Dale pulled his SUV into an open dirt lot next to her vehicle. Another stucco building, this one tan in an L shape, had a wooden OFFICE sign hanging on a post. A black and white husky wagged its tail and jumped up to greet them.

"Look at you," Lorelei crooned. The dog leapt all over her as if she were a long lost friend. "That raccoon mask on your face makes you look mean, but you're a gentle giant, aren't you?" She pet his head and rubbed his back.

Shannon emerged from the motel office. "She's at it again. I've never seen anyone get responses from animals that you do, Lore. Melissa saw Bandit greet you—he's never done that with anyone else. She almost fell out of her chair when she saw the dog's reaction to you."

"Shannon, stop making such a huge deal out of this."

"Have you always had a way with animals?" Ian asked.

"I guess you could say that. When I volunteer at the zoo, the antelopes and even the wolves sometimes come out of hiding to greet me. But it's not like I'm the fricking pied piper or anything." Lorelei glared at Shannon.

"Come on in everyone." A tall platinum blonde woman waved them inside the office. "I'm Melissa Harlow, owner of this ranch, though I don't have anyone staying here right now because of what's been happening lately."

Lorelei, Shannon, Ian, and Dale followed her into the office with a dark brown leather couch and a lime green Mexican-style rustic cabinet. In the middle of the room was a unique southwest wooden coffee table with six panels; each section hand-carved with various Native American symbols including sun, deer, bighorn sheep and stick figures. The décor provided a distinct warmth. A corner bar in the dining room was built around a mammoth round granite boulder.

"Wow! Cool that you would build your place around the boulder." Ian gazed at the unusual decoration in awe. Or was this one of the original buildings?"

"Yes it was, but I did do some remodeling when I first moved here five years ago." They were all distracted by the incessant scratching at the door. Melissa opened it and the husky almost knocked Lorelei down as Bandit jumped up in an effort to greet her.

"Did you baste yourself in bacon grease this morning?" Melissa asked. "That dog never reacts to strangers like that."

"This is Lorelei Lanier," Shannon said. "Besides being an animal magnet, she's our psychic and medium. And this is Ian Healy, our expert on Wicca, a healer and great with Native American history. Dale is our tech guru. He sets up our equipment, provides investigative training and is great at analyzing all of the audio and video we capture."

When Lorelei shook hands with Melissa, she sensed the woman was kind-hearted, devoted and hard-working. But there was something else about the ranch owner she couldn't quite comprehend. Was it related to the happenings at the ranch?

"Let me give you all a quick tour," Melissa said. The property is over sixty acres, but the guest ranch and other buildings are all in this vicinity.

As Melissa motioned for the four investigators to follow her, Lorelei caught the dark shadows that hung like curtains under her tired, hazel eyes—shadows that reflected the pale, unhealthy shade of stress.

"Annie and Jeff O'Shea, the original owners, established this guest ranch in the 1930's." Melissa walked up to a door labeled THREE. "As you can see, there is quite a bit of work to be done on the outside. I have plans to remodel next year. My first project was the restaurant, which you'll be visiting shortly."

There were cracks in the side of the structure, chunks of mauve tile had fallen from the roof, rain gutters were detached from the building, and slits underneath the doors resulted from years of settling.

"Both buildings have ten rooms. You guys will all be setup in the other building since I've been doing more remodeling over there. Feel free to take whatever room is more comfortable for you. I've left them all open so you can check them out."

"Did any of your guests ever witness anything unusual?" Shannon asked.

Melissa sighed, shaking her head side to side. "If any of them did, I wasn't aware of it. I've been keeping the Wagon Wheel, that's my restaurant, open for lunch and dinner. But I've been closing it by 6:00 p.m."

"You must have staff here—have they come across anything?" Shannon glanced around to see a young woman with dark hair walk into the log cabin-style restaurant.

"My chef has seen light anomalies in the restaurant, and my bartender has heard footsteps as well as noises in the cellar. Though I don't know if they could be associated with what I've encountered."

Shannon placed her hand on Melissa's shoulder. "When you're ready for an interview, let me know. I'd like to get some more information about what you saw and what the sheriff's department has been doing to help."

"Well, are you all hungry?" Melissa asked. "We can do an early lunch. My chef is awesome."

"Sounds good," Shannon said.

They all followed behind Melissa to the rustic structure with wraparound porch.

The smell of steak made Lorelei's stomach turn inside out and she realized how hungry she was. The team walked into the cozy restaurant. Tables with glass covered wagon wheels and supporting faux boulder stands gave the place its namesake.

"These murals are pretty lifelike." Lorelei gazed upon the right wall to a sunset that painted the sky brilliant colors of orange and pink. Horses were hitched to a post with their riders sitting by a roaring campfire drinking out of tin cups, laughing. She could almost hear the stories they told.

The opposite wall showed cattlemen in action, with reigns in hand and horses manes flying in graceful mid-stride. Hazy blue snow-capped mountains competed with the perfect round brilliance of the rising sun.

Her eyes followed the end of the mural to a bridge one foot in width. Built over an actual trickle of a stream with river rocks, it led to the western saloon. An old horse carriage with black benches, red paint and green wheels sat behind the bar.

Lorelei, mesmerized by the decor, jumped when Melissa guided her toward their table.

"Pretty cool, huh?" Melissa said. "That stagecoach is an original relic. It was found on the property over fifty years ago. Are you all up for some of the best steak you ever had?"

"Hell yes," Lorelei said. "I'm starving. Didn't have time to eat breakfast."

"Hey, Matt." Melissa motioned to a young, blond-haired waiter that came over to greet them and give them glasses of water. "Give my guests four of the thickest steaks you have with the complete fixings."

"Sure thing, boss," he replied with a smile. "Aren't you eating?"

"Not right now, Matt." He sauntered off shaking his head, looking concerned.

"Matt's great," Melissa said. "He's been with me the longest. I kind of have trouble keeping people, what with the distance from Tucson. Matt lives in Bisbee, an old mining town fairly close to here. He doesn't seem to mind driving the fifty miles to the ranch. I usually let my staff spend the night if they're too tired to travel."

"I understand you've already talked with the sheriff's department." Shannon took a sip of water.

"Yeah. Sergeant Jensen came over with a few deputies to scour the property." Melissa glanced around. "Business has suffered. Even during the week, the restaurant should at least be half full this time of day."

"So tell me about this man you saw," Shannon said.

"He was fairly tall—I'd say at least five foot eight, and thin. I saw him while riding one of my horses. He had short dark hair and feminine features. I'd say late thirties, early forties."

"Did you notice a foul odor, any other scent, or any other objects lying around him?"

"Not at all. He was lying face up. I didn't see any blood, either on the body or the ground. I looked at him for a few seconds in disbelief. Then I ran over to him and checked his pulse. There was none, so I rode back to the house to make the call. I didn't have my cell phone on me."

Shannon continued the questioning in a low tone as a waitress walked right by their table. "Did he look familiar?"

"Absolutely not. As a matter of fact, I remember thinking what a distinct appearance he had. He had rather striking features."

"Did the sheriff mention sending someone out to do a sketch of the man?"

"No. At least not yet."

"That's okay. Maybe I can get someone out here to create a profile based on your memory." Shannon shifted in her seat. "And you're absolutely sure there was no pulse?"

"Yes. I double checked. It's not like he could have gotten up and walked away." She sighed. "Well, I'm glad your team is willing to help. I haven't heard from Deputy Jensen since the day it happened. I think he thinks I'm playing a prank on them." Her eyes drifted downward, and she stared at the table somberly.

Lorelei noticed a petite, brown haired waitress grab the tray heaping with plates of food from Matt as he headed toward their table. Serving Ian more than just steak, she bent over to reveal ample cleavage from her v-neck top. She handed everyone else their plates, then looked at Ian one last time and said, "If you need, or want, anything else, just let me know."

Lorelei couldn't tell who was more embarrassed, Melissa or Ian.

Melissa looked at Ian. "I am so sorry. That's Kelly. She acts like that every time a good looking man walks in here. Considering there are three handsome men, she's going to have a ball. The poor thing's had it tough. She got pregnant at sixteen and her boyfriend dumped her when he found out."

"That is rough," Lorelei said. "How old is she?"

"Twenty-one, going on sixteen," Melissa said. "She's living with her parents in Sunsites."

As Kelly wandered around the bar, swaying her hips from side to side, Lorelei received an image that made her forget the conversation at the table, and who she was with.

Kelly was walking alone on the ranch—an evening stroll it seemed from her leisurely pace. Suddenly, the young woman glanced up in shock and vanished into a disturbing, shimmering force field.

Ian's voice called her back. "What other things have you been witnessing?"

"The sightings started before I saw the body," Melissa said. "I'm not sure if it's paranormal, supernatural or something in-between. As old as this ranch is, and as much history as this area has, my staff, visitors and myself have all seen and heard things, but nothing as terrifying as what I saw last week."

Melissa's trembling hand could barely open the packet of sweetener for her iced tea. Lorelei opened it for her, while Shannon reached out to hold her hand.

"I was reading in my bedroom late one night, about 11:00 p.m. The horses started going nuts—I have two paint horses and a quarter horse. They're normally such calm creatures. So I ran outside with my rifle and heard deep, throaty growling. It was coming from the barn."

Melissa let out a deep sigh. "I'm okay. Maybe I was more tired than I thought that night, but I didn't just catch a glimpse. I clearly saw a tall, broad shouldered 'thing' with really long fur. It turned to me and I saw dark orange, almost red eyes. I'm not a woman who is easily scared, but when it faced me I thought I was going to pass out. I got the impression it wanted to kill me."

This woman's terrified of something. Could this sighting and the body be tied together?

"How close were you to this creature?" Ian took a bite of steak.

"Not very far. It was standing at the other side of the barn, so I'd say twenty feet."

"My boss, Adam Frasier, mentioned there had been other sightings much like the one you experienced," Shannon said. "Have your neighbors seen anything?"

"Not that I know of. I don't really see Marie and Corbin too often. However, Matt knows a local family that lives closer to Dragoon Springs, not too far from here. The father witnessed something that scared the crap out of him. Matt mentioned this man is strict military and doesn't scare very easily."

"I'll be heading over to the sheriff's office to see what they can tell me. Maybe we can get someone to do a profile of that body, and try and find eye witness accounts of either the man you saw, or the creature."

"Matt and Kelly know I saw something," Melissa said. "But I didn't tell them what—I didn't want to scare them. But I'm wondering how safe it is here."

"Are there any particularly active areas as far as paranormal activity?" Dale asked. "Or are all of the strange occurrences primarily in the restaurant?"

"That's where most of it seems to be. At least before this 'thing' made its presence known. But there has been some odd stuff going on in the rooms. I was cleaning room number ten earlier this week since it was the maid's day off, and noticed an imprint in the bed I had just made. I went to straighten the comforter, but it wouldn't budge. Like someone was sitting on it. And it was unusually chilly in there."

Dale pulled out a pocket notebook and started writing. "Did you see or hear anything during that episode?"

No. The maid used to run out of the room screaming she was so scared. Now she just asks it to stop and it does. But she claims she still feels a presence. Thinks Annie and Jeff are still roaming the property, watching over everything."

"It's possible." Dale jotted more notes. "Many times there are those that haunt places because that's all they knew. Maybe they have unresolved business or died tragically. They could just be going about their duties as if they were still alive—it's what paranormal investigators call 'residual' hauntings."

"It's not the ghosts I have a problem with. I've had other mediums that have stayed here, and said they also sensed Native Americans, including Apache warriors passing through here. Such spirits and history actually add to the ambiance." Melissa's face darkened. "However, this male body and that dreadful wolf beast. I know the deputy thinks it's some sort of hoax—all of this. I just don't know who would do that sort of thing. Or why."

Lorelei still sensed Melissa was hiding something. Though she wasn't sure if it was because of the way the ranch owner averted her gaze, or something more.

"Guess we've got a lot to do this weekend," Shannon said. "Dale, let me know how you want to handle the investigation of the ranch."

"Excuse me," Melissa pushed her chair back and stood up. "I have some work to do in the office." She started to walk away, then turned back. "Oh, I almost forgot. I'm sure you'll want to check out the site where I saw the man. I piled up some smaller rocks in the general area—it's right off of the dirt road leading to the highway. There's no trail, but I did wrap a red handkerchief around a bush. The site is in a clearing about a quarter mile past that."

"Thanks very much for your help, and for letting us stay here," Ian said.

"No, thank you. I hope you can help figure all this out." As Lorelei caught Melissa's glance, she quickly turned and left the restaurant.

"Lorelei," Shannon whispered. "Did you get any weird or negative vibes from Melissa?"

"Actually, yes," Lorelei said. "I think she's struggling to keep the place going. As with many others who encounter the supernatural, she thinks she's losing her mind—especially since she found a body that disappeared right away. I don't think she's involved, but she's holding back."

"I didn't want to say this in front of Melissa." Ian looked around to make sure no one could hear. "It's possible she's encountered a skinwalker, or Navajo witch. At least from the description she's given."

Ian glanced at Lorelei while she was eating. Her hand started to tremble and the piece of steak on her fork grazed the side of her mouth. *Good Lorelei, show him what a dork you really are.*

But he didn't seem to notice. "Lore, are you getting the sense of anything dark or threatening here?"

"When we first pulled in, yes. I don't think it's a prank. Adam did mention this creature has been harassing others in the community. If this is some sort of joke, it's not just on Melissa. And I'm curious as to what this disappearing body has to do with these other sightings."

Shannon nodded her head in agreement. "So what's the deal with this skinwalker?"

"They are very powerful shapeshifters that will take on the form of an animal whose powers they want to obtain. They've been seen in the form of wolves, coyotes, bears—though most sightings seem to be in a wolf form. And I've talked with highway patrol officers who've seen them running alongside their cruisers at sixty miles per hour. They're as evil as you can get and are masters at mind control, and not above murder, even of their own family."

"So we're talking about real people transforming into animals?" Lorelei asked.

"There are different theories," Ian responded. "Some believe they are malevolent entities, but the religion and lore of southwestern tribes dictates they are shamans who decided to take the dark road."

"Melissa mentioned she didn't see any marks on the body," Shannon said. "If there were a murdering skinwalker in the area, I wouldn't think this mysterious man would have been left unmarked. But if that is what we're dealing with, how the hell do we get rid of it?"

"It depends on whether someone called upon the spirit of a skinwalker, or if there is a real witch out here terrifying the community," Ian said. "It might mean reversing a spell."

Lorelei shuddered thinking of such an inhuman creature wandering around such a peaceful and remote town.

If this beast or entity can change into any form, whose to say it won't take the shape of something familiar?

"Let's check out the scene first, and then head over to the Benson Patrol District to visit with Sergeant Jensen."

"I'll stay here." Dale removed his car keys. "I can go ahead and get some baseline readings and decide where to position the equipment. Maybe I can catch some clues as to what else is going on. It's possible Melissa witnessed an apparition rather than an actual body."

"But she mentioned touching it," Lorelei said. "To check his pulse."

"Spirits have been known to appear solid in form," Dale said. "Get some pictures, video footage and EMF readings when you're in the area where the body was seen, while Shannon checks for physical evidence."

Lorelei watched as Shannon bent down next to her chair and produced a briefcase-sized box on the table.

"Shannon's been holding out on us," Dale said. "She's put together her own ghost hunting kit."

"Not quite. This is a gift from the FBI for the team."

Lorelei and Ian pushed the plates and glasses aside so they could open the box.

Dale's jaw dropped when he saw the thermal imaging cameras.

"We can use them for the crime related investigations," Shannon said. "If Adam decides he likes what we're all doing as a special unit, then we get to keep them."

She barely managed to remove the first handheld camera when Dale's eyes flew wide open and he gasped in astonishment. "Holy shit!" Matt glanced up from the bar to see what the commotion was. "This is awesome, every investigator's dream."

"I figured you'd be the most excited. Though I'm sure Brandon will want to get his hands on these as well."

"How many did we get?" Dale took the device from the agent.

"Two."

"Isn't that a type of night vision technology?" Lorelei asked.

Dale turned the device on and viewed the interior of the restaurant through the lens. "Yes. Thermal imaging operates by capturing the upper portion of the infrared light spectrum, which is emitted as heat by objects instead of simply reflected as light. Hotter objects, such as warm bodies, emit more of this light, so you'll be able to identify them." Dale showed Lorelei the various colors reflecting from the people and objects in the room. "Of course it's not going to show exact details, just sources of heat and cold. But you can see that the bartender is showing as orange red meaning warmer, and the chairs and tables are blue. This number," Dale indicated a reading in the upper right hand corner, "shows you the exact temperature."

"The camera also has digital zoom, voice recording and the ability to take thermal and regular pictures simultaneously," Shannon said.

Lorelei glanced from Shannon to Dale. "How can these be used to detect the presence of spirits? I mean, ghosts aren't solid like humans."

"That's why it's just one of a number of devices that are used," Dale said. "There are people who think that ghosts can't emit heat. But I've seen these babies in use." Dale continued to scan the restaurant with the thermal imaging camera. "And I've witnessed unusual phenomena that did show up with a strong heat signature."

"These cameras were modified by the FBI for the purpose of

paranormal investigations. So they can detect EMF and density as well—though Dale and Brandon will have to figure that part out."

"This is friggin awesome." Dale's mouth opened in surprise as he played with the new piece of equipment. "I think I'm in love."

"Well, let's all go check out the site where Melissa saw the body." Shannon placed one of the thermal imagers back in the box. "Dale, keep that camera I just gave you. But be very careful with it. I need to take these back with me when the investigation's over."

"You're such a tease," Dale said.

Lorelei realized how working with the federal government could take their group to a whole new level. Helping with criminal cases and having access to the latest and greatest equipment could also help gain a better understanding of the paranormal.

Lorelei, Shannon, Dale and Ian got up from their table. Lorelei noticed the waitress had leaned up against the bar, revealing even more cleavage than she did at their table. She leered at Ian and licked her lips, while Matt rolled his eyes. Then he said something to the young waitress that Lorelei couldn't hear.

The group walked outside and Shannon unlocked her Jeep Cherokee with the remote. "Let's take my car to the site where Melissa saw the body so we can head right to the sheriff's office afterwards. Hey Dale, why don't you interview Matt and Kelly. See if they've witnessed anything Melissa might not have mentioned, and make sure to record the conversations. Shouldn't take too long, and then you can start setting up for the investigation."

"Sounds like a plan," Dale replied. "Let me know if you find any evidence out there."

"Absolutely," Shannon said.

A few minutes later, Lorelei, Shannon and Ian were pushing past mesquite branches, slipping on rocks and trudging through high desert grass where Melissa had marked the path.

Lorelei yelled when her foot caught under a rock. As she fell forward, she accidentally grabbed onto Ian's waist. She continued to slide to the ground with her hands on the back of his legs.

She glanced up briefly and saw Shannon cover her mouth, trying to control her laughter. "Now that was a classic fall."

Ian knelt down to help her up. "Are you okay?"

"I'm so sorry." Lorelei stood up wiping her hands on her jeans—she could not look at him.

"I'm glad you're all right. If you hadn't fallen on me first, your face would have hit that rock." Ian pointed to a plate-sized rock with an edge as sharp as a knife.

"Let's keep going. A few minor scratches—I'll live."

Ian prevented her from going any farther. He held her wrists to look her arms over, and her whole body shook. A burning sensation she had never felt rushed through her, and she gasped aloud.

"I, I'm fine," she stuttered, pulling her arms away.

"Hey guys!" Shannon yelled. "Over here!"

Lorelei and Ian followed the sound of Shannon's voice to a horizontal finger-like rock formation, which extended twenty feet. They all stood on the rock, overlooking a clearing.

Shannon closely inspected the surrounding area and took pictures of the expanse of land and a group of unusual boulder formations in the distance, which appeared to be a miniature city of rock. Ian walked further ahead on the narrow trail.

Lorelei headed toward two mammoth boulders, fifteen feet in height, right next to each other, allowing a shady retreat for her to pass through. Then she realized it had been one massive boulder at one point that had split in half. A grove of mesquite lay beyond and a large clump of beargrass erupted from the vegetation. Two flower stalks about six feet tall protruded from the plant's center.

Drawn through the tall boulders, Lorelei noticed more than mesquite trees. She approached a maze made of stones.

"Ian, Shannon, over here," Lorelei yelled. "Go through the two rocks."

Shannon observed the boulders in awe as she passed through.

"What is that?" Shannon stepped inside the maze of small rocks.

"A labyrinth," Ian said, walking around the circular-shaped object. "They are meant for meditation and contemplation, offering a single path leading into a well-defined center and then out again by the same path. It's a metaphor for the journey to the center of your deepest self and back out into the world with a broadened understanding of who you are."

Lorelei caught herself staring at him as he described what she had discovered.

"There are many different variations of the labyrinth." Ian stood back from the circle. "But they are a place for reflection and purification, and illustrate the human journey of life, and the twists and turns of the paths are the struggles one finds along the way."

"Impressive," Lorelei said, staring at him.

He smiled at her and she immediately focused on the ground. "It does look a little overgrown." Lorelei walked slowly around on the inside of the labyrinth. "And some of the rocks have been shifted around or removed."

Lorelei pulled her recorder from her back pocket and turned it on while roaming through the labyrinth. "There may not be any physical evidence, but since this is such a highly spiritual place, there might be an EVP to provide a clue."

"Good thinking," Ian said.

She halfway glanced over, still too embarrassed to look him in the eye. Turning away, she began to walk inward to the center of the circular labyrinth.

Shannon carefully scanned the grass and ground. "I don't see any imprints or blood in the foliage." Shannon let out big sigh. "Maybe the person was killed somewhere else and dumped here temporarily, where Melissa saw him. But there should still be evidence."

The killer could still be lurking nearby. Lorelei, Shannon and Ian walked back to the twenty foot long granite finger near where the body had been found.

"Are you both ready to head over to the Cochise County Sheriff's Department?" Shannon asked. "I'm anxious to find out if they discovered anything out here."

Hanging back to see if she could sense anything, Lorelei realized there was no sound at all—unlike a minute ago when the birds were singing and gentle breezes whispered by. The atmosphere was completely still and unsettling.

She jumped when Shannon screamed at her. "Lore, let's go!" She ran back through the brush and to the car. But she couldn't shake the feeling there was something back there.

***

Short dark hair parted in the middle and an upside down v-shaped mustache reminded Shannon of a western outlaw. *Take a black and white photo and this guy could be out of the pages of western history.*

"Can I help you?" asked the man standing behind the circular reception area.

Shannon looked around in the quiet, rural sheriff's office. Fake palm trees lined the beginning of four rows of cubicles with offices at the end of each row. And jars of leftover Halloween candy sat on desks.

"Yes. I'm Agent Shannon Flynn. And this is Lorelei Lanier and Ian Healy. They are investigators helping the FBI. I was here to meet with someone in charge of the case at Texas Canyon Ranch. I believe his last name is Jensen."

"Oh, yeah. FBI—Federal Bureau of Intimidation," he answered with a sly smile. Mr. Outlaw winked at the petite, perky blonde with the upturned nose who sat behind the desk.

Shannon faked a smile.

"Actually, that's me. Sergeant Jensen—Jack Jensen that is."

Even sounds like an outlaw's name.

Shannon extended her hand. "Nice to meet you."

He barely took her hand, shaking her fingers instead. "Let's head back to my desk. Elaine, hold any calls for now," he said to the perky receptionist.

"What calls?" She winked at Ian, looking him up and down.

Holy shit. He really is Mr. Magic. I can't believe how women react to him. Though there's only one woman he has eyes for.

Jack ignored the comment and invited Shannon, Ian and Lorelei to sit down inside a blue-walled cubicle, in front of a cheap wooden desk. Only one picture inside an 8 1/2 x 11 silver frame was in view—a tall, husky woman with medium-length brown hair and manly features stared back nonchalantly. Two chubby kids stood in front of her.

Though there were only two chairs, the sergeant didn't seem to notice. Ian quickly rolled another chair from the cubicle next door.

"As you already know, my team is staying at the ranch," Shannon said. "We're here to get any information you might have discovered regarding evidence or witnesses."

"Well, it's like we told Special Agent in Charge, Frasier is it?" The sergeant shuffled some papers on his desk. "I took some of my officers out there as soon as we got the call from Melissa. We scoured the area where she claimed to have seen the body, as well as outlying sections, and none of us found anything. And we haven't had any rain or windy conditions that would wipe away such evidence."

"Melissa mentioned she checked for a pulse but found none," Shannon said. "If this is a murder, the suspect could still be out there.

Have you at least contacted a sketch artist to come out? Then we would have something to go on, and someone in the community might know who the man is."

"My artist is on maternity leave right now," Jensen said. "And besides, we don't have a whole lot to go on. I did talk with many residents in Dragoon. None of them had seen anyone with the description Melissa provided."

"Guess I'll contact a forensic artist from the Sierra Vista FBI office. We need to get a solid representation for something to go on. Excuse me for just a minute." She reached in her purse and dialed the special agent in charge, but got his voice mail. "Adam, it's Shannon. I'm talking with Sergeant Jensen right now. They don't have a forensic artist available, so I need to get someone from Sierra Vista to help us identify the body Melissa found. And maybe even this creature that's been seen around here. I'm hoping you can get someone out here as soon as possible. Text me and let me know who it is and when they'll be out. Talk to you soon."

Jack had started tapping his pen on the desk from the moment she mentioned the creature. "All right sergeant. What's going on? You suddenly seem very uncomfortable."

"Dragoon's normally such a peaceful community. We just can't figure out where all this is coming from. I thought the body was a joke. Maybe it is. But these 'things' that are being spotted . . ." He shook his head back and forth and gazed out the window toward the mountains as if seeing a possible solution.

"Wait," Ian said. "What do you mean 'things?'" Melissa mentioned she saw something late at night, though she described it as a wolfman of sorts."

"That was what *she* witnessed," Jensen replied. "Another family living in the area claims to have seen a prehistoric bird perched on top of their garage. That sighting was yesterday at 2:15 p.m. They've lived here twenty years and I've never had any problems with them or their children. They're a church-going family and it's not like them to make stuff up."

A second creature – or is something capable of transforming into multiple forms?

"Ian was telling us about a skinwalker, or medicine men, that can transform into any form they desire." She turned to Ian. "Do you think the creature Melissa saw could be associated with the one this other family saw yesterday?"

"Some shamans are powerful enough to become anything. But it's not often you come across two different forms within days of each other. Usually shamans and skinwalkers will take on the shape of one particular power animal found in nature, like coyote, bear, wolf, which has the attribute they're seeking."

"There have been two sightings then?" Shannon stared at Jensen. "Melissa's wolfman and this other family's bird monster."

"Wait," Lorelei said. "Melissa mentioned that her waiter and bartender, Matt, knew of a family that saw something—the military guy in Dragoon Springs."

"That must be Jerry," Jensen said. "He used to be in the Army. However, I wasn't aware of any call from him. Could be he was afraid to let us know, fearing he would be made fun of." He paused and stared at Ian. "So you're familiar with whatever, or whoever, is terrorizing this community?"

"Possibly." Ian glanced over at the receptionist as she sauntered slowly by, giving him a flirtatious smile. "We need to review the interview details, or talk to the people that are seeing this stuff."

Shannon couldn't believe the responses Ian received from women. The man could have anyone he wanted. Yet he didn't seem to know it.

"Well, this one's all yours," Jensen said. "The deceased vanishing male and these outlandish sightings is a little out of our jurisdiction."

"Might as well," Shannon said. "Hopefully, Adam can send out a sketch artist. Can you provide me the contact information and addresses for the two families? I would like to take my team out there to talk with them."

"Sure. I'll give them a heads up that the FBI will be in touch, though I'm not sure ole' Jerry, that's the retired army general, will admit to seeing anything."

The sergeant printed out something from his computer and took a few seconds to write on it. Then he handed it to Shannon. "Here's a copy of the interview/incident form with the Collins family regarding the latest sighting. Jerry's home phone and address are on there as well. I'll also have my deputies' keep an eye on Melissa's ranch, and have them spend some time roaming the community."

Shannon stood up and shook hands with Sergeant Jensen. "Thanks very much for your time. I'll keep you advised. And if you hear of any other incidents, let me know right away." She gave him her business card.

"Gladly," as he shook hands with Lorelei and Ian. "Though I pray there won't be any more trouble."

CHAPTER FIVE

It was as if Lorelei had stepped out of Shannon's car and into another planet. The atmosphere was unusually heavy, especially for Dragoon where temperatures were normally in the seventies during the day. It was also quiet. Too quiet. Exactly like the clearing where the corpse was spotted. No breeze, no insects, not even echoes of traffic from the nearby freeway.

Lorelei noticed Melissa atop one of her horses in the distance. The owner of the ranch was riding slowly along a ridge—passing through a valley of mesquite and by a series of boulders that were shaped like the backbone of a mammoth dinosaur.

She remained as still as the very air around her. *Normally, silence is revered. But this is just creepy.*

"How did things go at the sheriff's office?"

Lorelei jumped when she heard Dale's voice.

He approached them from room ten. "I was doing a baseline in there and I setup a camera to cover the room. Maybe we'll catch proof of whatever spirits or creatures have been hanging out."

"It was interesting," Shannon said. "We found out there was another sighting, a prehistoric bird on top of a house. The incident Matt mentioned with the military family wasn't reported. The sheriff's deputy handed over both cases to the FBI—the male missing body and the supernatural case with these bizarre beasts. I contacted Adam to get a sketch artist out here so that we can at least determine what this guy looked like."

"I think you can call him back and cancel that request." Dale revealed the other side of the white piece of 8 ½ x 11 paper he held.

Lorelei watched as Shannon's jaw dropped. An articulate sketch showed a face of a man with feminine features, slightly sunken cheeks, thick, dark hair, sideburns and a small star-shaped scar that hung right below his bangs.

"Melissa drew this," Dale said. "It appears she has some

talents. She didn't think about doing this until you mentioned it in the restaurant. She even provided additional details, including estimated height and the location where his body was discovered."

Amazing. That's almost as good as what would be produced from a software program.

A few minutes later, Melissa approached the group on a beautiful black horse. Melissa waved, jumped off and walked over to meet the team. "This is my quarter horse, Night Sky. I've had her for ten years."

The animal stood next to Melissa and nudged her gently with its nose. Melissa stroked its side.

"Thanks for the picture," Shannon said. "The detail is incredible."

"It was a hobby. That's actually the first drawing I've done in a few years."

Lorelei crossed her arms and her eyes darted to three horses roaming in a paddock. All of them abruptly bobbed their heads up and down and stomped impatiently, creating plumes of dust. The black quarter reared up behind Melissa, blowing and snorting.

Looking closer, she thought she saw something wavy and shimmery in the middle of the paddock—a long, moving invisible field.

"Whoa baby, it's okay." Melissa stroked the horse's mane and neck, glancing around nervously. "Something's here. The last time they all acted like this was when I saw the wolf creature."

"Everyone, stay here while I check this out." Shannon removed her gun from its holster and headed cautiously toward the barn.

"We talked with Sergeant Jensen." Ian watched as Shannon approached the horses. "I can't be sure of what we're dealing with, though it sounds like a shapeshifter. If we're talking about one shaman, or witch, then they're choosing to take multiple forms. Though this sort of activity usually takes place on a reservation. They don't normally harass non-Native Americans. Is there any reason someone might want revenge?"

Melissa didn't get a chance to respond.

"Oh my God!" Melissa ran past Shannon toward a white horse with brown spots that was swaying back and forth precariously. As Lorelei, Ian and Dale ran over, it dropped on all fours and fell on its side.

"What the hell is going on?" Melissa cried. Blood protruded

from two lesions, both an inch wide. The animal's eyes were wide with fright.

Lorelei ran her hand over the puncture wound. *A snake bite. This can't be. The teeth marks are too large and far apart. This would have to be a fifty foot rattlesnake.* She looked around nervously.

"Snowcap, oh baby." Melissa sobbed. As she gently ran her hand along the horse's side in an effort to calm the beast, the nostrils flared in and out in a labored manner. The mare attempted to stand up, but could only lift her head.

Lorelei was familiar with pit vipers and knew she was seeing some of the affects of its venom—swelling, edema, hemorrhage and increased heart rate. Those were the visible symptoms.

Lorelei tried to hold back her tears as Snowcap's breathing worsened.

Melissa gently stroked her nose and side to calm her down.

This has to be another shapeshifter. How many more are there?

Snowcap's breathing stopped ten minutes later as Melissa laid over the animal's head, stroking its nose and sobbing into her horse's neck.

Lorelei, Shannon and Ian kneeled down to comfort the ranch owner. "Melissa, I'm so sorry," Shannon said.

"We all are." Lorelei wiped her tears away with her hand.

"Let's leave her for a minute." Ian led Lorelei and Shannon out of the barn, while Dale stayed with Melissa. "Whatever we're dealing with here isn't just frightening people anymore. It's killing. I plan on doing a small ritual here to help protect Melissa and her animals, but I can't perform a ceremony on the whole town."

"I feel like this is all my fault." Lorelei glanced back at Melissa mourning over her beloved horse. "I sensed something earlier and didn't say anything."

"Lore, you had no way of knowing what would happen." Ian took her hands in his. "None of us even saw this thing, and we were only standing twenty feet away."

"I did see something. Nothing solid," she sniffled. "But it was a strange heat wave-like effect."

Ian looked back into the paddock. "That doesn't sound like any shapeshifter I've heard of. I wonder what the hell these things are and why they're harming animals?"

"We need to try and get Melissa off the ranch," Shannon said. "It's too damn dangerous here between the wolf-like creature and now this invisible giant snake. Not to mention this prehistoric bird."

"Unfortunately, I'm not sure there's any safe haven right now," Ian said. "At least not in Dragoon."

Lorelei trembled as Ian continued to hold her hands. She stared up at him.

"Sorry," he whispered, letting her hands go. "I didn't realize..." Ian looked away in embarrassment.

Wracked with grief, sobbing and gasping, Melissa headed toward the Wagon Wheel. Lorelei started to walk over to console her, but Ian stopped her.

Melissa hesitated for a few seconds and turned to the group. "I plan on sending my staff home right now. I'll contact a friend who has a ranch in Sunsites. I've housed some of their horses before, and they've told me they would return the favor anytime. I'll take the other two horses and Bandit back to their place. But I'm not going anywhere. These beasts are not going to frighten me away from my home." Melissa turned slowly on her heels and headed into the restaurant.

Ian's mysterious, smoky eyes widened in surprise. "Tony Slaughter," he muttered. "I thought that face she drew seemed familiar. It just came to me. Shannon, can I see that picture again?"

"Sure. I laid it down over here." Shannon looked around outside the entrance to the barn to see if Melissa's drawing had blown away. She threw her hands up in frustration. "I set it on top of this old barrel before we went to look at the horse."

Dale wandered around the stable with Shannon. "That's strange. I saw you put it there. And there hasn't been any wind."

"Dale, you were closest to the barrel where I left the sketch. Did you hear or see anything?" Shannon asked.

"No. Oh shit. You don't think whatever killed that horse . . ."

"That makes absolutely no sense," Lorelei said. "Why would a creature intent on killing an animal steal a drawing?"

"There seems to be a lot out here that doesn't make sense," Ian said. "That profile showed a familiar image. The scar on his head looked sort of like a lightning bolt. There's a Satanic cult from the nineteen thirties that used that symbol. It was said that some of the most powerful people in the black arts were members. The man Melissa drew, Tony Slaughter, was a master in practicing dark magic. His cult disbanded by nineteen thirty eight. I can see if I can find an image of him on my laptop for a more positive ID."

"Wait," Dale said. "So he must have been an apparition since Melissa mentioned he was in his thirties or forties. I wonder if any of this could be connected to December twenty-first. This is 2012 after all—the year of Armageddon. Maybe there's a coven out here with some amazing supernatural abilities, creating havoc until the supposed 'day of doom.'"

"Yeah, maybe. I don't know of any coven practicing this kind of magic." Ian glanced over at the barn. "I'm going to grab my suitcase and laptop. I have some contacts that have been involved with paganism and Wicca for much longer than I have, and I'd like to check with them to see if they are familiar with what's going on."

"We can't assume it was an apparition," Shannon said. "Maybe there's someone who happens to look like Tony."

"If it wasn't for that distinctive mark on his forehead I would agree with you," Ian said.

"Okay," Shannon replied. "Let me know what you find out. I need to determine if this potential murder mystery is connected to these bizarre and deadly incidents. But I think we need to double up in the rooms. It will be much safer. Dale and Ian, and Lorelei and I."

Lorelei glanced up and caught Ian staring at her, his face flushed. And she wondered if he was imagining the pairing a different way—like she was.

CHAPTER SIX

Shannon opened the door to room twelve and immediately shuddered. Spiders hung silently in the corners and on the see-through maroon lace curtains. *Sure, you're all still right now. But as soon as I climb into bed and close my eyes, you'll be after me!* Carefully peeling back the thick floral comforter on the king-sized four poster bed, she closely inspected the sheets for any sign of movement.

"Shannon," Lorelei snickered, "they're granddaddy longlegs. They won't hurt you."

"I don't care. They have eight legs and hang on the ceiling. One will probably fall on me in the middle of the night." Shannon darted her eyes overhead from one corner to the other.

"You're something else. There are dangerous creatures terrorizing the community and you're worried about a few harmless spiders."

"Few my ass, Lore! There are probably hundreds in here hiding in all the cracks and under the furniture."

Lorelei shook her head in disbelief at Shannon's actions. "I wonder if this room had any activity, other than insects that is. I'll leave my recorder on overnight to see if we get any EVPs. Of course, I'll let you all know if any of my voyances detect anything."

They proceeded down two steps to another room with a dark red couch matching the curtains, a stone fireplace and an oval glass table on a southwest style area rug.

"I need to call Adam and update him." Before Shannon sat on the couch, she glanced down to make sure nothing was moving, then brushed off the cushion with a magazine. She hit a speed dial button. "Hey Adam."

His first response was a long, slow exhalation. *And yet another cigarette.*

"How's it going out there?" he asked.

"Very interesting. I left a message for you to send a sketch artist, but it appears we didn't need one. Melissa drew a picture—she provided more detail than the software I've seen other artists using."

Shannon observed the ceiling, watching for sign of movement.

"Besides Melissa's sighting, another family nearby spotted a prehistoric bird. And it's been a rather emotional day here as well. One of Melissa's horses died—apparently from a snake bite. The poor thing seemed to suffer from some of the symptoms of a venomous bite—convulsions, blood from the wound, labored breathing. It died within ten minutes. We were all standing right there and didn't see a thing. Except Lore did mention she witnessed some sort of invisible shape outside the barn."

"Wow. I wonder if the man Melissa saw fell prey to one of those things. There could have been markings she didn't see."

"That's another strange thing about the case," Shannon said. "Ian identified the man as Tony Slaughter—he was a master in the dark arts in the thirties."

"What? If the body she saw was really Tony, then we're dealing with a spirit sighting," Adam said. "Though I understand she actually touched him when she felt for a pulse."

"Yeah, she told us the same thing. Ian's convinced it's him because of the lightning shaped scar on his forehead. Apparently, the cult Tony was involved in used that symbol." Shannon pushed her hand through her hair in frustration. "Ian's doing some research to see if his contacts know about anything about Tony's cult, or if there's a specific type of magic we're dealing with. Initially, we considered the shapeshifter theory, but considering whatever attacked Melissa's horse was invisible, it doesn't add up."

Adam sighed heavily. "I don't understand what a spirit from the thirties would have in common with these other sightings. Looks like you've got a lot to figure out."

"The creature sightings and Melissa's discovery of Tony's body did start about the same time," Shannon said. "Oh, Cochise County decided not to deal with this case. Sergeant Jensen handed both over to us. Usually we have such power struggles with the local law enforcement."

"Can you send me a copy of that sketch?" Adam asked.

"That's the other thing. It disappeared—just like the body. But Ian thinks he can find a picture of Tony on the Internet." Shannon turned to see Lorelei staring out the window that faced the office.

"Seems like someone's trying to keep both secrets quiet."

Her boss let out a huge exhalation on the other end of the line. "Well, do what you can to keep Ian and Lorelei with you for the stretch. Sounds like this could turn out to be the case of the century."

As Shannon hung up, Lorelei still stood at the window, unmoving. "Lore?"

"Oh," Lorelei said, looking over at Shannon. "Sorry. I was sitting on the couch, and thought I caught something flash by the window. Not a person or wild animal. It was glimmering, though the sun is going down. Similar to what I saw in the barn. And I heard…"

"Heard what, Lore?"

She turned to look right at Shannon. "Something invaded my mind for a minute. A deep, gravelly, almost inhuman voice said, 'This is our home now.'"

"Did you get a feeling as to what it meant?"

Lorelei shuddered. "It wasn't pleasant."

"I think I'm going to head to the crime scene again and take a closer look before it gets very dark. Let's go get Ian. Dale will want to stay here and do an investigation."

Shannon glanced at her watch. "Crap. It's almost dinner time." They headed to Dale's SUV to get their equipment. "This shouldn't take too long, then we'll head somewhere for dinner. Maybe we can get Melissa to join us."

Shannon heard a door open and walked outside to see Ian coming out of his room.

"Hey Ian, we're going back out to the place where Melissa found the body. Do a more thorough search to see if there are any clues. I know the sheriff's department claimed to have scoured the area, but intuition's telling me there's something else we're missing."

"Do you want me to go?" Ian asked.

"Of course. I was going to leave Dale here to try and obtain some evidence. Who knows, maybe he'll catch something that will provide a clue as to these cases. Plus I don't want to leave Melissa alone here." Shannon looked toward the restaurant and then at Melissa's office and residence.

"Did you discover anything about the type of activity around here from your pagan contacts?"

Ian and Lorelei got their ghost hunting gear out of the back of Dale's SUV while Shannon removed a trace evidence kit from her Jeep.

"I did get a hold of one person who has extensive knowledge of the black arts and the Church of Satan. They've never heard of anything like this. But I do have a friend, Joe Luna, who's a shaman. I'll try to get him out here, if that's okay."

"Sure," Shannon said. "But what makes you think he can help out if you're other contacts don't seem to know anything?"

"He's a well-renowned healer throughout the four corners. And he's Native American, so he understands the concept of the shapeshifter. Actually knows people who can transform themselves into animals—himself included. Not sure if that's what we're dealing with, but shamans also have a tremendous grasp on magic and the supernatural."

CHAPTER SEVEN

Cool! Lorelei thought, as she walked down the dirt path with Shannon and Ian. A golden-yellow rattlesnake with brown blotches along its back, and a solid black tail slithered across their path.

Shannon backed away quickly.

Lorelei cautiously approached within five feet of where it had stopped. "Wow." She pointed her flashlight closer to the reptile. "A black-tailed rattlesnake. I haven't seen one of these in a long time."

Ian came and stood beside her, leaning over to see what she found. His face was so close she could feel his breath. Even though it was cool outside, Lorelei became flushed and warm. She totally forgot about the reptile.

"How long have you been interested in snakes?" Ian asked. But she didn't hear the question. Only the intense pounding of her own heart.

"What?" she whispered, looking into his eyes. *Did he get a little closer?*

His voice lowered a little softer as he gazed back at her. "I . . . uh . . . forgot what I was going to say. Something about snakes."

"Come on you two," Shannon yelled.

"Oh, yeah," Ian laughed. "I just remembered what I was going to ask. What got you so interested in reptiles? Most women don't want to have anything to do with snakes."

"My father and I would take a lot of backpack trips together throughout Arizona and the southwest." Lorelei began to take pictures to see if anything unusual showed up.

"He taught me a lot about nature. Certain trees and plants and animals, including reptiles. He would point out different species and tell me what they were. So I took that knowledge and decided to volunteer at the zoo educating the public on reptiles and other animals."

"That's pretty awesome."

When she glanced over and smiled at him, she could have sworn she saw purple specks in his irises—tiny dots that seemed to dance as their eyes met. He slipped his bomber jacket off.

"What are you doing?" Lorelei asked. "It's getting cooler out here."

"Apparently not where he's standing." Shannon smiled as Ian folded up his jacket and placed it in his backpack.

"Here we are at the crime scene again," Shannon said. "Let me know if either of you experience or discover something unusual. Oh," she removed the thermal imaging camera from her bag and handed it to Ian. "I figure we might as well try this baby out. You and Lore can work together." Then she winked.

Ian handed the thermal imager to Lorelei. "What do you think? Want to give it a try?"

Lorelei trembled as she took the camera. For a second, she thought she would drop it.

"This is pretty interesting," Lorelei said. "The EMF and temperature pop up in the corner, though no unusual readings."

Lorelei walked along the finger-like rock where Melissa had seen the body. Or could it have been an apparition?

Ian followed her as she looked through the viewfinder. "Seeing any warm spots?"

"No, not yet. Earlier, right before I went to Shannon's car to visit the deputy, I did feel something unsettling. It was almost as if time had stopped. One second, the birds were singing, there was a slight breeze, and I heard insects and traffic. The next second, it had all stopped."

Lorelei handed the camera to Ian after a few minutes. He carefully scanned the area for audio or video evidence, while Lorelei scanned her environment with her senses.

Twenty minutes later Shannon yelled for Ian while he filmed with the IR camera. Lorelei looked over to see the agent holding up a knife-like object with her gloved hand. "Do you recognize this?"

Lorelei and Ian approached Shannon, kneeling next to a hole big enough for an average-sized human to fit through.

"Yeah," Ian leaned over, gawking at what looked like a letter opener. "That's a ceremonial knife. It's used for channeling energy to cast circles during rituals." He scrutinized the potential weapon. "And that's an elaborate one."

The head of a pewter cobra perched proudly atop the long,

thin blade. The fangs dripped venom and its tiny, evil eyes glinted red. Its slender body was wrapped around the remainder of the blade.

"Where did you find it?" Ian asked.

"Right there." Shannon indicated a spot by a Palo Verde tree, just outside the hole. "I can see why the deputies missed it. It was partially buried in the dirt with branches over it."

Ian suddenly got on his knees and crawled through the aperture Shannon had found.

"Wait, Ian what the hell are you doing?"

Shannon squeezed past the Palo Verde and into the opening after him. "Ian, Ian!" She glanced back, "Lore, hang back a minute. I want to see what he's getting himself into."

Shannon disappeared after Ian. Then Lorelei heard Ian yell, "Over here!"

Heck with this, I want to find out what's going on. Lorelei slid through the opening and ten feet along the side of a long boulder. Ian and Shannon were at the intersection of three massive boulders, creating a triangular shaped area.

"Look who's here to join the party." He glanced up from whatever he and Shannon had been focusing on.

"Damn it, Lore! I told you to stay behind. There could have been danger in here," Shannon said.

"The way Ian yelled for you didn't exactly sound like trouble. So I thought I would see what was in here."

Ian passed a dirty look at Shannon.

"The fun never stops on this ranch. Come take a look." He pointed to a crevice where two of the boulders joined. "Now look down."

"Oh wow. Is that a tunnel?" Lorelei asked.

"Looks that way," Shannon said. "We're going down."

"How did you know this was here?" Lorelei snapped a few photos of the triangular space and the passage.

"When I saw that knife right near the entrance to this place, I figured there might be something here. Covens and cults have a tendency to operate underground and in remote places. This whole area definitely has a bizarre energy they can draw upon for rituals."

"I'm going in." Shannon started climbing down into the hole. She took her walkie-talkie from her backpack and spoke into it. "Shannon to Dale, over."

"Hey Shannon, what's up?" Dale's voice crackled over the

radio.

"We found a hole that leads underground. All three of us are going down to check it out. I'll give you a shout if we find anything down here."

"This place keeps revealing more secrets" Dale said. "I'm in the restaurant setting up the equipment now. Melissa's keeping me company. And the sheriff himself stopped by to see how thing are going—mentioned that deputies would be out here patrolling from time to time."

"That's good. How's she doing?" Shannon asked.

"Okay. Still in shock. We're waiting for her friend to come get her horses. I told her it might be better to keep Bandit around to alert us of danger."

"Great. Take care of her. I'll be in touch within a few hours. Shannon out."

Distinct whispers emanated from the subterranean darkness. Lorelei knelt by the entrance, listening as Shannon climbed down on the built-in rungs.

"Lore," Ian said. "Are you okay?"

Lorelei snapped out of her reverie. "Oh, yeah, sorry. Shannon, are you hearing anything down there?"

"No, nothing."

"Turn your voice recorder on," Lorelei said. "I'm getting something, but I can't make out any words. Sounds like multiple voices."

"Okay," Shannon yelled. "Hurry up, so we can get this party started!"

"How about you go next?" Ian asked.

"Lore, be careful," Shannon yelled up. "A few of those rungs are a little loose."

The vertical descent suddenly became a mine shaft—she envisioned herself alone and at the bottom with a broken leg—in pitch darkness and in pain.

The fear of falling overwhelmed her.

"Definitely tunnels." Shannon shined her flashlight in either direction. "But we'll have to find out how extensive they are."

"Lore, go ahead and climb in," Ian said.

Easy for you to say.

"Lore, come on." Shannon shouted impatiently.

Ian grabbed Lorelei's hand as she was about to swing her leg into the entrance. He yelled down.

"Shannon, I'm coming down with Lore right now."

Ian's face was within an inch of her own. His musky smell and his beguiling gaze threatened to overtake her.

"Would you like me to go first?"

"No, I'll be all right." Lorelei's face became flushed as she took a deep breath in and back out.

She threw her leg over the side. Her foot settled on the third rung down.

"Don't be embarrassed, Lore," Ian said. "We all have phobias. You're not alone this time. Nothing will happen to you."

Her eyes flew open. *Does he know about my experience at the mine? But how?*

Shannon's voice came from below, sounding slightly more muffled. "Come on guys, hurry the hell up!"

"Okay, okay," Ian yelled. "Keep your damn pants on."

Then he gave Lorelei a smile that made her feel as if she really were falling. He laid a tender hand on her cheek. "You'll be okay. I promise."

She didn't understand why, but her fear dissipated and she started her descent. Her eyes never left his until she reached the floor of the passage.

"It's about damn time." Shannon took Lorelei's bag as she got closer to the bottom.

Ian jumped off the last few rungs right after Lorelei. As her flashlight penetrated the blackness ahead, a sudden sensation of familiarity overcame her. Yet she knew she had never been there.

Shannon pulled an electronic device out of her backpack. "Another gift from the FBI—a GPS unit. These normally don't work underground because the satellites can't pick up signals under the earth. For some reason, I'm getting readings. Maybe it will come in handy to determine where these passages might lead."

"Great idea." Lorelei leaned over to get a better look at the handheld device.

"The tunnel heads southeast." Shannon indicated the direction. "Or northwest in that direction." She pointed the other way without even looking. "Lore, are you getting any vibes on which way to go?"

Lorelei turned and headed southeast.

"Ian, keep that thermal imager going. Lore, are you on to

something?"

"I don't know—I think so. Nothing evil though. I don't know why, but I have this sense of déjà vu. I got it the moment I stepped off the ladder."

"We should be filming down here." Ian removed the handycam from his bag. "And we also need to watch EMF and temperature."

Shannon took the thermal imager from Ian. "You've had enough fun with this. I'll use it for a little while."

"I've got my Mel-Meter ready and my audio going." Lorelei patted her behind to show them the recorder that was snuggly inserted into her jean pocket. It helps me track what I'm going through to see if it matches up to actual evidence."

Ian's gaze lingered on Lorelei's butt for a few seconds. He glanced away when he caught her looking.

They had continued through the tunnels for ten minutes when Lorelei stopped in her tracks. Clopping echoed throughout the passages. The sound came closer. Within a few seconds, she could see a white mane and tan markings.

Then she detected an overwhelming sense of loneliness, accompanied by shock, terror and suffering.

"Are either of you seeing anything unusual twenty feet ahead? I'm getting a reading of 3.2 and a drop of five degrees, which makes sense considering what's happening."

Ian focused the camcorder in the direction of her gaze. "No, I'm not seeing anything."

"I'm getting a very warm spot on this thermal," Shannon said.

Lorelei moved closer to see a human-shaped red heat signature on the unit in Shannon's hand.

Ian leaned over next to her. "What the heck? It looks like someone on a horse."

As soon as his words left his lips, the FLIR shut down. Shannon tried to turn the IR camera back on.

"Well, that's pretty indicative of spirit activity—to have our equipment stop working," Ian said.

Ian and Shannon stared in the direction where the entity had appeared.

"Is it still there?" Ian asked.

"No, she vanished right after the IR camera stopped working."

"Did it communicate with you?" Ian asked.

"Sort of," Lorelei removed the leather jacket from her backpack and slipped it on to ward off the damp air. "It was a young woman—mid twenties maybe. She was stunning." She glanced back at Shannon and Ian. "Somehow she found her way down here on that horse and came across something she shouldn't have. As she disappeared in front of me, I heard a piercing scream."

Shannon glanced at Ian. "Maybe we caught what you heard on EVP."

Try as she might, tears welled up in her eyes. *No damn it! I don't want to do this!* She could sense that the beautiful woman suffered, even before her demise.

Ian removed a handkerchief from his back pocket and handed it to her.

"Thanks." She glanced away, not wanting to get too immersed in his eyes. "This is so hard sometimes. Especially when it's someone so young."

"I understand." Ian spoke so softly. His fingers brushed against hers lightly in an effort to console her.

If that's how his touch makes me feel, how would his lips feel?

Then he leaned down toward her face, his mouth lingering briefly near her cheek.

"Get a room guys." Shannon sidestepped past them both, her flashlight beam slicing the darkness in an attempt to reveal additional secrets.

Ever since Ian discovered the entrance to this place, he's been reading my mind. Or has he been able to do that all along?

Lorelei concentrated on keeping her thoughts clear so they couldn't be invaded. She gasped aloud when she kicked a solid object.

"What was that noise?" Ian asked.

"I don't know." Lorelei bent over to examine the object that slid unseen across the ground. "I think we'll need an evidence bag." She stepped to the side to let Shannon investigate.

"A cell phone." Shannon bent over with a gloved hand to pick it up. "There's no juice," she said, dropping the phone into the plastic bag. "Our analysts can use a flasher box to extract all the details including names and numbers, appointments, e-mails and messages."

Shannon cocked her ears. "Do you both hear that?"

"Sounds like dripping water," Lorelei said. "Let's go check it out."

A minute later they arrived at the threshold to a mammoth cave. The smooth, round tips of the stalactites gathered moisture gradually, each drip echoing throughout the chamber. Golden stalagmites, some a foot thick at the base, protruded from the ground of the limestone cave.

"Wow. This is pretty cool," Lorelei said. "Hard to imagine such a moist environment considering the dry ground above us. This reminds me of Kartchner Caverns or Colossal Cave."

Ian continued filming again. "There are all sorts of hidden secrets under the ranch—paranormal and otherwise."

"We'll have to find out if Melissa knows about any of this," Shannon said. "Makes me wonder how many access points there are, especially if that young phantom woman Lorelei saw really did get her horse down here."

Lorelei stood next to Shannon to look at the GPS. "Are we still on Melissa's property?"

"We've come two miles, and considering the direction we're heading, that should place us across the main road. Her property is only on the north side.

Lorelei was drawn to the left side of the cave. A formation two feet tall looked like the bottom of a melting snowman, with an over easy egg sitting on top. The almost golden hues of the fried egg formation blended perfectly with the glinting earth tones of the cavern itself.

"I'm getting hungry for breakfast." The agent pointed upwards to a thin drapery-like sheet of orange and brown alternating bands which created an oversized strip of what looked like bacon.

"How tall do you think the ceiling is?" Lorelei gazed up to see they weren't alone. Part of the ceiling moved.

"At least twenty feet," Ian said. "I hope neither of you are skittish about bats.

"What?" Shannon shined her flashlight upward.

"Get down." Ian pushed them both to the ground as hundreds of Mexican free-tailed bats descended from their roosts.

"Oh, shit!" Lorelei flung her arms and hands over her head. Her left hand met a tough, leathery wing and part of a furry rat-like body. She glanced over to see Shannon screaming and swiping repeatedly in an attempt to remove a smaller bat that had embedded itself in her thick hair.

"Stop screaming," Lorelei said. "You're scaring it even more, and creating more havoc in here!" She crawled on her knees to help Shannon remove the terrified creature. Holding Shannon's hair down at the top, she placed her hand underneath the bat's belly and lifted, hoping to free it. But instead, it gave it the incentive to fly away with a chunk of the agent's hair. As if to thank her, the solid black bat hung facing Lorelei for a few seconds, then followed the rest of the mass into another hole in the back of the cave.

"Thanks, Lore," Shannon said in a condescending manner. "That fucking thing is going to build a nest with my hair!"

"Stop it, Shannon," Ian said. "It was your panic that caused the ruckus to begin with. And she got the bat out of your hair didn't she?"

Shannon let out a sigh and continued to massage the spot on the right side of her head. "Sorry Lore. Thanks for helping."

How can an FBI agent face drug lords, murderers and other hardcore criminals, yet be terrified of everything that moves?

Ian snickered.

"I hate to say this Shannon." Ian stood up and stared toward where the bats had disappeared. "But we need to follow them."

"I know, I know. I was watching them when they flew into that hole. If there's that many of them, it's got to be more than a small opening." Shannon got off of her knees and with her beam facing downward this time approached the aperture. "I can't believe I'm about to do this," she muttered. "Oh well, maybe I'll find my clump of hair."

Shannon climbed into the two foot tall by three foot wide opening.

"I'm right behind you," Ian said.

"Don't bother yet. There's nowhere to turn around in here. I'll give you a shout."

Lorelei waited anxiously, hoping her friend wouldn't come across the bats again. Or something much worse.

A few minutes later, Shannon's voice bounced off the stone walls. "Guys, come on! It's another passage that heads straight north. That must be where they went. Be careful. It's a little cramped at first, but it gradually opens up to another tunnel."

"I'll go first," Ian said. "Just in case I run across anything unpleasant."

Lorelei watched him place his handycam in his bag and slide it through the opening. As he climbed in, she made sure all of her ghost hunting gear was positioned securely in her backpack.

It was only the team's first day on the investigation, and they had already witnessed an attack on a defenseless animal, had found a series of underground passages, and discovered the spirit of a young woman in the tunnels. And for some reason, Ian was now able to read her thoughts.

Something told Lorelei this was the easy part of their adventure. Taking a deep breath, she started in after Ian.

CHAPTER EIGHT

"This is Dale entering room five at 7:10 p.m." He spoke into his audio recorder and pushed open the eighty year old door with the antique silver handle. "The creaking is the door, nothing paranormal," he said into the recorder.

Dale set his KII Meter, Trifield EMF meter, and laser temperature probe on the table so that he could monitor all of them at once. Then he removed his digital camera and the thermal imaging camera from his case."

"Don't worry, baby," he said to the thermal device. "I'll be with you in a minute." Then he began to snap pictures of the bedroom.

"Wow. It's getting warm in here," he mumbled, lifting his shirt away from his body. Placing the camera on the table, he picked up the temperature probe. "Shit! Eighty-six degrees with an EMF of 3.1? How can it be this hot when it's in the low fifties outside?" He walked around the room to see if the temperature fluctuated.

"Who's here with me?" Dale asked to whatever had caused the unusual readings. "Are you the person that's been heard walking around in some of the rooms?" The lights on the KII EMF Meter flashed all the way to red.

"If you are here, I'll be able to see you with this special piece of equipment." Dale picked up the thermal imaging camera. "But feel free to talk to me as well, so that I can hear you through my recorder."

Panning the bedroom first with the IR camera, he didn't see any warm spots that might indicate something paranormal. *Feels like the temperature is dropping back down*. The probe showed that the room was cooling back down to the baseline reading of sixty-five degrees.

"I'm going to sit on the bed now." Dale patted the comforter. "You can sit beside me."

Dale looked through the thermal camera at an orange-colored outline sitting next to him. He slowly turned in the direction of the apparition and lowered the IR camera. He couldn't see anything.

"Who's here with me? Are you the original owner of the ranch?" Right after he asked the question he flinched. "Ouch! What the fuck?" He rubbed his right cheek and got up to look in the mirror. A bright red handprint showed on his face. "What did you do that for?" He picked up the IR camera again, but didn't see the figure.

He started taking pictures when he heard a car's tires crunching over gravel, and looked out the window to see a sheriff's deputy pull up.

He walked outside to greet the man. "Can I help you?" Dale asked.

"Hi there. I'm Sergeant Jensen." He shook hands with Dale. "Is Agent Flynn around?"

"No. She's out roaming the property with a few investigators. "I'm Dale Sullivan, one of the investigators that's been assigned by the FBI."

"I tried calling her on her cell, but wasn't able to get through. We've had another report from two tourists that were driving down Dragoon Road. They saw a wolfman and a prehistoric bird—within seconds of each other." The sergeant glanced around as if expecting something to jump out of the mesquite trees. "Activity is picking up. And fast."

This is the most bizarre case I've ever encountered. A mysterious dead body that turns out to be a possible apparition. Terrifying creatures taking over a peaceful, small town. Could these have anything to do with Armageddon?

"I'll let Shannon know," Dale said. "Were these people injured?"

"No, just scared out of their wits. I escorted them back to Interstate ten." He paused, listening to another call that had come through on the car radio. "

"Sounds like more trouble," the sergeant said. "Hopefully, something simple like old Mike getting drunk and stealing chickens again." He shook his head. "God, how I long for those boring days again." Then he got back into his cruiser and left.

Dale wondered what he had gotten himself into, and if he would be placing his own family in danger by getting involved in such a dangerous case.

***

Dale sat in the living area of room five again to see if whatever had slapped him before would show itself again. Hearing a barking at the door, he opened it to see Bandit standing there wagging his tail. "Hey there, boy!" He ruffled the dog's black and white neck, until he rolled over, wanting Dale to rub his tummy.

"I'm on official duty right now," he said to the animal that now stood on all fours again. "Come on inside."

Bandit wouldn't budge. He stared into the room with his ears cocked. Then the hairs on his back stood straight up and he started to growl. A menacing sound that made Dale very uncomfortable.

"What's the matter boy?" Dale gazed into the room, but didn't see anything. "Something's still here, huh?"

When the investigator turned back around the dog was gone.

"That was weird," he said aloud. "Well, I'd better call Shannon and let her know about Jensen's latest report."

"Dale to Shannon, can you read me? Shannon, are you there?" He paused, his ear close to the speaker. "Damn." Picking up his cell phone, he called the agent's number. "Shannon, I tried to contact you on the walkie-talkie, but I guess you couldn't hear me underground. Hope you're all safe. Listen, we've had another incident with the shapeshifters, or whatever they might be, off of Dragoon Road—a mile or so from here. Though this encounter was a little different than the rest. I'm in room five now investigating some major activity that's been going on. I'll catch up with you all soon."

Dale jumped when the loud screeching of the motion sensors inside the Wagon Wheel Restaurant went off. Heart racing, he grabbed the IR camera and ran out of the room.

He raced up the stairs and in the dining room in time to witness multicolored lights zipping back and forth in the bar area, leaving iridescent trails of pink, blue and yellow. To Dale, it seemed as if they were playing a game, flying through and around the stagecoach behind the bar. "Holy crap." He ran through the dining area and across the footbridge and trickling stream. But the anomalies had vanished.

He picked up the audio recorder he had set on the bar. "What the hell?" The door to the battery compartment had been removed. The triple A's were missing. He looked down to see if the batteries had fallen on the floor or behind the bar, but couldn't find them. So he opened up the equipment case and grabbed a few more, inserted them and checked the unit.

"Who, or what, is here? Were you one of those lights I just saw?"

Dale snapped his head to the corner of the room when he heard something dragging across the floor. Flashlight in hand, he darted the beam around the room, and then stopped where the camera and tripod were now sitting. The equipment had moved a few feet from the taped X in the corner where he had originally placed them. "Okay, who's in here?" He received no audible response. "Why are you messing with my equipment?"

He moved the tripod and video recorder back into position and checked the settings. *Crap, this damn thing stopped half an hour ago.* Rewinding the video, Dale saw one of the light anomalies change into a blue mist. It floated in front of the camcorder, as if checking the equipment out. Dale continued to watch as the vaporous oddity darkened in color then vanished. "Amazing." Mesmerized, he replayed the scene a few times.

"How many of you are here?" Dale glanced toward the cellar. *Could whatever was in here have gone in there?*

He opened the door and started down the stairs. "Hello?" he yelled, but didn't hear anything. He went down a few more stairs, but didn't see the mysterious lights. Dale turned and went back upstairs. When he walked into the saloon, the lid to the equipment case had been closed, and the camera and tripod moved again.

"Oh come on." Dale moved it back into position for a second time. "You obviously want to play. I'm here now and would love for you to tell me about yourself. Feel free to talk out loud. Or find another way to communicate. I want to know who messed with our equipment and why. I'm going to stay here and make sure you don't do it again."

Dale sat at the bar for a few minutes. No more disturbances had occurred. "Come on. You're strong enough to move my camera and tripod, show me you have the balls to let me know you're here." He removed his digital camera, then walked around taking pictures of the saloon and restaurant.

After he finished taking shots of every section in the building, Dale grabbed the thermal imaging camera. *Oh wow. Wait a minute. Is that a person sitting in the stagecoach behind the bar?* The viewfinder revealed a dark orange human figure surrounded by yellow, staring at Dale.

The apparition's profile was of a woman in eighteen-hundreds clothing with very long hair and a hat tied down with ribbon. "Were you in an accident in that coach?" he asked. He lowered the camera, but couldn't see the spirit with his eyes.

He turned back to look through the camera. "Can you tell me what those lights were?"

Staring into the thermal's viewfinder, Dale caught a number that popped up in the middle, then ended up in the lower left corner. The EMF reading indicated 4.0 mG.

"This is so cool."

Walking cautiously over to the side of the coach, he reached in and felt a distinct cold spot. The spirit's form faded from view.

CHAPTER NINE

Shannon's flashlight lit up the craggy, earthen walls. Brownish-red stick figures, charcoal geometric designs, and a spiral shape of stars and nebulae wound outwards from a thicker, central bulge of stars.

"What are you looking at?" Ian asked.

"Looks like a rough drawing of the Galaxy," Shannon said, studying the image. "And I assume those nine round pictures are the planets—especially since that yellowish one has a circle around it."

Lorelei stared intently at the human shapes lying down under the representation of the solar system. Interspersed within the mass of stars were other stick-like figures.

"I wonder what that's supposed to represent," Shannon said.

"Astral travel." Ian and Lorelei said at the same time. Shannon gave them both a bewildered stare. But they didn't notice. They were too busy gazing into each other's eyes.

Ian managed to tear his eyes away from Lorelei. "Yeah, the figures lying down under the stars represent their physical bodies. The more abstract shapes within the solar system must be their astral bodies, since they're lighter in form."

Lorelei traced the stars and planets with her fingers, running them down in a straight line to the waiting horizontal figures on the earthly plane.

"Lore?" Shannon touched her shoulder. "Are you getting something?"

"Sort of. I had a very strong sense of déjà vu when we first arrived. And coming down into the tunnels, it was like I was coming home again. Now, it's even more intense." Lorelei turned toward Shannon. "I know that doesn't make sense. I don't know anyone here. But still . . . it feels safe somehow."

Lorelei pulled out her camera and took pictures of the ancient graphics.

"Ian, keep filming," Shannon said. "I want to see if we get any evidence, especially since these cave-like drawings weren't in the other passages. Maybe Lore's picking up on the tribe that used to live here."

Shannon glanced down at the handheld GPS unit. "Looks like this passage heads straight north, back toward the ranch."

The tunnel floor started sloping and a thin layer of moisture made the ground treacherous. "Guys, be careful. We're still going downhill and it's…" Before Shannon could finish the sentence, Lorelei's feet slipped out from under her and she fell on her back.

"Lore," Ian yelled. Ian took her hands and helped her up. "Is anything hurt?"

"I don't think so," Lorelei said. "My leather jacket absorbed some of the impact. How come I'm the one who always has to fall?"

"Oh shit. Lore, you're wet." Shannon ran her hand over the back of her jacket. She could hear her Lorelei's teeth chattering. "Did something push you?"

"No, I slipped. Fortunately, I came well prepared. I have a change of clothes and a towel in my backpack.

"Here, take my jacket and get warm for a few minutes," Ian said. "Yours is too wet." He took Lorelei's jacket off and draped his dry one over her shoulders.

"Thanks." Lorelei said.

Shannon rubbed Lorelei's shoulders and arms to warm her up. "I'll keep the flashlight on you while you get changed. Ian, I know it's tempting, but you'll have to turn your back."

"I don't know." He winked at Lorelei. "I think she might need some help. She is a little shaky."

Shannon rolled her eyes and watched Ian walk ahead of them as Lorelei took off her wet shirt.

"Are you sure you're okay, Lore?" Shannon patted her dry with the towel.

"Cold is all. I've been in worse situations than this." She quickly put her dry, long-sleeve shirt on.

"We can always head back."

"Shannon, I told you I'm fine."

"You're freezing and you don't have a jacket."

"She does now," Ian yelled from the darkness. "I'm giving her mine."

The chemistry between these two is unbelievable. Both intelligent, creative entrepreneurs. But there's something else I can't place my finger on.

"Thanks for the help, Shannon." She draped Ian's jacket over her shoulders. "I'm feeling better."

"But you're still trembling. It's fifty-five degrees down here."

Ian walked up to Lorelei and facing her, placed his hands on her shoulders. "She'll be fine soon."

He rubbed Lorelei's shoulders as he gazed into her eyes. But the next thing Shannon saw made her stop breathing. As they continued staring into each other's eyes, a mysterious glow surrounded them both. Pink light radiated from Ian's hands and the top of his head. The light became brighter with each passing second. Then Lorelei's hair turned a strawberry blonde, and a transparent red field emanated from Lorelei, extending from every part of her body.

Shannon slowly brought the thermal camera up to eye level so as not to disturb what was happening. She gasped as she saw the energy fields picked up by the IR camera. Brilliant rainbow displays originated from Lorelei and Ian—exploding yellow, orange, purple and blue.

Shannon didn't fully understand what was happening. She wondered if Ian were somehow manifesting the strange occurrence. Intuition told her they were both responsible. Was she witnessing physical evidence of the chemistry between them?

The longer Ian stared into Lorelei's eyes, the more she relaxed. Her jaw ceased quaking and her breathing became less labored.

Shannon stood completely still for what seemed like an eternity. As suddenly as it began, it was over.

"Wow! I feel amazing," Lorelei said. "How do you . . ."

"It's nothing—all in the hands." Ian picked up his backpack and Lorelei's and continued walking.

Lorelei followed behind him as if nothing had happened.

Shannon watched them both, shaking her head in confusion. "There's something big happening," she whispered. "And I have a feeling those two will be right in the middle."

CHAPTER TEN

Lorelei cocked her head and stood back while Shannon and Ian headed further into the darkness. "Did either of you hear that?" Lorelei asked as they all continued to wander through the underground passages. "It sounded like another language."

"No." Ian pulled his voice recorder out of his back jean pocket.

"Shannon, did you hear it?" Lorelei asked.

"No." She snapped some photos to see if she could capture evidence. "Perhaps we have a visitor."

"More than one," Lorelei whispered. She couldn't explain it, but somehow these unintelligible voices thought she was someone else. The only word she could understand was "Annie."

"Ian, are you seeing anything through the thermal?" Shannon asked.

"Nada. We'll see if your video shows anything unusual."

Ian glanced at his Tri-Field meter. "EMF says 1.6, feels like there was a slight temperature drop."

"I've contacted Joe Luna—he's the Native American shaman I mentioned. If you are hearing another language, he might be able to help identify it."

Lorelei placed her left hand quickly to her face as soft silky threads tickled her cheek. Using her flashlight, she looked around the tunnel for any movement. Then she gasped, and rubbed her left arm. *This feels like cobwebs*. She watched Shannon and Ian swipe at the invisible filaments.

"Shit. My EMF jumped all the way to 5.2." Ian turned in a complete three sixty, trying to see what was harassing them all. "Shannon, are you registering any hot spots?"

"Damn it!" She slapped and swiped repeatedly. "I can't even hold the thermal up to see anything."

"They're all around us," Lorelei said. "They're curious."

"What?" Shannon yelled. "Who's 'curious?'"

"The ancient ones," Lorelei whispered. She had ceased trying to rid herself of the cobweb-like sensation, and stood still. At that moment, all of their equipment stopped working, the batteries drained. All three were in total darkness.

"Feels like ectoplasm," Shannon said. "I had a very similar experience at an eleventh century castle in Ireland. But that incident only involved my arm and lasted a few seconds. This is much worse. This whole place seems alive with energy."

High-pitched humming reverberated all around them. They dropped their bags and backpacks, and put their hands over their ears for a few seconds.

The mysterious solar system drawings, the feeling of familiarity, and now the faint whispers of a foreign language…though Lorelei only spoke English, she somehow understood what they were trying to tell her.

"It's her," they kept saying excitedly.

Lorelei realized one thing—this was a celebration for her homecoming.

CHAPTER ELEVEN

Shards from a broken bulb in the cellar of the Wagon Wheel crunched under Dale's feet. A musty, moldy odor overwhelmed him. Looking up with his flashlight, he saw bare wooden beams and plumbing pipes diseased with large spots of fuzzy pea-green fungus. "Well there's moisture from somewhere," he said. "And breathing this stuff in can't be healthy, could even cause hallucinations."

His portable weather unit detected seventy-three percent humidity. Dale knew mold was capable of growing from sixty-five to ninety-nine percent.

He did a swift complete turn when an old barstool in the corner suddenly fell over. He tested the ground with his foot. "What the heck? The surface is pretty even—how did this happen?" His beam bounced from the stairs to the corners of the cellar. Placing the round stool upright, he made sure the metal legs were all level and that the chair rested firmly on the ground.

Dale sat down on the torn, tan colored upholstery. *Well it's not wobbling at all. And it's getting a little warmer.* As he looked, the temperature read seventy-five degrees with an EMF spike to 1.5 mG.

"Is there someone here with me?" Dale stayed in the same corner for twenty minutes, eyeing the dust-covered bottles in the wine rack against the wall, three fifteen-gallon round kegs of beer lined up against the cement block wall, and a huge black widow spider that disappeared into a crevice when Dale's light passed over it.

"Are you the one that messed with our equipment?" Dale walked up and down the length of the cellar, stretching his legs. That's when he heard it.

"What the hell." He cocked his right ear to better hear the strange humming sound. *That sounds like a swarm of bees.* Dale knelt down. *Feels like the cement floor is vibrating.* He quickly grabbed the Mel-Meter and placed it against the cold, cement floor. "Holy Shit! This damn thing maxed out to 50 mG. I almost forgot it read that high."

A few minutes later, the vibrations stopped. Dale got up and glimpsed something silver under the stairs. He hadn't seen the object before because it was hidden behind one of the kegs. "A tin box." It loosened itself from between the wooden beams after a few tugs.

The metal box emitted a single squeak of protest as the lid lifted. Scratched and dented, it opened to reveal a crinkled, yellowed newspaper article directly on top. Dale picked it up and unfolded it. "TRAGEDY AT TEXAS CANYON RANCH," was the headline and it was dated March 11th, 1940.

> *Annie and Jeff O'Shea, owners of the Texas Canyon Retreat in Dragoon, have mysteriously disappeared as of Friday, March 10th. The hired maintenance man stated he was tending to some odd jobs on the property, arriving back at their living quarters at 8:45 p.m., the day he was to be paid. But he couldn't find Annie or Jeff.*
>
> *There is still no sign of Annie or Jeff after an extensive search by neighbors, friends and the Cochise County Sheriff's Department. The maintenance man, Matt Weinart, made the following statement: "We just don't understand what could have happened. Annie and Jeff have lived out here for about seven or eight years and knew this place as well as they knew each other. It's so hard to believe something could have happened. We are all just hoping and praying that they will be found soon. Those two were so in love."*
>
> *The Cochise County Sheriff's Department is in the process of talking to local residents, family, and ranch employees.*

"Wow, I wonder if Melissa is aware of this history." The picture of the couple was too grainy to make out.

Placing the newspaper article on a shelf and digging through the metal container, he discovered a half burned votive candle and two four-inch tall wooden statues buried in smooth, round stones. "What the hell are these?" He removed the carved figures, inspecting them meticulously. He noticed a woman with long thin, curved etches for hair. The male was carved with very short hair and wire-framed glasses.

Placing the idols back in the box, he noticed the five palm-sized stones, all had the very same marking—a single, horizontal line with two slanted lines on either end.

Then he saw another carved symbol on the opposite side of the stones—insignias unique to each, made out of triangles.

I'll have to see if Ian is familiar with any of these signs. The hairs on Dale's arms stood up and he shuddered as a frigid blast of air blew by. Turning quickly around, he could see nothing. Yet he felt like he was being watched. He placed the stones and idols back in the container and closed the lid. The temperature in the room returned to normal and whatever presence had been in the cellar seemed to vanish.

CHAPTER TWELVE

Lorelei, Ian and Shannon had run into a brick wall. Literally. Their flashlights revealed various sized, reddish, flatter stones cemented with clay.

Shannon's flashlight flickered on and off three times, then went out. "Oh great." Shannon smacked it against her hand. "I just replaced the damn batteries this afternoon."

This is, or was, their home. Lorelei gently ran her right hand along the surface, where Ian's beam spotlighted. "Indian ruins." Then her eyes scanned upwards and she guided Ian's hand with his flashlight. "Look, there's an old wooden ladder about ten feet up in that doorway."

"Hey, those look like ventilation holes," Ian said. He scanned his light twenty feet up. "Engineered for rooms where there's a fire pit—you can see they're in a horizontal line."

"Yes, I recognize them from other sites I've visited," Lorelei said. She didn't comprehend how she knew. But Lorelei realized this place represented so much more than history. It was her past.

"Follow me," Lorelei said. Then she started climbing up the ruins, using the protruding bricks as support.

"Lore, wait." Shannon shouted. But she didn't stop. Five minutes later, she pulled herself into a room where the cave wall extended over to meet the opposite manmade stone and mortar wall, which formed a triangular doorway. Collapsed wooden beams, used at one time as a roof, now threatened to topple down onto the blackened dirt floor.

Lorelei helped Shannon, then Ian up into the structure.

Lorelei ran her finger over a large black smudge covering the cave wall, indicating soot from a fire pit. Then she proceeded through the open, triangular doorway.

"Jeff and Annie O'Shea," she said. "They were more than land owners. I'm getting a strong tie to this place for them."

Lorelei looked down into the valley below at five monstrous granite monoliths lined up in a half circle.

"Watch your eyes." Shannon snapped a few photos of the ruins they were in and the unusual formations.

Lorelei noticed the flash on her own camera enhanced the whiteness of the rocks, creating an eerie glow.

"No way," Shannon said. "This can't be."

"What?" Ian asked.

She showed Lorelei and Ian the digital image of the five mysterious monoliths—all were highly distorted on the viewfinder.

"You did focus on the right thing?" Lorelei asked.

Shannon sighed and looked at her like she were nuts. "Of course. You can clearly see the five rocks. And I didn't move when I took the picture." Shannon pointed at the granite fence-like barrier on the screen. "They seem just as they are now. But watch." She snapped another picture.

"That's weird." Ian took the camera from her. "They're all misshapen. And you weren't shaking when you took the picture."

"And none of my other pics have come out like that."

"I wonder if anyone knows about this place?" Ian removed a bottle of water from his bag. "I can see why people might not know about these passages. But this is such an open place."

Open, but with a secret so hidden . . . until recently. Now they're in danger – and so is everyone else.

Lorelei wandered down into the valley below. Rocks, boulders and debris that normally would have tripped her, were only objects. Though she had her flashlight, she didn't use it. She heard Ian and Shannon scurrying after her.

"Lore," Ian said. "Can you tell me why I'm getting a reading of 4.5? You seem to know you're way around out here."

"They're all still here," she responded. "Afraid to leave." Hundreds of voices spoke to her at once." Though she couldn't distinguish what they were saying, she realized things weren't the same—the ancient ones had a threat to deal with. Something, or someone, was attempting to take over their land.

She couldn't take her eyes off of the Stonehenge-like formations. She reached up to touch a symbol embedded into the rock—a six inch horizontal line with two one-inch slanted line on either end.

"Holy crap." Ian said. "That's a travel rune you're seeing. It's one of many symbols Wiccans use for prayers and rituals. This one is used for those who wish to represent safe travel, whether that is the physical, or another plane."

Shannon stared at the monolith next to hers.

"Which sign are you referring to? I'm seeing two."

Glancing further down the boulder, Lorelei noticed another mark. "These weren't here before."

Shannon leaned in closer to see the marking. "You're right. They do look newer than the travel runes." She glanced over at Lorelei. "How did you know?"

Lorelei walked from one stone pillar to another, looking at the signs on the bottom of each. "There's a different symbol on each of the five."

"Yeah, you're right." Ian said. "The travel rune is the horizontal line at the top with the two shorter lines at either end. It appears that they are at the same level on all the rocks. The lower markings are distinct on each one, but I have no idea what they represent. They do all incorporate triangles."

"What's with these damn triangles?" Shannon asked. "Did you both notice that where we entered that first tunnel was a triangular shape? And that doorway up there." She pointed back toward the ruin. "And now this?" She leaned down, indicating the two small triangles on top of a half moon shape. "Ian, is there some sort of significance cult wise?"

"The pentagram, or pentacle, represents a star, however, the shape of the pentagram does sort of look like five triangles in a circular formation. Not sure if that has significance here." Ian stared at the monolith in front of him.

"What the hell?" Shannon said. "These boulders are red on the thermal. Come see this."

Ian and Lorelei stood on either side of Shannon, gazing at the screen, the bright red heat signature reflecting off of the granite monuments.

"They're cool to the touch." Lorelei placed her hand on the center stone. Glancing down at the glowing green display on the Mel-Meter, she saw a temperature of twenty degrees, even though the baseline reading for this November night was forty-five. She started to shiver uncontrollably and backed ten feet away. But the freezing temperature followed her. Frost escaped from her lips as she gazed at the mystical formation.

How can these be showing as warm spots on the thermal? Especially when the readings are just the opposite.

"Well, I think we should try and find a way back to the ranch," Shannon said. "It's past 8:00 p.m., and it might take a few hours to get back."

Shannon looked at Lorelei. "Are you warm enough?"

"Yeah, I'm fine." Though she was still confused about Ian's recent ability to read her thoughts and her discovery of a race she was strongly tied to.

"Listen," Shannon said, "Something really strange is happening with the two of you. I'm not sure what it is but. . . "

Ian looked over at Lorelei, and then down at the bear grass and rocks beneath his feet. "I'm so sorry, Lore," he whispered. "If I could stop reading your mind I would. Hopefully, we'll get this case wrapped up quickly and get the hell away from here. It only began right before we went underground."

"Before what began?" Shannon asked.

"I don't know how, but Ian is able to read my thoughts," Lorelei said. "He knew I was afraid to descend on that ladder. And he probably knows about the fall I had in a mine shaft a few years ago. I fell while hiking and I ended up spending the night there before anyone found me. Guess that's why I was hesitant about going underground."

"First of all, that must have been horrifying." Shannon said. "I'm sorry you went through that. I wish you would have told me. I would have been a little more patient."

"It's okay. I think being involved in the paranormal has actually helped me overcome my fear of the unknown. I didn't want either of you thinking I was afraid."

"Newsflash, Lore," Ian said. "We're all afraid at one time or another, and considering what you went through, I'd say you had damn good reason. And trust me, I don't like being able to invade someone's mind—it's like you don't have any privacy."

"I know it's not intentional," Lorelei said. "We'll have to see if it keeps happening when we're not together."

"Telepathy or not," Shannon said. "You both have major chemistry between the two of you." She patted Ian on the butt and jabbed Lorelei lightly with her elbow.

"Shannon, you definitely should get laid," Ian said, laughing. "Give that boyfriend of yours a shout."

Shannon's flirtatious smile vanished and she walked ahead at a faster pace.

Lorelei whispered to Ian, "He broke up with her." Ian smacked his forehead with the palm of his hand and whispered, "Crap, I have such a big mouth sometimes."

Glancing over at him, knowing he could read her thoughts, *yes, yes you do Mr. Magic.* Then smiled teasingly. Ian's sensuous mouth turned upward slightly and he playfully pushed her shoulder.

As they left the ruins, Lorelei wondered why she hadn't revealed what else happened on that January day in 2009—the night in the mine shaft that led to her first and only out of body experience.

Afterwards, the man that found her said, "It was so strange. I was sitting around the campfire last night around 9:00 p.m. It was as if something told me to come to that spot. I even had an exact image of the place."

That's when she knew she hadn't merely left her physical form. She had managed to communicate her plight to a complete stranger.

"Stop!" Ian screamed. He had stretched both hands out wide so that Lorelei and Shannon could not go any farther. Shining her flashlight, Lorelei looked straight down into a large chasm they had almost walked into. Their gaze followed the length of the mini canyon. The deep arroyo stretched from where they stood to the back of the ruins, to the other side of the valley and behind the five monuments.

"We're surrounded," Lorelei said. "This is an island."

CHAPTER THIRTEEN

"What are you still doing up?" Shannon asked. Melissa approached her, Ian and Lorelei as they arrived back at the ranch at 10:00 p.m. The dark circles, her unkempt hair and her tired, red eyes were just the beginning.

"Are you kidding? A disappearing body, a fucking wolf creature, a horrible, invisible monster kills my damn horse, and who knows what else is on my property. How could I possibly sleep?"

Shannon glanced over at Ian and Lorelei. *How is this woman going to react to all this other stuff we found?* Shannon wondered.

Melissa sighed. "I can see from that look you all just passed each other, that there's something else. Dale told me you found an entrance to some tunnels. Is there a cave under my property?"

"It's much more than that, though I'm not sure it's a bad thing. Were you aware you had passages and caves on part of your land?"

"No. I've never seen any indication, and haven't heard about such a thing from anyone in the area."

"I'm not sure anyone else would know either." Shannon yawned. "The entrance we found was almost impossible to discover. I think we should all turn in for the night. But we do have some stuff to discuss."

Shannon looked at Dale. "I did get your voice mail about the latest incident with the wolfman and dinosaur. The sergeant left a message as well. These sightings might have something to do with some of our other discoveries from the adventure tonight."

Melissa began to turn away. "I'll catch you in the morning. I was thinking we could head over to Bisbee for breakfast at 8:00. Don't have much of an appetite, but I really need to get away from this place, even if only for a few hours."

"Melissa, maybe you should room with Lore and I tonight."

"No, I'll be okay. Dale said he would crash on my couch in the living room."

"Good idea," Shannon said.

"Dale, do you need any help with the equipment?" Ian asked.

"No, thanks man. I'm going to leave the equipment setup overnight. I've already experienced some interesting stuff."

"Glad you said that because I'm pretty damn tired anyways. I'm heading off to bed. Good night." Ian glanced back at Lorelei.

"Night, Ian. Thanks for the help today." Shannon waved as he headed to his room. She turned to see that Melissa had already started walking back to her living quarters.

Shannon looked at Dale. "Don't ask. Melissa's going to have a lot more to deal with. You, Ian, Lore and I will meet in the courtyard at 7:30 tomorrow morning so we can fill you in on what we've found."

"Sounds good," Dale said. He pulled out his cell phone. "See you all then. I better call my wife and let her know I'm okay."

Shannon couldn't help but wonder what else awaited—above ground, below ground, and between Lorelei and Ian.

CHAPTER FOURTEEN

The scent of bacon, eggs, waffles and biscuits wafted throughout the quiet streets of Bisbee, Arizona, artist colony and retirement community. Lorelei gazed at the steep hillside dotted with restored Victorian and European homes. "Melissa, I know this was a mining town, but do you know when it was first founded?"

Lorelei, Ian, Shannon, Dale and Melissa walked into the restaurant.

"It was in eighteen eighty – named after Judge DeWitt Bisbee, financial backer of the Copper Queen Mine. It was proved to be one of the richest mineral sites in the world, producing nearly three million ounces of gold and more than eight billion pounds of copper. By the early nineteen hundreds, Bisbee was the largest city between St. Louis and San Francisco with a population of over twenty thousand. The town was considered a rather cultural hub with the state's first community library and a popular opera house."

"Pretty impressive there Melissa." Lorelei glanced around the busy restaurant. The walls of the soda fountain style diner were covered with pictures of the now inactive mine. Old pickaxes rested on nails between some of the photos as a reminder of the arduous labor. A long counter with bar stools was on the right-hand side and old-fashioned ice cream makers adorned the shelves.

"Yeah well, you don't live in such a historic part of Arizona without learning a lot about the past, and what led to Arizona's present. If I can find the time, I'd love to volunteer as a historian or docent."

Melissa sighed. "It's nice to be served for once. I'm so busy between administrative stuff, cleaning rooms, maintenance and helping out in the Wagon Wheel." They sat down at a table by the window.

Shannon took a drink of water as the waitress arrived to take their orders. After she left, she glanced furtively around to make sure no one was listening. "Melissa, as I mentioned briefly last night, we found an access point to some passages and a large cave. The first passage was uneventful, though it did lead to a rather impressive cavern, what you would call a wet cave with some stunning formations."

"Really? I want to check that out. All the years I've lived here, and I've never heard of anything like this being on the property."

"Well I'm not so sure it's all on your land," Shannon said. "I've got GPS measurements, and it appears that these passages crossed Dragoon Road at one point."

"Then that's not my land. I'm only on the north side. But you mentioned 'the first passage.' That implies another one."

"You got it. When we were inside the cave, we inadvertently found another passage. And you couldn't even tell what it was at first. We all had to crawl through a tight hole which opened up into a larger area."

"That's not all," Shannon continued. "There's some unbelievable energy flowing through those things, and that could be contributing to the problems the community is having. But we don't think the passages are the reason for this energy. We believe it could be the Indian ruins and Stonehenge-like formations."

Melissa's tired eyes sparkled for a second. She sat there stunned. "I don't know what to say. I knew this was an awesome place when I moved here, but I had no idea. Have any of you contacted the local universities, or the archaeological society to see if they're aware of any of this?"

Lorelei noticed an attractive group of women a few tables away, staring intently at Ian and snickering. "We haven't exactly had a chance." She glanced over at the women, rolling her eyes. Ian didn't seem to notice the attention. "That passage from the cave headed straight north—they ran right into the Indian ruins. The pueblo looked down on a valley with some bizarre rock formations. Sort of like Stonehenge I guess you could say. Not that type of stone, or in that placement, but they definitely seem like they were put there for a reason since they were in a half moon formation. This place is only accessible through the tunnels. We didn't get to the area until it was dark, but there was a deep chasm surrounding the ruins and monoliths. So I'm not sure too many other people would know about the site."

Lorelei took Melissa's hand. "I know this is all overwhelming. We came here to help with the body you found and these terrifying monsters. Instead we announce there's more to the puzzle. But I don't think the cave, tunnels and ruins are negative. The energy Shannon mentioned could be feeding these creatures.

"Where do you think they came from?" Melissa took a small bite of toast. "And what else, or who else, are they going to harm?"

"Unfortunately, we have more questions than answers," Shannon said. "

Dale stabbed his fork into a ham, cheese and hash brown omelet. "Sergeant Jensen said the latest witnesses saw a prehistoric bird that flew right in front of their vehicle and a wolf-like creature. Either there were two creatures in the same spot that appeared one right after the other, or this freaking thing transformed very rapidly."

"That is rather odd," Ian said. "I've never heard of a shapeshifter transforming in such a manner. I've placed a call to Joe Luna, and he's able to make it out here. He should be here later this afternoon. Joe's a Navajo shaman himself and is very well known throughout the four corners."

The four women continued to stare at Ian. Then they would glance over at Lorelei and whisper. She was tempted to move closer to Ian to irritate them, but didn't think it would look very professional.

"The good news in this, if you could say that," Ian said, "is that there might not have been a real body at all. Shapeshifters, if that's what we're dealing with, and mind control go hand-in-hand. It might have wanted you to think there was a body. Or we could be talking a real apparition. That picture you drew looked exactly like Tony Slaughter—a black arts magician from the thirties."

When Ian mentioned the black arts, Melissa stared down at her plate, playing with her scrambled eggs.

"Maybe it just happens to be a coincidence," Dale said. "It might not even be associated with these other sightings."

"I plan on doing some research to see if anyone knows about what we all found underground," Ian said.

"Someone knew," Shannon said. "We did find that ceremonial knife right by the entrance to the tunnel, and the mobile phone underground. Which reminds me." She picked up her BlackBerry. "I need to see how soon I can get those objects analyzed. Excuse me."

While they waited for Shannon to return, a petite, dark haired woman walked up and stood next to Ian. "Sorry to bother you, but I was wondering where you all were from?" She only eyed Ian.

Like you care where the rest of us are from.

"Well Melissa here," Ian pointed to the ranch owner, "is from Dragoon, but the rest of us are visiting from Phoenix."

"That's awesome. I was hoping you would say that. Here's my card—feel free to give me a call anytime." She winked at him.

Ian looked over at Lorelei, then handed back the card. "Thanks, that's very flattering, but I'm not interested."

Did he do that on my account?

"Are you a man under those tight jeans?" Shannon approached from behind.

"Excuse me," the woman said. "What's that supposed to mean?"

"Just asking because you have a lot of balls coming over here and hitting on him. I mean, how do you know this beautiful blonde woman sitting next to him isn't his girlfriend or wife? The chemistry between them is pretty damn obvious."

"I, I..."

"Yeah, that's right. It's all about you. Just go back to your friends. This is official business here." Shannon flashed her FBI badge, and sat back down, leaving the stranger standing there with her mouth open and hands on her hips.

Lorelei thought the woman was going to say something else, but then she walked off in a huff, whispering to her friends back at their table. "Shannon, that was harsh."

"No it wasn't. She was just trying to show off for her friends. That slut had her eyes on Ian ever since she walked in here."

Ian started to reach out to her. "Lore told me what happened with your boyfriend."

"Please, I don't need any pity. My own way of getting revenge, I guess." She glanced over at Melissa, "I apologize."

"None necessary, I was thinking the same thing when she came over."

Shannon pushed her plate of food away. "Dale, did you have anything interesting happen while we were underground? Other than what Jensen mentioned about the tourists."

"That experience was probably more exciting than what I encountered. But yes. I saw the same light anomalies the bartender has seen. I think that's what set the motion detectors off. When I ran in to check it out, I noticed something had messed with our equipment. The camera and tripod moved again when I was in there. And the audio recorder had its batteries removed."

"Are you sure no one was in there pulling a prank?" Shannon asked.

"I didn't see anyone when I went down into the basement. And there was a strange blue mist when I played back the video. Even if someone had snuck in there and had a cigarette, the smoke wouldn't have been royal blue. When I investigated the cellar a while later, the bar stool in the corner was knocked over, then I started hearing this weird humming noise—I thought I felt a vibration when I laid my head against the cement."

"I've heard that as well," Melissa said. "It was always sort of faint, so I thought maybe I was hearing things."

"Wait a minute," Lorelei said, staring at Dale. "What time was that?"

"Sometime after 9:00 p.m. I would have to check my audio and thermal data."

"Isn't that about the time we encountered that cobweb-like substance, right before we found the ruins?"

"Lore's right," Ian said. "Dale, sounds like you might have experienced part of what we did underground, which means that that particular tunnel that heads straight north passes under your restaurant, Melissa."

"I don't know if I should be frightened by all this, or excited. I mean, I've always been fascinated by that stuff, but when you throw in monsters and dead bodies, it puts a whole new perspective on things."

"Don't worry," Shannon said. "The FBI only brings in the best. I promise. We'll get this figured out."

A half hour later, they were ready to leave the restaurant.

"I want to stop and interview Marie and Corbin Metast, Melissa's neighbor," Shannon said. "They are in between two sightings, so I'm hoping they can help us. Maybe even tell us if they've seen any of the creatures, or the person from your sketch."

"Oh that reminds me." Melissa bent down and removed a piece of paper from a folder. "I drew another one up for you last night. I couldn't sleep anyways."

"Thank you so much. You've been a rock considering all you've been through. And to do this? It's not even your job."

"Hey, I've got a very personal stake in all this. I want to open my guest ranch again and continue with my life."

Lorelei could feel the cold stares from the women that had

been eyeing Ian as they finished their meal. She figured Ian must have felt it as well because he reached out and put his arm around her waist.

Is he being protective, or just making those women jealous? Ian tried not to react, but Lorelei noticed he had a hurt look on his face. He was still reading her mind.

Shannon handed the sketch to Ian. "You mentioned you were familiar with this guy. Did you ever find an actual photo of him?"

"Yes, but the websites I found had much older pictures where Tony's face was more filled out, his hair was lighter, and he didn't have the scar. There were some articles pertaining to black magic and he was mentioned in a few as a powerful magician."

Melissa cringed when Ian mentioned the black magic. Lorelei knew she was hiding something.

"Do we know anything else about this character?" Shannon asked.

Ian pulled out cash and put money down for his bill. "Tony Slaughter was from Gallup, New Mexico. It's just over the state line, so it wasn't that far to travel here. He could have known about the spirituality of this place. Joe is aware of him through contacts that are into the dark arts. Tony's coven always found the most remote locations for their rituals. Who knows where he might have practiced—the cave, the passages, the ruins. Tony was highly respected, but not for the right reasons. People were terrified of him."

"But that was so long ago," Lorelei said. "Why would Melissa be seeing his body now?"

They all got up from the table. Ian ignored the group of women and opened the door for everyone as they left the restaurant. She pulled her jacket closer as the chill of the early morning air greeted her.

"Residual haunt possibly." Ian replied. "Perhaps that's where he died eighty years ago. Joe mentioned he died a tragic death."

"But I didn't see any markings on him." Melissa shivered. "I can't believe he was a spirit. I mean, he felt solid when I touched him."

Dale opened the car doors. "That's not that unusual. I've heard of many instances where people have deceased relatives or friends pay a visit, and they seem as normal and real as any of us right now." He hesitated. "Okay, who said I was normal."

Lorelei's heart ached, remembering the appearance her

mother had made after her death.

"It's so strange that Tony's ghost shows itself at the same time that these monsters begin terrorizing the community." Lorelei climbed into the SUV.

"Not necessarily," Ian said. "Someone might have deliberately brought him back, messing around with things they had no understanding of, and enticed Tony, and these creatures, here without knowing it."

As Dale drove them back to the ranch, Lorelei saw Melissa gazing at the canyon-like Lavender Open Pit Mine.

"I wonder if the tunnel's you've all found could be connected with any of Bisbee's mines," Melissa said. "The Queen Mine is just one. There are more than twenty-five hundred miles of tunnels around here."

"These didn't look like mining tunnels," Shannon said. "There were no wooden support beams."

Lorelei already knew the underground realm they had discovered had nothing to do with mining. Her astral experience during her time in the mine shaft three years ago, the feeling of familiarity in a place with out-of-body petroglyphs and the archaic version of the solar system—she didn't know how, or when, but she knew there was much more to uncover on this case. And much of it would have to do with her.

Ian placed his arm around her.

Don't let go, she thought.

He pulled her closer.

CHAPTER FIFTEEN

A two-story forest green house with white trim and wrap-around porch welcomed Shannon and Lorelei amidst rolling hills and a spectacular backdrop of harsh, cragged peaks of the Dragoon Mountains. A short, rotund woman with medium length brown hair shaped into a bob stood by the stairs of the home to welcome them with a warm smile and a watering can in her right hand. Yellow and purple petunias adorned window sills. Spider plants and pothos vines hung from the porch ceiling.

"Hello, I'm Marie, nice to meet you." She took turns gently shaking hands with Lorelei and Shannon. "Melissa mentioned you'd be stopping by. Won't you please come in? I have iced tea and the best cookies. Not that I need to be eating such stuff." She patted her stomach. "But cookies and chocolate are my two favorite things."

The interior of the house was as "country charm" as the exterior. The brightly lit great room revealed sage and off-white checkered valances draped on the large bay window, supported with metal bird hooks. A farmhouse style country bench sat in the entryway.

Marie sat them around a square country wooden table with four perfectly placed whitewashed chairs. The glass pitcher of tea was poised in the center. And a stir-stick with a one-inch rooster at the end floated freely among the ice cubes.

A ceramic plate in hues of moss, rustic red and mustard sat next to the pitcher. And Marie's hand delicately swooped up a cookie to show a peek at a rooster's face.

Could there be anymore damn roosters in the kitchen? Shannon wondered. Just then, she thought she heard a rooster's crow.

"Oh, that's Harold making all that noise." Marie said. "A little off, he never crows during the morning, occasionally in the afternoon and always late at night."

Shannon gave her a brief smile. "You've got a very," slight

pause, "interesting place."

"Thank you. We've been here for ten years now. Can you believe this place is over eighty years old? My husband and I spent the first few years or so remodeling. Corbin is in town getting some feed and such. Hopefully you'll get to meet him if he returns in time."

"Marie, I'm an agent with the FBI, but Lorelei here is one of the team members with the Arizona-Irish Paranormal Research Society, a special group of investigators who are hired to help us out. As you already know through Melissa, we're at her ranch this weekend for an investigation—providing Cochise County with assistance for a very unique case."

"Oh yes. That place has had stuff going on forever." Marie shoved another cookie into her mouth. "But nothing too serious." She chewed in a muffled voice. "Typical shadows, mists and bumps in the night."

Shannon glanced at Lorelei, who seemed to be thinking the same thing—how the hell could Marie not have heard about the creatures terrorizing the area?

"Have you ever experienced anything on your property?" Lorelei asked, taking a sip of the sweet tea. "Or witnessed anything out of the ordinary in the past few weeks?"

Shannon tried not to laugh out loud when she saw Lorelei's face suck in after taking a sip of the tea. Lorelei pushed the glass out of the way.

"Like what?"

"Animal-like beasts," Shannon said. "Trust me, you would know if you saw one. Your neighbors on either side have seen some rather terrifying things. So figured whatever these things are might have crossed your property."

"You know," Marie said in a gossipy tone of voice. "I've been hearing tales from people in the community about such stuff. I just can't believe it! I'm sure they're seeing a large dog or some sort of bird of prey."

"I don't think so." Shannon stared into Marie's eyes. "There's a very frightened military family that reported such an incident. Someone like that is as straightforward as you can imagine. My investigators and I have witnessed some pretty scary stuff, and we've only been here one day. There's even been an unexplainable horse death related to this case."

There's something about this woman's demeanor. Sickeningly sweet, just like her iced tea.

"I'm so sorry to hear that. But as I mentioned, Corbin and I haven't seen anything like that."

Shannon noticed a slight tremor in Marie's left forefinger as she held her glass. Her grip was tight enough to pop the vein on the back of her hand.

"There was another incident last night," Shannon said. "A few tourists had a rather disconcerting experience." Then she calmly picked up her iced tea and eyed Marie as she forced a long gulp. She put the tall glass down on the table. "But that's not all."

Marie's cell phone rang, piercing the uncomfortable moment. "Excuse me," she said, getting up from the table. She snatched the phone from the kitchen counter and walked down the hall and out of sight.

"What do you think?" Shannon whispered.

"She's a little too nice. She seems very uncomfortable, and I'm getting a very peculiar vibe. As if all this," Lorelei motioned her hand toward the spic and span, too charming atmosphere surrounding them, "was somehow a lie."

"So sorry." Marie walked back into the dining room. "Don't mean to be rude, but I have to run. A friend called and she needs me to take her to the doctor. Last minute, I know, but her husband isn't able to take her."

"Okay, thanks for your time," Shannon said. "Here's my card. Please let me know if you can think of anything else."

"Of course. It was great meeting you both. Good luck with your investigation." Marie quickly walked them to the door, escorted them outside and closed the door behind them.

"Well that was rather abrupt," Lorelei said.

"Yeah, did you notice that she started getting that way after I mentioned the unusual occurrences? She knows something all right."

"Maybe they have seen one of those things."

Shannon climbed into the driver's side of her jeep. "Or perhaps she knows more about what's going on than the rest of us do."

CHAPTER SIXTEEN

Ian, Joe and Melissa gazed down into the arroyo that he, Lorelei and Shannon had almost fallen into the previous night. Cottonwood trees lined a stream that meandered northeast. *And yet another explanation for the extreme energy levels,* Ian thought. *Water.*

"This explains why no one's been here," Joe said. "It's virtually impossible to get to. "Unless they find the same entrance you all discovered last night." He glanced back at the ruins.

"This definitely isn't my property." Melissa brushed dirt of her jeans and sweatshirt with her hands. "It's too far east."

"What about your neighbors—the Metasts?" Ian asked. "Is this on their land?"

"I don't think so. This should be state land."

"This place is pretty remote," Joe said. "It's always a possibility that someone could climb down into the arroyo and back up into this little valley, but it would be risky."

Ian gazed into the chasm—the bottom was at least fifty feet below.

I would prefer it that way," Melissa said. "It's such a peaceful respite. And I almost feel as if we shouldn't be here. Maybe that's because of those intimidating looking boulders."

Joe slowly walked over to the middle monument closest to the cliff. *He touched, no caressed it,* Ian thought, his hands slowly working their way outward.

"We were getting some high EMF readings around here," Ian said. "And the thermal imager showed these stones as heat sources." Bending down, Ian showed Joe the mysterious marking on the bottom. "I know the sign in the center is a travel rune. But I've never seen anything like this one, or any of the other symbols at the bottom. They all have triangles incorporated into them."

Joe stared, transfixed, at the unknown etching—two triangles with the bases facing each other and two parallel squiggly lines running between them. Then he glanced back at the ruins above.

Is Joe connecting the triangular door at the ruin to these signs?

"Guys, sorry to interrupt, but I'm not feeling so well," Melissa said.

Ian turned to see her collapse to the ground, nearly hitting her head on a sharp rock. "We need to get her back to the ranch."

"I'm okay," she said, trying to get up. "Haven't had much of an appetite lately. Suppose I shouldn't have insisted on coming here."

"Whoa, sit right down for a few minutes." Ian guided her to a large round boulder. Then he put his hands on her shoulders and stared into her eyes. Like he did with Lorelei, he focused intently, and imagined the specks in his irises transforming and in motion.

It was this animosity in his steel grey eyes that captured the attention of those he healed. Melissa relaxed in his gentle grip, becoming lost in his gaze. A minute later, she closed her eyes tightly, and opened them again.

"What a difference," she said. "Thanks."

Ian glanced at Joe.

The only people who never reacted to his unusual healing abilities were those familiar with magic.

CHAPTER SEVENTEEN

A scream caught Lorelei's attention. But this wasn't from the present. It was the past that came rushing in as Shannon interviewed the family that saw the prehistoric bird. Humongous wings folded in, a long, knife-like beak, and a crest above its head…a pterosaur. It sat perched on top of the garage, watching the daughter.

Lorelei shuddered, staring at the top of their garage. *God, it looks so intelligent. And those eyes.*

The girl froze in fright. She couldn't move. Her terror turned to curiosity, as she seemed to listen to something it was saying. Then the monstrous creature extended its wings, covering the garage and the house.

The Jurassic bird leapt off of the roof and toward the sixteen year old. The father came running out of the house as the creature flew into a transparent heat wave, then vanished.

"Thanks for your time," Shannon said. "If you can think of any details, please let me know."

Lorelei had been in a daze, seeing the vision through the daughter's eyes. Why didn't the giant bird attack? Could her father have scared it off?

Lorelei could see the frustration on Shannon's face. The parents or their daughter weren't talking about what had happened. They didn't need to.

"Thanks for your time," Shannon said. "Please let me know if you remember anything."

"Shannon, I witnessed what Elena did while you were talking to her. I saw the damn thing sitting on top of their garage. It went right for her—the father came out and it just disappeared. I saw the shiny force field, or whatever it is. I think all of these creatures have that in common. This particular beast took a flying leap off their house and into this weird force field."

"Did you see where it came from?" Shannon asked.

"No, I just saw what Elena did. It was already perched. Her face was so strange, quizzical almost. It was as if she were listening to it. I couldn't hear anything in the vision, but Shannon, it looked so intelligent."

"What about the first couple we talked with? Did you get the same thing with them?"

"I don't think I had enough time. I mean, they didn't even invite us in. They said the sergeant had the information all ready. The people in this community are terrified."

"Oh, I almost forgot," Shannon said. "Ian texted me during the first interview. Said his shaman friend was here. He's probably taken Joe and Melissa to the ruins."

"Did you get that cell phone and knife we found to a lab?" Lorelei asked.

"I have someone from FBI's Sierra Vista location to come and get them. Said they would put a rush on it, but that could mean a few days, or a few weeks."

"Shannon, do you really believe that a person is responsible for all of this horror?"

"I don't know Lore. Ian said there are instances of shamans transforming into such creatures. But it's not normal for a community to be harassed by a variety of shapeshifters. Being an FBI agent, I have to be analytical, yet the only clues we really have are what seem to be a description of a dark arts master from the thirties, a cell phone and a knife used for rituals. Maybe this is cult related. Like Dale mentioned, it could be related to the Armageddon on December 21, 2012. If so, I don't know where in the hell someone would get this kind of power."

Lorelei barely registered what Shannon said. The dark-haired waitress from the Wagon Wheel that had been flirting with Ian flashed vividly through her mind. She didn't get an image, yet something told her the young woman was in trouble.

A minute later, Shannon was waving her hand frantically in front of Lorelei's face. "Earth to Lore."

"Call the ranch," Lorelei said. "We need to find out if Kelly's okay."

"Melissa said she doesn't have any staff onsite."

"She may not be working, but she's there, and in trouble."

Shannon immediately tried to call Melissa on her home phone. But there was no answer. Another call came in right after she disconnected.

Staring at Shannon's shocked face, she listened intently. "Okay Ian, we're on our way."

"You've done it again. Kelly vanished right in front of Matt—I guess they were there visiting Melissa."

They jumped into Shannon's Jeep and drove back to the Texas Canyon Retreat.

When they arrived back at the ranch, Melissa was in hysterics. Lorelei and Shannon ran over to Melissa, Ian, Dale, Joe and Matt.

Dale and Ian sat on either side of Melissa on the front porch. Matt turned to face Shannon. "She's gone," he said. "Kelly saw Ian and wanted to go talk to him. She went into his room and was in there for awhile. So I figured she'd be safe."

Matt's face paled even more. He trembled so fiercely Lorelei thought he would collapse. "I was over there." Matt looked back at the office and living quarters. "Melissa and I heard a loud scream. When we came running outside, Kelly was there, then suddenly gone."

"Did you notice anything unusual?" Lorelei asked. "Like a shimmering effect?"

"As a matter of fact, yes." Matt sat down on the step next to Dale. "It was as if someone threw an invisible cloak over her. She was approaching the office. I didn't see what caused her to scream."

"Ian, where were you?" Shannon asked. "You know how dangerous it is around here."

Ian sighed heavily, placing his hands on his forehead. Lorelei knew he was in major distress.

"Ian," Shannon said. "You could have prevented this if you were with her."

"No." Dale yelled back at her. "Kelly went into his room and threw herself at him. I walked into the room and found her with her arms around his neck, kissing him. And she was trying to undo his pants. Ian desperately tried to get her off. She didn't handle the rejection too well and went running. That's when it happened."

"God, Ian I'm sorry. I should have known."

"I could have chased her," Ian said. "But I was in total shock."

"On the way over here, I called in additional forces from Cochise County and the Sierra Vista regional office. We'll do what we can to find her."

But Lorelei knew it was a waste of time. They weren't going

to find her—at least not on the earthly plane.

CHAPTER EIGHTEEN

The red stagecoach behind the bar of the Wagon Wheel Restaurant contained two passengers—a man in a dark suit and black bowtie and a woman wearing a tied-down hat. Lorelei noticed them watching Joe, Dale and Ian as they analyzed some of the evidence from the recent underground excursion. She started to say something, but the couple vanished.

"You just saw her, didn't you?" Dale asked.

Lorelei turned her head away from the direction of the stagecoach. "Yeah, but they're gone now."

"What do you mean, 'they?'" Dale asked.

"I saw a man and a woman. They appeared to be watching us."

"Wow. I wonder if the guy was there last night, and I couldn't see him. Could it be Jeff and Annie O'Shea?" Dale asked.

"No," Lorelei said. "These two were dressed in eighteen hundreds clothing. They were in a stagecoach accident." She focused on the conversation between Ian and Joe.

"The voices Lorelei heard do have a slight Navajo inflection, but it's not any Native American language I'm familiar with. I'd send that to a university or linguist," Joe said.

"Are you sure?" Ian asked.

Joe nodded. "Those rock formations and symbols aren't typical either. We could be talking about a whole new race." He held the headphones tighter against his ears to hear the next part of the audio. "What happened down there?" He glanced up at Lorelei and Ian. "I hear a humming noise in the background."

"We all experienced some rather strong activity," Lorelei said. "We were attacked by what felt like cobwebs. Then that humming noise started."

Joe stared at her. His intense gaze made her uncomfortable. "You're not doing your fellow investigators, or Agent Flynn any favors by holding back."

Dale and Ian both looked from Joe to Lorelei.

"Okay. That familiar feeling I mentioned was so much more than that. It felt as if I was being welcomed home. Extreme warmth and caring overcame me down there. And that rough drawing of the solar system—I've seen that exact map before. I just can't remember where."

"Lore," Ian said, "Joe and I think this whole area is deeply engrained in the concept of astral travel. The symbol of the travel rune, the map that we found of the universe. . . " Ian took her hand in his. "And the fact that you rescued yourself from that mine shaft a few years ago through your first out-of-body experience."

"Great Ian." Lorelei stood directly in front of him, looking up at him. "It's not enough that you're able to read my mind, now you're telling everyone else experiences from my past."

"He had no choice," Joe said. "You weren't confiding in anyone. You were holding back what could turn out to be pretty important information. Did you stop to think why he might be able to read your mind? There's a purpose for all of this, and for what's happening between the both of you." Joe got up from the table and walked over to Lorelei. "I believe someone's trying to get you to admit what you're really capable of, since you're too damn afraid to admit it to yourself."

"Lore," Dale said. "There's a section of video you need to see. This happened at the same time you all encountered those vibrations and the ectoplasm. Here, you'll see it begin in ten seconds, at the same time the vibrations start."

He handed her the headphones and hit play. She gasped when Dale turned the volume up. *It can't be.* But Lorelei could not deny it. She was seeing it for herself. While Ian and Shannon were holding their ears to block out the noise in the tunnels, she was standing there, smiling. Then she started talking—the same unusual language emitting from her own lips, as if she were responding to the unseen spirits."

"That can't be," she said. "I don't know any other languages."

"It's you," Ian placed his hand on her shoulder. "Dale has voice recognition software. And we confirmed your voice on this audio to a piece from the Vulture Mine investigation. Not that we need that with the video. But since the vibrations were so loud, neither Shannon nor I could hear what you were saying."

"So what the hell are you all suggesting? That I was part of this unknown race of people?"

Ian moved in closer to her. She didn't want to, but she became lost in his eyes. "We don't have the answers, Lore. You do. You just have to want to hear them." Before she knew it, Ian had reached his arms out, pulling her to him. "It's okay. I can help you with all this. Help you bring these memories to the forefront."

At first, Lorelei wanted to push him away. Instead, she found herself putting her arms around his waist, her head against his chest. Suddenly, she wished everyone would vanish.

Ian smoothed her hair with his hand. His breathing became heavier and he held her tighter.

"Shit, I almost forgot with all of the stuff going on." Dale presented a newspaper article with pictures of Annie and Jeff O'Shea. "I found these items inside this metal box." He picked up the container.

Lorelei removed the box from Dale's hands and opened the squeaky lid while Ian read the article.

Lorelei removed a smooth stone from the top of the pile. Sliding her finger over the etching of the travel rune, she turned it over to reveal a marking matching one of the granite monoliths. "These symbols match up to the obelisks at the ruins." Lorelei passed the small stones to Shannon.

"Dale, where did you find this box?" Joe asked.

"In the cellar. I noticed it when I was down there investigating. The article mentions the disappearance of Jeff and Annie O'Shea. *The Tucson Citizen*, which was in operation during the thirties, is the publication that printed it. I looked online for any follow-up articles on the couple's disappearance, but couldn't find anything. Maybe local law enforcement can provide more detail on their case."

"Has Melissa seen this box before, Dale?" Lorelei asked.

"I asked her right after I found it, but she said no."

Lorelei noticed Ian's stunned face. Glancing over, she saw him staring at a four by six black and white photo of the couple. Dale slid the photo out of Ian's hand. The seventy year old picture could not conceal the striking similarities between Jeff and Annie O'Shea, and Lorelei and Ian.

"It was too dark in the cellar to notice this before," Dale said.

"That's a very rough image," Lorelei said.

"Are you kidding?" Joe asked. "Look at her face. Look at Jeff's face. I have a feeling Annie had quite a bond with whoever lived in those ruins. I believe you were Annie O'Shea." Joe held up the article and photograph. "You're desperately trying to hide it, but you're falling in love with Ian. And now you're coming face-to-face with your original identity. Like it or not, you and Ian have found each other for the second time. Maybe to fix something from the past."

Lorelei pulled two wooden statues out of the box. The features of the idols were similar to that of the man and woman in the photo, the wood intricately carved to reflect the long strands of Annie's hair. The male idol even had eyeglasses and the same wavy lochs as Jeff.

Dale turned the smooth stones over in his hand. "What do you think all this is for? Could this stuff have been used for rituals?"

"I would say yes," Ian said. "Traditionally, rocks themselves represent earth." Ian dug in the container. There's candles for fire, and this is another big clue that this box contains secrets." He held up a pentagram-shaped pewter necklace with an emerald crystal in the center.

Lorelei took the necklace from Joe, enclosing the charm tightly in her palm. She closed her eyes and saw Annie and Jeff. Or was it her and Ian? No, it couldn't be. The woman had strawberry blonde hair. But there was sadness surrounding the charm—a deep melancholy about love lost.

Joe laid the five stones out in front of him. "These are talismans."

"What are you talking about?" Dale looked over his shoulder at the unusual rocks.

"A talisman is a natural object, like these stones. It can also be a ring or any other object engraved with figures or characters." Joe indicated the unusual etchings representative of the five monoliths. "Such symbols can be observances of gods or goddesses."

Lorelei picked up the first stone in the lineup. There was an inscription of a triangle with two smaller shaped triads for eyes, and two pyramid-like ears. Then she closely observed the signs on the others. "I can't believe we missed this."

"Missed what?" Dale asked.

"These talismans—look closely at the designs. Yes, they're all inscribed with triangles, but the shapes they're forming seem to represent the creatures people are witnessing."

"She's right." Ian picked up the center stone. It had been carved with long, slender triangles extending outward, a shorter triangle in the middle. There was also a triangular "crest" and tail with a smaller triangle at the end. "This must be the prehistoric bird that's been seen by the tourists and the military family. Lorelei's holding what must be a wolf."

Ian picked up another smooth stone. "There's a serpent-shaped carving inside a triangle on this one."

"That means," Joe said, "there are two more monsters out there. One of which is a Gila monster from hell with the rounded head and knife-like appendages extending from the small bumps on its back. And the other is a demon." They gazed at the two stones with representations of the as yet unseen monstrosities.

"Joe, do you actually think these things are treated as gods?" Dale asked. "Don't tell me this innocent looking couple," he threw down the newspaper article next to the talismans, "are responsible for all the strange sightings in the community?"

"No," Lorelei said. She gripped the emerald charm tighter. "Remember, the matching symbols on those formations at the ruins were much newer than the travel runes. They weren't as weather worn. Whatever's causing all this is just as evil as the malevolent beasts they've created."

"Are you getting that from the stones?" Ian asked.

She shook her head. "The idols. And those Stonehenge-like formations have been around for centuries. But the stuff in the box Dale found is a lot more recent."

Joe glanced over the objects from the container. "Sounds like someone is concocting the spell of the century. The question is why."

"It's a mystery to all of us," Shannon said. "This is a bizarre puzzle with multiple pieces and I don't know how they fit together. There's a black arts magician that's been dead for years. Melissa supposedly saw the apparition. Or maybe there's a Tony Slaughter look alike. But I don't know how that would connect with a modern day supernatural nightmare and an abduction."

"I prey to God," Ian said, "that Kelly's all right. I know she's pretty messed up, but she doesn't deserve to die."

"Well, are you ready to begin the cleansing of Melissa's property?" Ian asked Joe.

"Not sure a cleansing is going to help in this situation. But it's better than doing nothing."

Could that be how Tony Slaughter met his maker? Did he delve a little too deep and discover something he couldn't manage? And if Kelly is alive, where the hell is she?

CHAPTER NINETEEN

Ian walked cautiously into Melissa's empty barn. The smell of horses and hay lingered in the air. The atmosphere still felt oppressive, and he noticed Bandit standing at the entrance. The dog would not come in.

"Do you think this ritual is going to keep these things away from Melissa's property? We don't even know what we're dealing with—spirits or monsters. Or they could be a combination of both."

Joe lit the stalk of dried herb and handed it to Ian. "The strange force fields indicate that these definitely aren't typical skinwalker incidents. I think the creatures might represent other dimensions."

"This sage will cleanse all negative energies and spirits." Ian held his head high, waving the smoking herb into one of the stalls. "All negative energies and spirits must leave now and not return. I banish you to whence you came." Bandit barked, then ran off.

While they worked their way through the barn, a scream sliced through the late afternoon silence.

"Where did that come from?" Ian asked.

"The living quarters, probably Melissa," Joe said. They both ran out of the barn, toward the office.

Ian noticed Shannon and Lorelei darting out of the restaurant.

"What the hell?" Shannon asked.

"We don't know," Ian said. "The scream came from Melissa's place."

"Wait," Shannon yelled, her hand on the butt of her gun. "You can't just go in there—it might not be safe." She slowly, cautiously opened the door and walked in. A minute later, Shannon came to the door and motioned for the others to follow.

"Melissa doesn't look good," Shannon said.

Joe, Lore, Ian and Dale followed Shannon through the lobby and down the hallway to the master bedroom.

Melissa was still in her clothes, lying on top of her bed. She thrashed and moaned, then let out another loud yell. "No, please don't."

"Melissa." Ian rushed over to the other side of the bed, and shook her arm to wake her, but his arm slid off. "She's soaking wet, so are her sheets."

The owner of the ranch sat up in bed, startled and breathing heavily.

"Melissa, it's us," Lorelei said. "You had a nightmare." Melissa sat straight up, not moving, eyes wide with terror.

Joe looked briefly at Ian. "Extraction," he said. "Ian, I'll need some help from you."

"Of course. Are you sure it's necessary?"

Melissa's wet bangs clung to her forehead. Her well-tanned skin perspired profusely, drenching her light blue t-shirt.

"Yes," Joe said. "Whatever this is has gone a step further. It's not only invaded her property. It's invaded her mind."

CHAPTER TWENTY

She's still in the nightmare. Shannon held Melissa's hand. Her pulse was rapid and her eyes wide with terror.

"Keep a watch on her," Joe said. "I need to get some things from my car."

Shannon saw him run down the hallway and heard the front door open and close.

"What's he talking about, Ian?" Shannon asked. "What's Joe planning on doing?"

"Extraction is removal of negative energy from the body." Ian held Melissa's other hand. "These things could have done more than take over her property. Something's probably taken over her dreams. She'll be okay. If anyone can help her, it's Joe. He's known as one of the most powerful shaman's in the four corners."

"Do you need us to leave?" Lorelei asked, as Joe ran back into the room clutching a duffel bag. She stood at the end of the bed.

"It's up to you." Joe removed unusual items of clothing from his bag. "If you stay, you must make no noise whatsoever. I'll be locating the misplaced energy initially. The next step is to merge with my guardian spirit to bring out my powers. That's what allows me to remove the energy."

Joe placed a headdress with large brown bird feathers on the top of his head. A brown leather skin with feathers attached, positioned in the shape of two wings, was draped over his shoulders.

"This power animal also protects me from taking this negative energy into my own body, so it's imperative there are no distractions. This cannot go wrong—for me or Melissa."

The room became silent. Joe removed a small round drum and a drumstick. He handed a chalice to Ian with a bottle of water. Without any explanation, Ian poured half into the pewter cup and placed it on the nightstand.

I can't believe this. Melissa hasn't budged—she barely seems to be breathing. Shannon helped Ian gently push Melissa into a prone position on the bed.

Lorelei barely seemed able to breathe herself as she watched Melissa.

As the drumstick met the rawhide of the instrument, a steady deep staccato emanated throughout the bedroom.

A wolf's head decorated Joe's instrument. He stopped the drumming. And raised his long, broad wings skyward, creating a slight gust that blew everyone's hair. He raised his head heavenward.

Shannon could have sworn Joe's eyes changed. The shape remained the same, rather the iris transformed into a black orb, while the outer portion turned into a light yellow.

As soon as Joe looked at him, Ian took the drum, then continued the rhythm of the ritual. Joe twirled and hopped in circles around the room.

The beat of the single drum increased—Joe's movements became frenzied and frantic. Sweat droplets flew from his forehead and hair, the moisture reflecting as it passed by the mid-afternoon sun through the window.

Suddenly, Joe ceased all movement and placed his hands above Melissa's body, starting below her neck. He slowly slid his palms within an inch from her skin.

Ian picked up the gold chalice and after a few moments, the shaman seemed to have found something as he lowered his hand below her heart. Shannon did a double take as Joe removed a bright red ball of energy. He then placed it into the chalice of water on the nightstand as if he were holding a baby.

Lorelei's eyes flew open and her jaw dropped.

Joe removed his headpiece.

Melissa shook her head rapidly a few times. She looked up at Joe, Ian, Shannon and Lorelei. "What's going on? What are you all doing in here?"

"Not so fast," Ian whispered to Melissa. He gave her a kind smile and gently encouraged her to lie back down.

"You were having some rather serious nightmares," Joe replied. "There's a lot of negative energy on your property, and it's getting worse. Your high stress level has made it easy for these things to take control of your dreams."

Ian removed a smooth, olive green, oval shaped stone from his pocket. "We finished a ritual. This is a mineral called moldavite.

It will help ensure the bad vibrations become positive. I'm going to place this where Joe performed the extraction." He held the smooth rock against her skin and looked into her eyes.

"You don't remember anything about your nightmare?" Joe asked. "I hate to stir up such things, but it might help to solve some of this."

"No, not right now." Melissa struggled to sit up. "Listen guys, I think I'm going to leave this place for a while. I thought I could deal with all this, but it's just too much."

"That's a good idea" Joe said. "Ian and I will complete the blessing over the ranch. The process will take a while and might stir up things, so it's best you stay with someone."

"I realize how hard this is for you." Shannon took Melissa's hand. "You're settled in a slice of heaven, trying to make a living, and all of a sudden you're involved in a total nightmare. But I promise, we'll all do what we can to figure this out."

Melissa responded with a weak smile. "Well, I better give my friend a call and let her know she'll be having extra company, in addition to my horses." She glanced at Ian and Joe. "I'm not sure what happened, or what you both did. But thanks. I actually feel quite calm now."

"Promise you'll do what you can to find Kelly." She took Ian's hand as she got up from the bed. "I know what she did to you wasn't right. But she and Matt have been very helpful to me here."

Shannon glanced at Joe every few seconds. She had never seen an extraction ceremony in action. Nor did she completely understand what happened. But Shannon did realize how powerful the Native American man standing before her was.

CHAPTER TWENTY-ONE

Green rolling hills merged with the early morning mist. A herd of red deer grazed next to the spectacular lake, their vermillion bodies reflected in the placid waters.

The vision switched to a used bookstore café with worn leather sofas, endless rows of books and a small corner coffee bar. A handsome man with shoulder length light brown hair peered repeatedly at a woman from behind a hardcover book. The young woman somehow seemed very familiar. Light strawberry blonde hair with an oval face and porcelain skin.

She flashed a sensual smile – a deliberate enticement. He approached her table almost immediately.

"Excuse me," he said in a hesitant, yet somehow seductive voice. "I noticed your beautiful pentagram amulet." He stared at her soft, supple skin. "Can I take a closer look at the emerald crystal?"

She held out the necklace so he could get a closer look. "It's a pewter pentacle bordered in Celtic knotwork. It's set with a Swarovski crystal."

"Stunning." He gazed into her eyes as he said it.

She stared back at him. "It represents…"

"Growth, prosperity and fertility," he finished the words she intended to say.

"That's not all." She slipped her ankle out from under the table and watched his gaze drift from her well-toned leg to her slender ankle with the Celtic spiral tattoo.

"Please sit down," she said, using her long leg to push out the opposite chair. "So, are you pagan, or Wiccan and pagan?"

"Both. I grew up in a pagan home, though my sister chose not to pursue the religion. We're all solitary though, no covens."

"Of course not." She leaned toward him. "The most powerful are those that are *solitary."*

Out of nowhere, he produced a perfect single yellow rose.

"This is for new beginnings. After all, it is a Gibbous moon, rather appropriate, don't you think?"

"Absolutely." She inhaled the sweet scent of the flower. "New ventures, new relationships."

A similarly seductive male voice woke Lorelei. Ian leaned over her. Dale and Shannon stood behind him. Lips slightly parted, Ian's breath warmed her from the inside out. His palms rested on both sides of her face.

Shannon sat next to Lorelei on the bed. "It was strange. I heard you muttering in your sleep. Sounded like you were flirting with some guy. The last thing I heard you say was 'new ventures, new relationships.'"

Lorelei sat up slowly and blushed. "You really don't miss much, do you?"

"That wasn't the weird part." Shannon glanced at Ian who stared down at his feet, then looked away. "While you were having that dream, Ian had a sudden urge to come see you."

Lorelei glanced at the necklace she had slipped over her head. "Wait." She held out the charm. "I put this on. I had the strongest vision I've ever had—of Annie and Jeff, when they first met. Though I have no idea what that has to do with the case."

"Probably nothing," Shannon said. "Just a vivid dream due to the commonalities that you and Ian have with them. Not to mention the chemistry between the two of you."

"Why don't you lie back down and rest?" Ian said.

"No, that's okay. I really don't feel like being alone right now."

"You won't be. I can bring my laptop over here and do some research while you're resting." Ian left her room to get his things.

"Did you find out anything about Kelly?" Lorelei asked.

"No," Shannon said. "I didn't expect to based on what you were telling me, and what Matt witnessed. I hope that she's still alive. But whatever, or whoever this is, is pretty bold. Kelly disappeared out in the open between the guest rooms and the office—and in broad daylight. And Melissa's horse was killed during the day." She shook her head in frustration.

Ian came back into their room, setting his computer up at the desk. "Joe mentioned these monsters might be connected with other dimensions and the wavy effect people are seeing is a portal."

"I wonder if there are five different gates—one for each of the beasts. Or if there's only one," Shannon said.

"I don't know," Ian said. "But if those things do lead to

another realm, it can't be good."

Lorelei yawned and threw her legs over the side of the bed. "Melissa's horse didn't get abducted."

"Snowcap wasn't human." Ian said, as he came back into the room. "Perhaps the creatures need people and need their victims alive."

Lorelei shuddered, staring out the window into the courtyard.

"Damn. So now we have to wait for another disappearance or killing," Shannon said. "In some ways, this isn't much different than a serial killer case."

"Serial killers do it for the thrill," Ian said. "I don't think that's the purpose behind all this. If those rocks are talismans, then those inscriptions, and these creatures, could represent gods. If this is associated with the dark arts like it seems to be, then it's for power."

"The whole shapeshifter theory is definitely out the window." Shannon glanced down at her phone at an incoming call.

"Like I said before, this isn't typical shapeshifter behavior to turn invisible and kidnap people."

Shannon's exhausted demeanor and confused expression frustrated Lorelei. She wished she could provide more assistance as far as the reason for the sightings and destruction. But all she seemed to be receiving were clues from a possible past as Annie O'Shea.

Lorelei placed her forefingers on either side of her head to alleviate the dull ache.

Shannon reached in her purse, opened a bottle of aspirin and handed a few to Lorelei. "Lore, get some more rest. This investigation has been particularly rough on you because of your talents being tested and the discovery of your relationship to Annie and this ancient race. We can all go get some dinner later. And please, I don't want any of you wandering around alone."

"I'll keep a close watch on her," Ian said.

"I'm sure you will." Shannon winked. "I'm going to follow up with Sergeant Jensen to see about any more sightings and have a conversation with Joe to see what he can do to help. I've also contacted Sierra Vista to have them send over an evidence response team."

Ian came over and took the aspirin from Lorelei. "I don't think you'll need those." He placed his hands on either side of her face.

"It's okay, it's not that bad," Lorelei said. Every time he touched her, fire emanated throughout her body. She had enough to deal with lately without the complicated emotions of an affair.

Rather than seeing his beautiful, healing eyes staring into hers, Lorelei received an abrupt vision—Jeff and Annie O'Shea making love on a lush green hilltop, the morning mist and overhanging Magnolia branches providing a romantic, mysterious backdrop.

She gasped and pulled away, imagining her and Ian instead.

"Lore, is everything okay? Another vision?" He sat next to her.

"You could say that."

"I saw Annie and Jeff." She hesitated, as if telling him what she saw might embarrass him.

"Lore, stop holding back," Ian said firmly.

"Annie and Jeff. They were making love." She glanced down at the bedspread.

"Oh," he said, his face flushing crimson. "Well, get some rest. This should help."

He gazed into her eyes and she watched the violet specks in his iris dance and swirl until she became completely calm. She felt as if she had meditated for two hours. Drawn to his sensuous lips, she leaned in. *I want you, Ian.*

"I'd better go," he said breathlessly. Then he rushed through the French doors that led into the living area. For a few seconds she thought he was going to say something else, but he merely smiled and vanished behind the glass door.

CHAPTER TWENTY-TWO

When Lorelei awoke, it was three hours later. Purple and pink streaks painted the sky in brilliant hues as dusk settled in. She saw Ian's reflection through the French doors, sitting in the front room on his laptop.

That's the best sleep I've had in a long time. How did he learn to heal with his eyes? She continued watching him, but he didn't turn his head or acknowledge he read her thoughts.

A knock on the front door startled her. She jumped off the bed and opened the door.

"Hey, Lore. Hope I didn't wake you," Dale said.

"No." She heard Ian come up behind her.

"Oh good. I hesitated coming over here. Guys, I have to head back to Phoenix. My son and wife are both sick. "Dale handed the thermal imaging camera back to Ian. "Make sure Shannon gets this back. I'm tempted to run off with it, but I think my wife would get jealous. I found myself calling it 'baby.'"

"I'm sorry to hear about your family," Ian said.

"Nothing serious. My son started out with a cold, and now my wife has it."

"Okay, be careful." Ian shook Dale's hand. "It's getting dark and that's over a three hour drive."

"Bye, Dale," Lorelei said. "I'm sorry if I seemed a little irritated about the unusual video footage you found."

"No worries," Dale said. "I can't believe how well you're handling all this. I'd be a complete nutcase. What am I saying? I already am." His boyish face broke out into a mischievous grin.

"I wasn't able to find Shannon, so tell her bye for me and give her my apologies. I'll e-mail her anything else I find."

Lorelei turned around to see that Ian had his shirt undone.

"Oh, s, sorry," Ian stuttered as he fumbled over the small buttons. "I forgot."

Her back up against the door, she closed her eyes, holding the knob so tightly she thought her wrist would break. *Okay, Lore, get your mind off this.*

The itsy bitsy spider went down the water spout…Down came the rain and washed the spider out.

A slight smile crossed Ian's face. But the smile quickly faded when the screeching of tires surprised them both.

Lorelei threw open the door. "Where's Agent Flynn?" Sergeant Jensen jumped out of his car. "I tried calling her but there's no answer. There's another emergency. A little girl is missing from her grandparents' property on the other side of the freeway. A different monster's been spotted."

"I'm right here." Shannon came running from the direction of the area where Tony's body had been seen. "Your message went right to voice mail." She caught her breath. "I was showing a few crime scene techs the tunnels."

"I'm heading out there now." Jensen ran to his patrol car. "I need for you all to follow me—it's only about fifteen minutes from here. The grandmother saw a creature she described as 'the devil.' It showed up out of nowhere as Tanya was riding her horse. Then the child vanished right in front of the grandmothers' eyes."

"Get in my car." Shannon yelled, looking around. "Where's Dale?"

"He had to leave," Ian said. "His wife and kid are sick."

"Get your equipment—I'll wait by my Jeep." Shannon raced toward her car parked in front of the office.

Shannon contacted the ERTs to let them know she had to go.

Lorelei and Ian ran back into each of their rooms for their backpacks then jumped into Shannon's vehicle.

"Sounds like a repeat of Kelly's case," Lorelei said.

"Don't know if it's the same creature," Shannon said. "No one ever saw what took *her*. Jensen said the grandmother described Tanya's abductor as having tall horns very thick at the base, very wide greenish body, and an evil grin with extremely sharp teeth."

The sergeant's voice came through Shannon's walkie-talkie. "Tanya, their granddaughter, was here visiting from Michigan for the week. They saw her riding one of their horses an hour or so ago. She heard a scream and looked out the kitchen window to see this creature that looked like the devil. That's when she saw Tanya disappear. The horse didn't vanish with her, even though she was on its back."

Lorelei drew in a deep breath. "I'll bet her grandmother saw a shimmering field when this happened, just like I did, and the same as Matt."

Jensen went silent for a few seconds before he said, "Actually, yes. Listen you all have to figure this out. Everyone here is terrified. I've decided to send my family to Tucson until this gets figured out. And many other families are abandoning the community."

"We've got the best people on this case," Shannon said. "We *will* stop this nightmare.

Fifteen minutes later, Lorelei, Shannon, and Ian arrived at the crime scene. They followed Jensen to the back of the property where a small group had gathered. One man in particular stood out. His two long braids, black cowboy hat, and black long-sleeve shirt with a turquoise bolo tie in the shape of an eagle made him stand out.

"Joe," Ian said in surprise. "I thought you were roaming the property with the FBI."

"I was."

Lorelei wondered why Joe was so elusive. *How did he find out about this new case before Shannon?*

"The sheriff here mentioned you were on your way," Joe said.

Shannon stared at Joe in suspicion.

"Agent Flynn, glad to see you." A tall gentleman in a white cowboy hat with short gray hair and ruddy cheeks held out his hand. "I'm Sheriff Guilford. I understand your team's been staying at Melissa's ranch."

"Yes. This is Lorelei Lanier and Ian Healy, two of my investigators."

"Pleased to meet you." The sheriff nodded at them. "We have a few deputies from the Benson substation out there right now."

Lorelei looked into the distance to see two deputies roaming among the tall grasses, yucca, creosote bushes and acacia trees.

"Where are the grandparents?" Shannon asked.

"Their names are Sam and Joan. They're out looking for Tanya." The sheriff removed his hat and wiped his brow.

"What? We already have one missing person. With all that's going on here, Sheriff, I don't think they should be out there alone. Especially considering how damn fast these victims are vanishing.

"Listen agent, I don't know exactly what the hell is going on out here. But I do know it's getting rather serious. And those two aren't the kind to sit idly by and wait for their young granddaughter to return. They both know how to use a rifle."

"Sheriff," Joe spoke up. "That's what I've been trying to tell you. A rifle, or any other modern weapon, isn't going to help. Something's been stirred up, and it's not likely to go back into hiding on its own."

"Sheriff," Shannon said, "have there been any other incidents like this in the past? These creatures, the disappearances..."

"Yeah, but it was so long ago. The nineteen thirties, after the ranch was first built."

Lorelei, Ian, Shannon and Joe stared at each other.

"Tony Slaughter," Ian said. "His spirit was seen by Melissa on her ranch, and he used to be a rather infamous dark arts magician."

"He might have been responsible back then. But who, or what, is causing it now?" Shannon slipped on her sunglasses. "Sheriff, was the case ever solved?"

"Not that I know of. I heard the sightings stopped within a few days. The person that disappeared was found within twenty-four hours, wandering aimlessly in the valley where they vanished. But that victim died ten years ago."

"Where did Tanya disappear?" Shannon asked.

"Right by that stream over there." He pointed to a clump of cottonwood trees.

"Lore, let's go take a walk," Shannon said. "Thanks for your help Sheriff Guilford."

Lorelei and Shannon headed out toward the scene of the crime.

"Thanks for not sending Ian out here with me. It's getting rather suffocating with this whole telepathy thing."

"I got the impression the mind reading was getting pretty serious. But so are his feelings for you, Lore. I'm wondering if this special bond between you has something to do with all of this. It seems too bizarre that both of you resemble Jeff and Annie. And you may not admit it, but I know you have the same feelings for Ian. I can see it when you're close to him."

Though Lorelei found herself caring about Ian more and more every minute, it made it hard to concentrate, knowing her thoughts were never her own when she was around him.

Could that have been what my mom meant in her parting message when she said not to deny love? Could she have known about Ian?

The pale windswept grass sighed. Horses neighed and whinnied in the background. The narrow stream meandered past a thick stand of golden cottonwoods. And this quiet town in southeast Arizona continued to be harassed by something they couldn't comprehend.

Lorelei recognized a tiny voice, barely audible in the wind, "Help me. Where am I?"

"Did you hear that?" Lorelei asked.

"Yes." Shannon turned to her in shock. "Either I'm picking up your psychic abilities, or that poor girl is here somewhere."

Lorelei did a slow three sixty degree turn, scanning the area. "She's not dead. That's why we're both hearing her. I think whatever took her has Tanya in limbo, in another realm like Joe and Ian mentioned. That's why we can't see the victims."

"Sounds like Tony Slaughter started this whole thing when Annie and Jeff were here." Shannon looked at Lorelei. "Or maybe Annie and Jeff were responsible."

She couldn't explain it, but Lorelei knew the couple wasn't responsible. Annie O'Shea had been tightly bound to the ancients. And they wouldn't have such a relationship with someone so evil.

"Tanya, my name is Lorelei. I'm here to find you. Can you hear me?"

"Yes." Tanya's distorted voice seemed to come from within a few feet.

"Can you tell me what happened?"

"I, I don't know. It came out of nowhere—this shiny, clear wall. Then that monster was there, in front of Magic. It grabbed me hard, pulling me off, and it all felt weird when I went through."

"Went through?" Lorelei asked.

"A milky cloud," Tanya said. "Sort of like water, but I didn't get wet. Everything seems so strange now. I want to see my grandma!"

A tear ran down Lorelei's face. *What can I tell this little girl? I have to walk away from here not knowing if she can be saved.*

Shannon waved the deputies over. "Stand here and listen. "Tanya, talk to me honey. These nice men are here to find you. Let them know you're here, and that they need to stay here with you."

"Hello," Tanya answered.

"Is this a fucking joke?" asked the bald-headed deputy, spinning around so rapidly that he almost lost his balance.

"Please, help me," the little girl's voice said again.

"This is crazy," his partner said. "She sounds like she's right here." He looked around in amazement.

"She is," Shannon said. "But not in the earthly plane. Trust me, I understand that this is all a little hard to comprehend right now, but it's important you stay in this area. Tanya could be caught in another dimension, and she needs company until my team can find a way to stop all this."

"Tanya, are you still here?" Lorelei asked. There was no answer. "Tanya, are you okay?"

"She's gone."

Ian, Joe and the Sheriff came running over.

Lorelei noticed everyone staring at her chest. She looked down at the emerald embedded in the pentagram necklace, radiating brightly. A triangle had formed within its brilliance.

"I think Lore and I need to head back to the ranch," Ian said.

Somehow, Lorelei knew he was right. They had to go back to where the ancients had resided, where Tony's spirit had been seen and the tin box had been found—back to the source of the mystery.

"Of course." Shannon eyed Lorelei warily. "Please stay close to each other…" She started to remove the keys from her front jeans pocket.

Lorelei didn't wait. She yanked the keys, almost dragging Shannon with them. "Hey," Shannon yelled. But Lorelei was already halfway to the Jeep.

She threw open the vehicle's door and got behind the wheel as Ian slid into the passenger seat.

"Ian, did you hear her? Tanya?"

He sighed. "I wasn't there to hear when it happened. Joe was talking to the grandparents and I came over when I saw you all gathered. I heard it through you."

"Damn it, Ian. Can't you focus on something else besides me?"

"I've already told you I can't fucking help this!" he yelled. "Lore, I've tried meditation, I've had Joe bless me, I don't know what else to do. Even when I'm not thinking of you, which isn't often, I can't stop hearing your thoughts. It's as if you're talking only to me."

He turned to the window, watching the moonlit boulders as they drove in silence. Lorelei pulled onto the ranch property and parked in front of the Wagon Wheel.

Walking to the door, Ian took her hand. "I'm sorry for yelling at you. I don't know why the telepathy started here. You and I both know something pretty amazing is happening between us. And I have a feeling you're going to be part of the solution to this mystery. I don't want you to hate me. I want so much to help you."

She didn't know if it was his vulnerability, his honesty, or his feelings for her that made her do what she did next. She pulled his face within inches of hers and whispered, "I'm sorry." Then Lorelei kissed him softly on the lips. She reached up and ran her hand through his wavy locks. He kissed her back with an intensity she had dreamed of for months. He drew her closer into his determined arms, lifting her off the ground.

Suddenly, he let go. "Lore, you can tell how much I want you," he said breathlessly. "The effect you have on me—you drive me to the brink."

She could feel him trembling as he held her close. His warm kisses, his obvious desire, and her hand on his chest, she knew she couldn't go back. "I'm sorry. For everything. I've wanted you since I first met you. I've been so afraid. Since you've been able to read my mind, you probably know why."

Ian tilted her chin up so that she faced him. "Your ex-husband. I'm so sorry for what you've been through—with him and here at the ranch. Most people wouldn't even be sane after all this."

Ian got down on his knees and took her hands in his. "I promise you, when this is all over, I'm going to show you how much you're worth. Please let me care about you."

"All right." Lorelei wiped a tear away. "I don't think I would be able to stay away from you anyway."

Lorelei stared toward the spot where Tony's apparition had been seen. "Kelly, Tanya—they're both in some sort of portal. Someone started all this when Annie and Jeff were living here, probably Tony. But who's doing it now? And why?"

Ian hesitated. "Lore, what if it *was* the O'Shea's?"

Lorelei lifted the pewter pendant off her neck. "It can't be. Intuition tells me they were so in love."

"That doesn't mean they're not capable of something like this. They could have started out as decent people, and then turned to the dark arts. Maybe they were in a cult with Tony."

"Do you really believe that?" she asked.

"I suppose not."

"How do we figure this out?"

"I think someone's trying to help." Ian placed his hand around hers as she held the necklace. "The answer's somewhere up there." He glanced up into the sky.

Lorelei let go of the charm so she could see what it showed. Stars shimmered within a triangle, though three were the most brilliant. As with the image of the universe below ground, she became immersed in the changing scene within the pendant.

"Triangulum Australe," she whispered. "And Ara."

"Say what?"

"They're constellations." She stared into the same eyes that had healed her hours before. "Two of many. The three brightest stars within Australe are the Three Patriarchs—Abraham, Isaac and Jacob." As if in response to her comment, the trio began to pulsate. "Ara, the other constellation means 'the altar.'"

He put his arms around her again and she held her face against his chest. "Your astral abilities helped you save yourself from a mine. Now those same talents will help you save this town."

CHAPTER TWENTY-THREE

Shannon rang the doorbell to the elaborate, light pink southwestern home, sprawled out across half an acre with stately wooden logs decorating the doorframe. "Come on, answer the door. I know I heard someone in there." After not hearing the pitter patter of footsteps, she rang the bell again, then three times in succession.

A female voice from inside the home yelled, "Hold on, I'm coming! Take a chill pill!"

The door swung open wide to reveal a petite woman with very short black hair. She didn't look happy. She glared at Shannon and Joe. "How can I help you?"

"Agent Shannon Flynn. I'm with the FBI." She flashed the woman her credentials. "And this is Joe Luna." She nodded her head to indicate the dark haired man standing next to her. "Sorry to bother you, but Melissa, the owner of the Texas Canyon Retreat, told me she was staying here. Are you Jennifer?"

"Yeah, but she's not here. I've been keeping her horses, but she didn't mention anything about staying here. Melissa was supposed to stop by and give me some money to take care of her animals."

Shannon glanced beyond the woman's shoulder at the clutter—a couch hidden by jeans and sweaters, dirty plates and glasses on the kitchen counter and living room table, and dog toys scattered throughout the front room. "Do you know of anyone else she might be staying with?"

"Other than Vincent, her ex, I have no idea. Though I can't imagine her doing that."

"Oh, why's that?" Shannon asked.

"For one thing, she loves it around here, absolutely hates the big city. For another, he's the reason their daughter Sarah ran away. He was into some very strange stuff. Sarah was marked for the cult from birth. Melissa even suspected that Sarah was brought into the cult, raped and tortured." Jennifer watched Shannon quizzically. "I take it she didn't tell you any of this."

Shannon glanced at Joe in frustration. "No. Was Melissa involved in any of that as well?"

"She's always had an interest in witchcraft. That's part of the reason for their initial attraction. They were in a coven together. Then her ex formed his own a year or so into their marriage, and that's when things got worse. Vincent got into the dark arts using spells and rituals to deliberately harm others with mind control, astral projection, and poisonous herbs and potions. That's when she said enough was enough."

"Is Harlow her married name? Or did she go back to her maiden name?"

"The latter. She refused to keep that man's name. Her married name was Joiner."

Vincent Joiner. Dark arts…could this be the connection?

"Where does Vincent live now?" Joe asked.

"Not sure. When they were married, they lived in New Mexico."

"Thanks very much for all of the info." Shannon removed a card from her pocket, handing it to Jennifer. "You've been a big help. Please let me know if you hear from her. She only left her ranch this afternoon. I thought she was heading here."

"She might just be taking care of some stuff," Jennifer said. "She never mentioned anything about staying with me, but she knows I'd let her in anytime."

As Jennifer shut the door, Shannon turned and walked to Joe's truck in a huff. "I can't believe she didn't tell me any of this. Joe, does the name Vincent Joiner sound familiar to you?" She glanced over at him as they climbed back into his Chevy pickup. His hands were tight on the steering wheel, and she noticed his gaze focused intently on the two greyhounds in Jennifer's side yard.

Joe shifted in his seat and avoided Shannon's gaze. "Yeah, I know him." He pulled his truck out of Jennifer's long driveway. "Like Jennifer mentioned, he's into the dark arts. The last I heard, he was in prison."

Shannon searched for any detail on Vincent through the National Name Check Program for DNA and fingerprint files. She stopped her search for a split second.

"How do you know Vincent?"

Joe didn't answer.

Shannon searched for a few minutes. "I came up empty on Melissa Harlow, Melissa Joiner, or Harlow-Joiner. Vincent isn't so clean. Three counts of kidnapping and two of molestation—cult related. And all of this occurred while they were married. No wonder Melissa didn't mention it. She must have been too embarrassed. Or maybe she figured we'd peg her and her ex as the responsible parties."

Shannon stared over at Joe. "But I have a feeling you already know what's in this database." She suddenly realized how good looking he was. Unlike Ian, the Native American had more rugged features, including a slight dimple and broad nose.

He didn't reply, but intuition told her he knew much more about the case than he was letting on.

Shannon stared down at her phone in shock. "Were you aware Vincent was released from prison right before all this shit started?"

"What?" Joe yelled. "That son-of-a-bitch was supposed to put in twenty years." He slammed on the brakes in the middle of the highway.

"Uh, Joe." Shannon turned her head to check for traffic. Another car was bearing down on them. "We can't sit here like this. Either pull off or keep going."

His jaw muscles and hands relaxed, and he released the brake. He let out a big sigh as the truck gained speed. "I was involved in his cult case five years ago. I helped put Vincent in jail."

"Are you saying you were a witness? Were you in his cult?"

"Sort of. Yes," he said in an irritated voice. "But it was an infiltration."

"I'd be the one slamming on the brakes now if I were driving. You're with the FBI!"

"I was, but I retired a few years ago."

"I thought you were a shaman and a healer."

"I am. I've always been into Reiki, healing, Native American religion. I mean, it's an important part of my past. The FBI thought I had a rather unusual ability to get along with people, to make them cooperate. But Vincent was another matter. He's extremely dangerous, and if that man is here, I can guarantee you he's involved in all this."

"So you already knew about Melissa and her daughter? You must have met them both."

"No," replied Joe. "I never met either of them. They were both placed into Witness Protection, but I didn't have details on the location. I didn't piece all this together until Jennifer mentioned

Vincent's name."

"What if he came back to get vengeance on her?" Shannon asked.

"It's possible. But I think he would have before now. That man spent years studying the most dangerous aspects of black magic," Joe said. "He was obsessed. Every waking moment involved evil schemes, perfecting toxic potions and even manipulating other people's thoughts and actions."

Joe pulled off onto a dirt road that seemed to go nowhere and turned to face her with a stern look. "Agent Flynn, I participated in a ritual involving astral travel. I didn't do it myself, but I watched as Vincent went through the meditative process—I even saw his soul rise from his body and vanish into the heavens."

She could only sit there, a captive listener, knowing the worst was yet to come.

"We all waited for hours. Finally, he came back. But he wasn't the same. I found out his motive during his out-of-body journey."

He paused, though she wasn't sure if for effect or because he didn't want to remember the incident. "Vincent used astral projection to convince a man to commit suicide. A once very happy man that suddenly decided, without warning, to slice open his arms and remove his veins. And how do I know that this unfortunate family man was the victim of Vincent's astral abilities and mind control? Because one of Vincent's minions held up the man's picture as the ritual began. Then I saw his lifeless cadaver the very next day."

Normally, there wasn't much that shook her up, but Shannon had to press her right hand on top of her left to stop from trembling.

Joe leaned close to her. "I'm sorry Shannon. For not telling you any of this earlier. I had no idea who Melissa was."

"Do you think he used mind control to get himself out of jail?"

"It's highly possible."

"Ian never mentioned that you were an FBI agent."

"I told him not to. I didn't want to make you feel as if I were taking over your case." He leaned a little closer and reached out to touch her hair. Her phone rang. Joe turned his head toward the window.

"Agent Flynn."

"Agent, this is Jensen again. You'd better get out to the Metast place." He paused for a few seconds. "And prepare yourself." Then he hung up.

Joe pulled back out onto the main road. “I heard. Let's go.”

Ten minutes later, Shannon and Joe arrived at the once serene ranch house. They drove by a deputy and a crime scene investigator who were emptying the remains of their stomachs under a mesquite.

Joe parked next to the CSI van and Shannon jumped out of his vehicle. She ducked under the yellow crime scene tape attached to the front of the porch railings and showed her badge to the well-built six foot tall deputy at the door. "Jensen's waiting for you inside." He pointed to the men throwing up. "But it's not pretty—both Marie and Corbin were brutally murdered."

She glanced at Joe. "Perhaps you should wait here."

"Don't worry about me," he said with a wink.

The warm tones of the quaint, country interior were replaced with bright red splatters. A male arm lay on the couch—the hand resting up against the arm of the sofa, as if ripped apart while lounging. Intestinal matter had splattered against the beige walls and slid down in a heap on the wooden floor. The living and dining areas were newly painted with the couple's body parts, and the pungent scent of cinnamon potpourri mingled with the scent of death.

She couldn't believe it was the same house. The scene was more than even Shannon could handle. She ran back outside and down the front porch stairs, almost tripping over the crime tape. Barely making it to the dirt, she threw up the sandwich she had for lunch. Joe was right beside her, holding her hair back.

She stood up, still holding her stomach. "I was at a bank robbery where the suspects killed five victims at point blank range with an AK47. But this makes that crime scene look tame." She looked over at Joe. "How come you're not sick?"

"I told you. I've dealt with my share of violence."

Shannon got on her cell phone, dialing Adam Frasier. "Agent Flynn. Listen, we need a few more members from evidence response. We've got a brutal double murder here that looks like it could be related to these creatures. Tell them to prepare themselves. The address is 2502 Stagecoach Pass."

Shannon touched Joe's arm. "I need to go back in and find Jensen. I should be okay. Thanks for watching my hair."

As they walked back inside, Jensen was waiting. Shannon could tell the sergeant desperately tried not to look around.

She glanced over in the kitchen as a deputy stepped over an

elongated dark organ. Shannon shuddered when she realized it was a liver.

A breeze from the open sliding glass doors blew through the house. "Crime and trauma scene decon will be picking up remains for quite a while after evidence response gets through," Jensen said.

"They're on their way," Shannon said. "This definitely isn't a one man job. In this case, guess we could strike out the word 'man.' I'm wondering if one of those creatures were responsible. Joe and I will take a look around. So far, there haven't been any human deaths associated with these things." She glanced at the arm balanced on the couch. "But this definitely isn't a typical murder scene."

"Have at it," Jensen replied. "Just try not to slip on anything."

Shannon walked into the master bedroom with Joe. Suitcases were splayed out on the king-sized bed. Dresser drawers were flung open and clothes tossed into luggage as if the packers' lives depended on it.

Joe showed Shannon a note lying on the bed. "Looks like this might be the reason for Marie and Corbin trying to leave in such a big hurry."

> *You didn't believe me. You should have known. Thanks to the ruins, I am the God of black magic, of everything evil. Tony's minions are now under my control. You both thought you were so above it all, but I know things – things the law enforcement of Cochise County don't even know. But you won't have to worry about your past sins much longer.*

"No signature," Shannon said. "I'm guessing it's your good friend, Melissa's ex-husband." She slid on a rubber glove, then picked up the note and slipped it into a plastic evidence bag. "'You won't have to worry about your past sins much longer.' Not sure what that means."

"If that note's correct and those monsters are under Vincent's control, he probably had one of them kill Marie and Corbin," Joe said. "I hope you can get some prints from the slip of paper."

Shannon looked around the room. "I wonder how Vincent knew Marie and Corbin? He wasn't in touch with Melissa, at least that we know of. And Melissa claims not to know them that well."

"Not sure. Maybe the couple was into some of the same stuff

he was," Joe said. He placed his hand on her shoulder. "I'll go get Jensen."

As Joe went to retrieve the sergeant, Shannon walked across the hall.

"What did the Metasts have to do with Vincent Joiner?" Shannon whispered to herself. "Could Corbin and Marie have had blood on their hands? Damn it. Every passing minute only seems to initiate even more questions."

She flipped on a switch in the spare bedroom and a glass tiffany lamp revealed ocean blue with swirling waves of color. A queen-sized poster bed sat in the middle of the room, matching white-washed nightstands on either side. She opened the closet door to find an old computer monitor and some clothes hangars and boxes.

A few minutes later Jensen popped his head in. "There you are. I heard about the note." Shannon handed him the plastic-enclosed piece of notebook paper. "Sergeant, Marie mentioned they'd been living here ten years during my interview with her."

"At least. They were here when I started with the sheriff's department in two thousand two."

"And did you ever have any issues with either of them?" Shannon asked.

"No. Ideal citizens if you ask me. Corbin was involved in the search and rescue for Cochise County. And Marie has led a few local charity drives to collect toys and food for the holidays. She's been rather busy." Jensen glanced down and shook his head. "Was busy I mean, for tomorrow actually. Hard to believe it's Thanksgiving."

For Shannon, she could care less about the holidays. At first, she was glad they had this case to help her focus on something else besides being dumped. But now she wished she were back in town feeling sorry for herself."

Sergeant Jensen observed the note in his hand as if it were coming to life. "Wait a minute," he whispered. "You asked if there were anything suspicious about Marie and Corbin."

Shannon looked at him quizzically.

"There was a young woman visiting from Phoenix, Karen Acevedo. She was here for a long weekend a few years ago. She was a rather young woman, twenty-six years old. She went missing the day before she was supposed to head back to the city. She was last seen riding a horse near Dragoon Springs. Nothing ever came of it because there was no evidence, and no one saw anything out of the ordinary."

"I see a 'but' coming." Shannon waited patiently for him to continue. She thought about the woman Lorelei had sensed in the passage, and the shape they had seen through the IR camera.

"It's funny," Jensen said. "Corbin was on the search team for her case. He and five other men looked for days. I didn't think about it 'til now, but the other searchers mentioned he would wander off on his own, whereas the rest of the group would pair up and stay within a certain distance of each other. Corbin would end up miles away from the team. No one thought about it much at the time because he was head of S&R."

"Wait," Joe said. "Who reported Karen missing?"

Jensen hesitated a few seconds. "Corbin. I thought it out of the ordinary because she was almost a complete stranger. Except he said the girl stopped by their house asking directions to the site of the four confederate soldier graves at Dragoon Springs."

Joe glanced at Shannon. "Perfect alibi for a murderer or kidnapper. If you're an ideal citizen on the search and rescue team, no one would suspect you were capable of such a crime."

"Until now," Shannon said. "This could be what Vincent referred to. Maybe Corbin and Marie killed Karen, then reported her missing. Looks like Melissa's not the only one who had secrets. I need to follow up with the lab. Hopefully, they've been able to identify prints on the knife and the cell."

Shannon pulled out her phone and dialed the forensic analyst. "Hey, John. Tell me you've got the results. I'm going to place you on speaker phone so that Sergeant Jensen and another investigator, Joe Luna, can hear you."

"You're a mind reader, agent. I finished the analysis an hour ago. But then another hot case came up, and well, you know how that goes."

"Now that you've got me on the phone, consider mine the priority."

"You got it. That ornate knife turned up prints for a Vincent Joiner, a rather disturbed individual with a dark past. But Corbin Metast's prints were on the cell phone *and* the knife, though Corbin's were on the weapon first."

She looked up at Joe and the sergeant. "Were there any traces of blood on the knife?"

"Yes. DNA matches to an unsolved missing person's case in Cochise County. Her name was Karen Acevedo from Phoenix."

"Thanks, John," Shannon said. "Anything else?"

"We extracted the messages from the cell. There was one suspicious message recorded November 20th. It said 'Will be arriving tomorrow. Remember the deal.' It was an anonymous number, but I did trace it back to a land line in New Mexico."

She sighed. "Whose number was it?"

"The land line was registered to Sarah Harlow. Voice recognition matched the message itself to Vincent Joiner."

Her mouth dropped.

"Agent, are you there?"

"Uh, yeah. Send me a soft copy of everything you've found, including her phone number."

"It's on its way," he said.

"Thanks. Have a great Thanksgiving, John."

"If Corbin did kill that girl, he's definitely gotten what he's deserved," Jensen said. "It's so hard to comprehend that someone who spent so much time trying to find loved ones, would deliberately harm innocent people."

"Many sick minds think that if the community perceives them as incapable of such deeds, that it makes them immune," Shannon said. "Maybe he used the search and rescue work to find potential victims. The fact Corbin's prints were on the knife, or athame`..."

"Vincent might have found that knife somehow and his psychic abilities instantly identified Corbin as the owner," Joe said. "But we still don't know the motive behind Karen's murder."

"I'll have to continue this later," the sergeant said.

After he left the room the dull pain in Shannon's head that started a few hours ago had become an intense throbbing. She pressed her fingers to her temples.

"Here, let me help." Joe's voice softened. He massaged her temples with his palms on the upper part of her head.

She closed her eyes in response to his touch. He was so close she could feel his breath. Then she pulled away. "Thanks, that's much better."

"Anytime." He moved his hands so that he was cupping her face.

Walk away Shannon.

The ERT members had arrived and were filing in with their equipment. Katrina Graham, a petite brunette, and Don Wilson, a husky man in his forties, stopped inside the door.

Don looked at Shannon. "You really know how to make a guy feel welcome."

Don had a tendency to be gruff and to the point, but he was the best crime scene investigator in the state.

"This murder could be associated with the recent abductions," Shannon said. "I found a note in the master bedroom." She held up the plastic bag. "I'll hand this to you to include with any other evidence."

Shannon headed to the door. "We'd better get back to the ranch. I want to see what Lorelei and Ian are up to."

Joe placed his hand in the small of her back as he escorted her outside. Images of him flashed through her mind. She envisioned his dark, naked body covering hers, his hands running through her hair. As if it would eliminate the impure vision, she shook her head vigorously back and forth.

"Joe, what if the Metasts told Melissa about Vincent being released from prison? They were neighbors after all. Maybe that's why Marie seemed so damn nervous when Lore and I talked with her. That might explain why they were murdered."

"That *would* piss him off. With Vincent's powers, there are a number of ways he could have found out Melissa lived here. And I don't think he would want Melissa to know he was in the area, especially if he wanted to surprise her."

"I'm beginning to think Melissa didn't end up here on accident," Shannon said. "Her friend Jennifer mentioned she was into witchcraft. Even though she wouldn't admit it, Melissa might have known about the underground passages, the ruins and valley, and all of the power and energy this area fosters."

"You could be on to something," Joe said. "That didn't elude my mind either. Though I can't imagine her working with Vincent in all of this. She went to so much trouble to ensure he was completely out of her life."

Joe opened the passenger door for Shannon. "If Vincent really is controlling these moving portals, things could get much worse before they get better."

CHAPTER TWENTY-FOUR

Lorelei jumped, distracted from the display on necklace, as a loud crashing sound emanated from the Wagon Wheel Restaurant.

"Ian, I just saw a man moving around in there."

Lorelei followed Ian into the guest room he was staying in. He removed a pistol from the dresser and loaded bullets into the handgun.

"I didn't know you were familiar with guns."

"I wasn't until a few years ago. I decided it would be good to be prepared, especially after having my house robbed twice within a month. And I was home the second time it happened."

"Oh, Ian."

"Let's go." He held open the door for her and they ran up to the entrance of the restaurant. Peeking in the window, he said, "Shit, whoever's in there trashed the place."

Lorelei looked through the glass. The beautiful murals had been slashed repeatedly, the glass tabletops overturned and shattered, and bottles of liquor thrown up against the walls and paintings.

Ian attempted to open the wooden door, but found it locked. "Stand back," he instructed. He broke the glass with the butt of his gun. Taking his jacket off, he laid it on the sill so that neither would get cut by the shards. "Let me go first. I want to make sure it's clear."

Lorelei watched as he leapt through the window. Holding his gun at arms length, he cautiously moved through the dining room, and then the saloon. The door to the cellar was open. Ian vanished into the basement, and reappeared a minute later.

"There's another way underground from the cellar. Looks like that's where the culprit went." He went around and opened the front door to let her in.

"You didn't see anyone?" she asked.

"No. Only heard rustling in the cellar. By the time I got down there the person had already descended into the tunnels."

Ian removed a flashlight from his coat pocket draped on the sill. "We'll need this." He led her down the stairs. "I think you should stay here. We have no idea who or what we're dealing with."

Lorelei placed her hand on the side of Ian's face, her other hand on her necklace. "We both know I have to go."

Ian let out a heavy sigh. A four by four foot panel, which had been removed from the wall, lay on the basement floor. They both peeked into the waiting darkness. "There's a built-in ladder," he said. "I'll go first, it's not far down, then I'll wait for you at the bottom. Make sure you stay behind me in case we run into them."

"How did the intruder get in?" Lorelei asked. "I didn't see any signs of forced entry. And how did he know about this entrance underground?"

"Could be someone who works here," Ian said. "Or someone who was able to get a hold of the keys. Did you get a close look at the man you saw?"

"No. It was from fifty feet away."

Lorelei climbed down after Ian. The passage became colder closer to the bottom—much colder. Frost burst from their mouths—bright swirls of white hanging briefly before dissipating. Though she had a leather jacket on, her teeth still chattered. But when Ian took her hand, it was as if she had just stepped into a thermal spring.

They walked cautiously ahead with Ian's gun at the ready.

Within ten minutes, they were standing at the wall to the Indian ruins. He turned and said, "Lore, I don't know why all this is happening. Why we both ended up on the same team. Why we have this amazing connection, not just to each other, but to Annie and Jeff. I just know that when this is all over, I'm going to take you in my arms and never let go."

She could barely breathe. And for the first time since her ex-husband's tragic death, Lorelei knew she would love again. *If I didn't have these talents, I would still be stagnant—in life and in love.*

Holding his fingers to his lips to indicate to Lorelei to keep quiet, he stared up at the open rooms.

She heard whispering. Not the mysterious whispers that emanated from the large stones, but distinct voices coming from the pueblo directly above them.

"Vincent, I told you I don't know anything about the box."

Melissa. But who is Vincent?

"You lying bitch." Lorelei gasped as a slap echoed throughout the ruins. "You tried to hide my own daughter from me. Did you think that would actually work, knowing my powers, my connections?"

"Owww, stop it!" Melissa began to cry.

"Oh God, Ian, he's hurting her," she whispered.

"Shhhhh." He climbed up the stone and mortar wall alone to the open rooms overlooking the valley. Lorelei watched him disappear into the ruin.

Her heart stopped with the sound of an unfamiliar male voice.

"Glad you could join us," boomed the unseen man. "Get her up here."

"Who?" Ian asked. "I'm here alone."

"Don't fuck with me! The blonde—get here up here now. I know she's waiting below in the tunnel."

Ian, I have to. I'm sorry. Lorelei had already started climbing up. She didn't want to lose him, not now. That's when she heard the whispers—the same exact voices that she had communicated with—the ancients.

"I'm coming," she yelled. As she got to the open room, Vincent yanked her right arm, pulling her up into the pueblo. She screamed in agony, and Ian came up behind the vicious, dark-haired man in fury.

"Don't hurt her!" Ian grabbed Vincent's arm to pull him away from her.

Lorelei stood helplessly as Ian was thrown against the stone wall with such force that it took the wind out of him.

"Ian," she yelled, rubbing her right arm.

"Two lovers, huh?" Vincent forced her on her feet, looking her up and down, within inches of her face. "So tell me, what's so special about this guy?" He nodded toward Ian. "I can do things for you that you couldn't possibly imagine." He leaned in and attempted to kiss her.

Still holding her arm from the pain, she kicked him in the privates to get him away from her, but he didn't even react.

High cheekbones, pale, gaunt face, and the lightning-like symbol on his forehead…Vincent looks like the same man Melissa found lying in the clearing on her property. He looks like Tony Slaughter.

"This was soooo easy," he said.

His rancid breath made her want to vomit. Pure evil emanated from every inch of him. Uncontrollable flashes of torturous rituals ran rampant through her mind—innocent victims spread-eagled on stone tables being carved alive. Others forced to drink concoctions from a gold chalice that would cause instant agony. Horrifying screams of pain echoed constantly. It was a horror movie she tried to put out of her mind. She bent her head and mashed her hands against her temples. But the visions wouldn't stop. He yanked her chin up, forcing her to look him in the eyes.

He's doing this on purpose. He wants me to know what he's capable of.

"I knew you would both follow me here." Vincent glanced over at Ian. "But it's your sweet girlfriend here I really want." He sneered as he played with Lorelei's hair.

Repulsed, she attempted to withdraw, but couldn't. Ian's frantic face looked at her. Then she noticed that he was banging on an invisible force field.

"You really don't have any idea what powers you hold, do you?" Vincent asked.

She closed her eyes. *Ian, can you hear me?*

"Don't even try to communicate with him," Vincent said. "He can no longer hear your thoughts."

The dented, scratched silver box Dale had found lay on top of the altar.

"You're the missing piece. I started out as Vincent Joiner. But now?" He emitted a disturbing, malevolent laugh. "Now I'm something stronger, more indestructible. And you?" He stroked her face and neck. "You're going to complete my transformation, and ensure this realm he created so long ago becomes a permanent feature of this landscape."

The temperature in the ruins abruptly increased. A stifling wave of heat overcame her.

The valley below shimmied, undulated and glistened.

"They're all here." Vincent swept his arm to indicate what was occurring below them. "Tony was their creator. And once you help me complete my transformation to his greatness, they will all be mine, along with the dimension Tony stole so long ago."

He picked up a silver knife, slowly slicing his forearm without wincing. Then Vincent laid the knife against the oozing blood. He approached her with the same knife, grabbed her arm and quickly sliced a three-inch long cut on her left forearm in the same place.

She screamed. Her shaky right hand grasped her wounded arm. Then Vincent picked up a chalice from the altar.

She vaguely saw Ian frantically pounding and yelling, his eyes wide with terror through the invisible shield. She couldn't hear his pleas.

As she stood bleeding, a distinct clicking in her ears preceded light-headedness. Then her body collapsed. There was no panic—even as she looked back down at her still form.

For the first time, she felt completely free and at peace. The cord on her back stretched to allow her to ascend even further into the heavens. The twenty foot long travel rune on the roof of the pueblo and the triangular trail surrounding the valley reminded her what talents she possessed. She was home again.

Lorelei ascended quickly on her celestial journey—earth in its blue and green splendor gradually became but a dot as she rose further into the stars. She floated by the ion and dust tail of a comet. Distracted by the comet's brilliance, she found herself passing directly through a massive solid object. Glancing back, Lorelei saw an irregular shaped brownish object a few miles wide.

An asteroid!

But it was the sun's splendor in the midst of this universal darkness that took her breath away.

The souls of the ancient ones gathered around during her out of body experience, reminding her who she was and celebrating her return. In a language that only she could understand, they spoke to her. "Our celestial dimension has changed. It is no longer peaceful. It represents the worst evil possible. Vincent has your blood, but not the true secret. This can be stopped."

Her necklace had also made the astral journey. The stars in the constellation Ara awaited, as did the altar of the centaur Chiron. She knew that since the ancients believed they originated from the skies, their realm had to be rescued from within the stars.

This celestial ritual had to happen. Or there would be mass destruction.

Among the millions of stars and the many inhabitants that honored the solar system, it was all coming back. Unlike Tony, Lorelei could project at will. That had always been his weakness.

Annie O'Shea had dealt with Tony. Now Lorelei had to confront him again eighty years later as Vincent Joiner. This time the battle was much easier. Because it wasn't her husband Jeff she had to fight—once loving and devoted, he had turned to the dark arts, and to a new personae called Tony Slaughter.

Annie had confided to Jeff about the talents and powers of the people that shared their land. She never knew what made him transform into something so evil and use the information against them. Jeff thought he had killed her through sacrifice to the beastly Gods. He was wrong. Annie knew much more than he could possibly understand. True immortality was not found on the earthly realm. Real power, real knowledge resulted from the ability to connect to something greater than yourself, to develop an inner connection to your spirit, and expand perception far beyond physical limits.

The luminescence from the pendant attracted hundreds in numbers of the once earthly race. They gathered in front of Lorelei at the astral altar.

"Tony is reborn through another," Lorelei said. "And so are his weapons of destruction. They are more dangerous than ever because with every rebirth, they become more indestructible. They are becoming true Gods in their own right. Youth, strength, skill and power are merely objects for their taking—from anyone they choose. They appear where they want, when they want, and can walk the earth unseen."

As Lorelei concentrated in an effort to communicate with Ian, the emerald in the pendant exploded in a brilliant play of light. She focused on the ruins and the triangle of the three patriarchs that surrounded the valley.

Ian, get rid of the small stones from the box. She projected with all her will. *They belong in a place where no one can ever get to them. A place as dark as coal, yet holds the promise of light. You are not alone. You will have help.*

CHAPTER TWENTY-FIVE

Ian watched Vincent squeeze Lorelei's blood into a gold chalice. Her eyes became vacant and she collapsed to the ground.

"You bastard," Ian screamed. But Vincent was in a trance.

Lore, please be okay.

Ian didn't know how, but Vincent had managed to become Tony Slaughter—the infamous dark arts magician. Or at least most of the way. Now he planned on completing the transformation with Lorelei's blood.

As Vincent continued with the ceremony by tracing the carvings on the stones with her plasma, Ian felt the purest form of love go through him.

Within minutes, a stunning emerald radiance reflected from far above. *Lorelei!*

He realized at that second what she was truly capable of. Then he received her message. *A place as dark as coal, yet holds the promise of light.*

Melissa had not regained consciousness. Ian would have to leave her at the altar while he helped Lorelei end the madness. He knew she would be all right. It was Lorelei Vincent really wanted. The ritual had to end before Vincent completed filling the smooth stones with Lorelei's blood. Or the monsters that had been terrorizing the community would become permanent fixtures.

Each time Vincent traced the red substance into a stone, he would extend his hands out as an offering to each of the five pillars. Then an outline of one of the hideous creatures would appear and his eyes would close for thirty seconds, as if soaking up their energy.

Ian's gun lay ten feet away, directly under the triangular doorway. While Vincent extended his hand with the third stone and closed his eyes, Ian dived for the pistol. Apparently, the black arts master couldn't maintain the force field that originally held Ian apart from Lorelei while he performed another ritual.

"Stop right there, Vincent," Ian yelled. He grabbed the pistol and leapt to his feet.

"Who is this Vincent you speak of?" His voice roared, inflected with hatred, greed, and pure iniquity.

Ian could feel the presence of the ancient ones. But Vincent/ Tony didn't seem to hear their indistinguishable whispers. Whispers Ian recognized from the first night at the ranch.

"Give me those stones or I'll kill you. Like it or not, I'm not going to let you use Lorelei's blood for your own greed." Ian glanced over at her body, slumped against the altar.

If you can hear me Lore, please come back to me. I know where you really belong, but I can't live without you.

Tony glanced at her helpless form, then back at Ian. "You won't have her much longer. I hope she likes it up there because that's where she's staying."

Vincent's voice grew deeper, and each word echoed, sending chills down Ian's spine. As Tony picked up his athame` and turned toward Lorelei, Ian heard someone scrambling up the side of the ruins.

"Stop. FBI!" Shannon yelled. "You're under arrest, Vincent Joiner."

Joe was right behind her. All three had their guns pointed at the dark arts magician.

Shannon gasped when she saw Lorelei's lifeless body.

"She's okay," Ian said. "He cut her arm for her blood, but she's not dead. I can't explain this all now. I need to get those stones somewhere that will help end all this."

Joe cautiously walked up to Vincent, never taking his eyes off of Melissa's ex. He grabbed the knife from him and handed it to Shannon. "Ian, come and get the stones."

Ian realized Joe was using his own talents to keep Tony at bay. The ex-FBI agent and shaman had the ability to mesmerize even the most dangerous criminals. But this talent also took a lot out of Joe.

Vincent's eyes reflected hatred, even as they were held captive by Joe. Ian grabbed the stones and idol, tossed them into the box and ran down the narrow pathway into the remnants of a small ruin. He was being guided.

He approached a foot wide hole level with the ground. A brief, brilliant display of white light illuminated the depths.

This has to be it. The blowhole, a connection to the supernatural.

Shannon yelled from the ruins. "Ian, they're coming for you."

Glancing behind him, Ian noticed the whole valley shimmered and seemed to be in motion. "What the fuck."

Is Vincent still able to get creatures to do his bidding while being held captive? Or did the nefarious gods know what Ian was about to do?

Ian quickly removed the smooth stone representing the devil since it was the closest to where he was.

"I release the first of Tony's minions into the depths of the earth where it belongs." Immediately after Ian pitched the stone into the darkness, a reddish-orange flash originated from deep underground. The intense flame pushed its way up and through the hole, illuminating the darkness into day. Ian's hair blew back as a fierce blast of warm air exploded through the hole.

A piercing, inhuman scream came from somewhere nearby. Nothing like Ian had ever heard. He glanced behind him to see the hulking figure of hell transform into the shiny portal, back into solid form then burst into flame.

Ian dropped the next stone. "I release the second of Tony Slaughter's minions back into the bowels of the earth. Let this creature never see the light of day again." Ian dropped the stone with the bird-like symbol.

He placed his hands over his ears as a thundering cry, sounding like a cross between an eagle and a lion, echoed throughout the valley.

"Ian!" Both Shannon and Joe yelled out. The last three gods Tony created eighty years ago suddenly turned from translucent to solid form. The gigantic pit viper, the Gila monster with knife-like protrusions, and the massive wolf on two legs. . . Ian fell backwards in astonishment. The snake was the closest to him—it's forked tongue whipping in and out. It opened its mouth as if to scoop Ian up. Two foot fangs dripped with yellowish venom.

Hands shaking and eyes wide with terror, Ian fumbled through the metal box for the stone with the snake symbol. The pit viper hissed loudly, lunging its heart-shaped head at Ian as he grabbed the stone.

"Back to hell demons! You have no more connection to earth!"

He dropped the third, fourth and fifth stones in within seconds of each other.

The last three monsters glowered at him, then howled and threw their heads back before disappearing in flames. Ian closely watched for any sign of shimmering motion, indicating they might have only turned invisible.

There was nothing. He glanced up at the altar in the ruins to see Vincent on top of Joe, pinning him down on the ground.

Ian raced up the hill to help. That's when he saw Lorelei and Melissa both coming around.

Vincent was on top of Joe, the athame` pointed at his heart. Shannon dragged Lorelei out of the path of their struggle. That gave Ian the clearance he needed. He darted toward Joe and kicked Vincent off of him.

Knife still in his hand, Vincent scrambled for Lorelei. He pulled her against him and lifted the weapon high in the air, staring at Ian. "With my blood on this knife, Annie will never be able to live again." A victorious grin crept into the corner of his mouth as he started to bring down the blade.

Ian realized he only had a split second. Or he would lose Lorelei. Inches from penetrating Lorelei's heart, the athame` flew from Vincent's hand, seemingly on its own. The weapon landed next to Joe, who dove for it. Ian ran over to Lorelei and gathered her in his arms.

Vincent started to pull something else from his jacket.

"This ends now dirtbag," Joe said. Then he shot Vincent in the head.

A growling laughter emitted from the ruins. "We are invincible. We are one. And our souls will live on for eternity. We will be back."

"No. No you won't," Lorelei whispered.

Within seconds, Ian watched as Vincent's soul rose from his lifeless body, traveling into the valley below.

Ian was about to ask Lorelei what she meant when an intense ray of emerald green light descended from the heavens—revealing an illuminated triangle, which extended from the top of the Indian ruins to the top of the five granite pillars.

The base of the triangle hovered behind the five monuments. He could only imagine the triangle point behind the ruins where they now stood.

Vincent's spirit appeared in the middle, below where the beam of light originated. He seemed to be trapped. His soul began to split apart under the heightened luminosity. Moaning turned into the worst, most painful screams Ian had ever heard.

If it's possible for souls to die, then that's what's happening here. Glancing at Lorelei, he knew she was somehow responsible. In order to do what she did—complete an astral journey without any sort of preparation and then end that journey and the nightmare Tony Slaughter had started so long ago. . .

Lorelei is an astral goddess.

Ian, Shannon, Melissa and Joe were all transfixed as they witnessed the last of the evil black arts master being obliterated. Within less than a minute, the pulsating light had completed its mission.

CHAPTER TWENTY-SIX

Lorelei saw a beautiful light tan horse trot into view in Dale's video footage—exactly like the one she had seen in person the first day of the investigation. The mare had a long white mane and tail, white socks and a white stripe down its nose. But even more stunning than the horse, was the woman riding it. Tight fitting jeans emphasized her long, slender legs, and the peach top she wore accented her olive skin. Her long black hair flowed freely as she sat proudly on top of the palomino.

A piercing scream echoed throughout the black void. The woman and the horse vanished.

That was definitely Karen," Sergeant Jensen said. "This is pretty amazing stuff you've all captured. I have to admit, I wasn't much of a believer until this case. I never had any experiences. Though I would have preferred to start out with one ghost, rather than monsters and evil black arts people."

"This case has been a shock to all of us," Dale said. "I had planned on emailing Shannon this evidence. "But when she called me with all the details of last night, I had to come back."

Lorelei looked down at the pewter pendant with the mystical emerald hanging on her neck. For her, the last few days were a haze. She barely recalled the out-of-body experience. Maybe they wanted it that way. She only knew she looked forward to getting on with her life. And she hoped it wasn't going to be by herself anymore.

Ian came over and placed his arm around her waist.

"Karen's is classified as a residual haunting." Dale glanced over at the sergeant. "The spirits relive their last moments, or some part of their lives, over and over. They might be afraid to pass on because of unfinished business. It seems like this might be when Corbin killed Karen, though he's obviously not in the video."

"Justice was served in the end." The sergeant continued to stare at the video. "Those were definitely Corbin's and Vincent's prints on that knife, and Karen's DNA. I prefer not to think how she died. My deputies are down there now to see if they can find any remains."

Shannon sat down next to Dale. "Appears Vincent discovered the knife since he had been roaming the property, and with his psychic ability, he knew about the couple's crime. He used that knowledge to threaten Corbin and Marie to watch over Melissa. We think they were both supposed to deliver her to Vincent because Melissa said she received an urgent phone call from Marie before the extraction ceremony saying she needed help. For some reason, Marie phoned back a few minutes later telling Melissa she was all right. Apparently, they decided to back out and hit the road. That's why they were murdered."

"I wonder why Marie decided to forgo luring Melissa to her demise?" Ian asked.

"Melissa helped out with some of Marie's food drives," Shannon said. "Plus Melissa did take Marie to the emergency room when she had a heart attack two years ago. The doctor said if she hadn't made it there when she did, she would have died. I'm sure Marie and Corbin felt they owed it to Melissa."

Lorelei took a sip from her mug of hot chocolate. "Interesting, considering Corbin used his connections with the search and rescue team to abduct victims and then initiate a false search party."

"Looks that way," Jensen said. "Never knew he was such a sick bastard. One thing I didn't tell you all until now is there was another missing person's case."

Shannon, Dale, Lorelei and Ian all glanced over at Jensen. "There was a homeless male seen roaming the Metast property from time to time. No one thought much about it at first, thinking he had moved on." He sighed. "But maybe we'll run across his remains, if there are any."

Lorelei wondered if Corbin and Marie knew about the ruins and its history. If so, no one would ever know. Melissa had confessed to the team that she ran because the Metasts had tipped her off about her ex-husband being released from jail early and that he was seeking revenge. Marie let Melissa know when she called her back to cancel the request for help.

"I'm still seeing that massacre at the Metasts," Jensen said. "The worst any of us have ever seen. My deputies and I have been having nightmares. There were prints on the note Vincent left and in other parts of their home to back up what the rest of you experienced."

Shannon yawned and took a sip of her coffee. "Vincent could have transformed into a skinwalker. Melissa mentioned Vincent did have the ability. Or he could have commanded one of his horrible minions."

Lorelei was grateful Shannon didn't mention how the case ended. Communicating with beings that she never knew existed, finding out she's the reincarnation of Annie O'Shea, and possibly finding the love of a lifetime and performing astral travel to eliminate a powerful magician. . . she barely understood it all herself, let alone explaining it to someone she barely knew.

Soon after the confrontation with Vincent, Ian could no longer read Lorelei's mind. Perhaps his temporary ability was for the sole purpose of communicating to him while she gathered the ancient ones together. Or maybe to make her understand how strong of a bond they had between them.

"It's so bizarre Melissa chose to move here," Dale said. "I mean, think about it. The same damn thing happened to Annie O'Shea. Her husband turned to the dark arts. At least Melissa didn't turn out to be a victim."

"Maybe Melissa's daughter will move here," Ian said.

"Not sure she's going to stay here though." Shannon threw herself on the couch. "Melissa's talking about selling the ranch. Too many bad memories."

"Speaking of bad memories," Lorelei glanced up at Jensen. "How are Tanya and Kelly doing?"

"As well as can be expected, I guess. Tanya's grandparents found her wandering around in shock, right after you all caught Tony." He sighed heavily. "Unfortunately, they'll be having some serious nightmares for a while."

Lorelei sat quietly, staring at the bandage on her arm where Vincent had sliced her. Though it had been a deep cut, the healing had progressed so fast that the wound was all ready scarring. She had Joe asked and Ian if they were responsible, but they both insisted it was beyond their capabilities.

Dale had a contemplative look on his face. "So this all started with Tony Slaughter, who was really Jeff O'Shea?"

"Yeah," Lorelei responded. "Jeff changed from a loving husband to a master of the dark arts. Annie confided the secrets of this place to him, so he used that information to transform this astral realm into another dimension for his own power. That's where those stones come in—he performed a ritual that included etching the five monstrous 'gods' into both the smaller stones and the pillars in the valley."

Joe came over and placed his arm around Lorelei. "And Vincent knew about this place all ready. I think he might have connected with Tony, or Jeff, in a spiritual way, since they were both so dark minded. It's hard to say if Jeff's spirit initiated the idea, or if Vincent used his abilities to see the past and what Jeff had accomplished."

Sergeant Jensen glanced down as his cell phone buzzed. "Sorry guys, have to head out on a call. Thanks for getting rid of Tony and getting this community back to normal. Please feel free to come back anytime. I'll make sure the sheriff's department pays for your stay."

Jensen waved goodbye and rushed out the door.

Ian looked at Shannon after the sergeant left. "What does Jensen think happened to Vincent?"

"Told him the culprit was shot in order to save Melissa." Shannon winked at Lorelei. "At least that will be the cover story. I think we need to protect our secret weapon."

Lorelei rolled her eyes and looked at Joe. "So Shannon mentioned you had infiltrated Vincent's cult?"

"Yeah. Let's say I have special talents that help me gain confidence with criminals. The other agents were completely amazed by it. But after some of what I witnessed . . ."

His voice trailed off. Lorelei knew he was reliving the more horrifying moments with the cult. And his witnessing of the OOB experience that led to a man's suicide.

"What about the body Melissa saw?" Dale looked from Shannon to Joe. "Since Vincent had actually become Tony, could that be what she saw?"

Shannon stretched her arms. "A tourist staying at a bed and breakfast in the area identified Vincent Joiner—not Tony Slaughter. Vincent was seen the same day we arrived, but in his true form—brown hair, fuller face than Tony's and no mark on the forehead." A few witnesses mentioned two residents were talking peacefully on the street, then when Vincent came around, the conversation between the locals suddenly escalated to an all out battle. One witness said Vincent got this strange look of satisfaction when they started fighting. Both men suffered broken bones, and one a broken nose. And both reported feeling totally out of control, for no reason at all. If Vincent's capable of such mind control, then maybe he was playing mind games with Melissa."

Lorelei threaded her arm through Ian's. "Or it could be that Tony, or Jeff, actually died in that spot. For some reason, that was one thing I couldn't pick up on."

"Joe, you mentioned Tony died from a tragic death," Ian said.

Joe stopped texting and put away his cell phone. "I guess you could consider expiration from an out-of-body journey a tragic death."

"What do you mean?" Lorelei asked.

"My contact in the FBI." Joe glanced at his cell phone. "I checked on his cause of death as soon as Ian mentioned Tony's description. As we all ready know, Jeff took on the personae of Tony Slaughter."

"But how the hell would you know he died during OOB?" Shannon asked.

"Because he wasn't alone when it happened. There was another person that took the astral journey with Tony. Only he came back, and Tony didn't."

"You can actually be killed if someone cuts your silver cord, the thin fibrous strands that connect to your physical self." Ian started to pack his ghost hunting equipment. "Joe, who did he perform that out-of-body with? Whoever it was must have severed his cord during travel, explaining why there were no marks on the body."

"Annie O'Shea's brother—but Jeff didn't know that. He had never met him."

Lorelei gasped. "Oh my God. He knew. Annie's brother must have known what Jeff did." She looked up at Ian. "She did get her revenge. Damn it Joe, when did you find this out?"

"Just now, sweetie. That was the text message."

She wasn't sure what to feel anymore. Originally excited by the romantic connection between Jeff and Annie, Lorelei now wondered if Ian was a reincarnation of Jeff. And if so, would he turn to the dark arts?

Joe interrupted her thoughts. "My contact also mentioned that Tony always did his astral rituals in remote places. Since Jeff *was* Tony, I could easily imagine him performing his journey in the clearing where she saw him since the labyrinth was nearby."

"That makes sense," Shannon said. "But why wouldn't he have done such a thing at the ruins where he created those *things*? I mean, between the pueblo and the mystical monoliths, the valley does have more of a spiritual meaning."

Her question went unanswered.

"Vincent seemed so jealous of your power." Ian pulled her close and kissed the top of Lorelei's head. He was pretty intent on. . . " Overwhelmed with emotion, his voice choked.

Reaching up, she draped her arms around his neck. "Thanks to you, he didn't." Then she kissed him softly on the lips. He responded by pulling her close.

"Did Shannon tell you how we managed to find you both? And just in time," Joe said.

Lorelei lifted the pendant off her neck. "It was them. The ancient ones."

"Seems that way," Shannon said. "When Joe and I arrived back at the ranch, we heard those same voices from the tunnel that goes to the ruins. Not that we understood what they were saying, but we were both physically pushed toward the restaurant. I thought we were going to fall down the stairs with the force. That's how we found the entrance."

Joe smiled. "Actually, we didn't have much of a choice. They were making it very clear where we needed to go."

Ian laughed. "Dale, close your mouth or you'll let all the spiders in."

"I've been so focused all these years on the paranormal. But I had no idea there was so much more. I mean, this whole case could make one hell of a novel." Dale stared at Lorelei. "And it's so hard to believe that Lorelei is still sane after what she's been through these past few days."

"There's quite a bit of evidence left to review from Dragoon," Shannon said. "Dale, you have over twelve hours of audio and video, not to mention the thermal, right? Adam said he would pay for your hours of analysis, so you have clearance to keep going with the investigation."

"Woo hoo," Dale yelled. "Awesome." He hesitated. "Maybe we can find more solid proof of the people that lived here. We know they based their beliefs and existence on the heavens. But were they a tribe among themselves? Was this where they originated, or did they migrate like other Native tribes in order to survive?"

"I didn't get all the answers during that journey," Lorelei said. "But I know they used the universe to put things into perspective. After all, when you're up there," she glanced up at the cracked ceiling. "Things, problems, people, seem much, much smaller. Sadness, anger, daily frustrations don't matter as much."

Ian placed his hands on her shoulders. "Lore's just as anxious to find out more about them as the rest of us. What if we contact universities in Arizona, or historical and archeological societies and show them the proof we found?"

"Joe and I started contacting some places in the state. So far, no one's heard of these particular tunnels, ruins, or the cave," Shannon said. "One professor said the underground passages could be associated with leylines—the straight, often geometrical lines that run across landscapes, connecting ancient or sacred features."

"There are those who feel that leys are probably lines of energy, of magnetism even, and associated with UFOs and psychic experience," Ian said. "One of the most dramatic examples is at Chaco Canyon in northwestern New Mexico where the Anasazi used to live. Those roads stretch sixty miles beyond the canyon and link ceremonial Great Houses."

"Wait," Joe said. "The word Anasazi means 'Ancient Ones' or 'Ancient Enemy.' Lore, do you think they're the race you've connected with? They were Puebloans who were said to have emerged around 1200 B.C. They lived in the four corners region. And no one knows what language the ancestral Puebloans spoke. The culture was widespread in space and time, so it is likely that different languages were spoken."

"I, I don't know. Dragoon isn't part of the four corners. And the ruin doesn't exactly reflect the type of style or size of their architecture. It's not on the scale of Mesa Verde or Chaco Canyon."

Lorelei felt there were other unexplored tunnels. Other lost entrances that may never be discovered. But she also knew that she, and this ancient race, preferred it that way.

Joe walked up to Lorelei, giving her a hug. "We've all learned how truly amazing you are, Lorelei Lanier. You've made it through one hell of an odyssey these past few days—both on earth and up there. But you have to let Ian and I help you learn more about your past, and what you are really capable of. Lore, you are Annie. And this is your second chance at love. Forget the past with Patrick—and Jeff."

Three loud knocks drew their attention to the door. Shannon opened it to find Melissa standing there with an attractive girl with light brown hair and an unusual mark on her forehead.

"Melissa. How are you doing? I thought you were in the hospital."

There were bruises in the shape of fingers lining both her arms where Vincent had grabbed her and pushed her around. And deep scratches on her face, throat and arms.

"No, I, I'm fine." She glanced down nervously at the wounds on her arms.

Lorelei noticed Melissa could barely look any of them in the eye.

"Just superficial. I wanted to make sure my daughter was okay, so I left the community hospital in Willcox early this morning. This is Sarah by the way."

"Nice to meet you all." Lorelei had seen that smile before. It was the same one that Marie Metast had used during the interview. Sarah turned and stared at Lorelei with a quizzical yet annoyed expression—as if she had read Lorelei's thoughts.

Melissa gave them all a quick hug. "I wanted to stop by and give my thanks before you all leave. You've been wonderful. If I decide to keep the place, you guys can come back at any time, no charge."

"Oh mom, you know you'll keep the ranch. It's too special—to all of us." Sarah shook Shannon and Dale's hands then walked over and stood in front of Ian and Lorelei. "I've heard some interesting things about the both of you."

Ian put both his hands on Lorelei's shoulders. He suddenly seemed protective, pulling her against him and away from Sarah.

Lorelei gazed at the cult scar on her forehead. She could barely breathe the longer she looked at Sarah. Something wasn't right about Melissa's daughter. She felt as if the young girl were drilling into her mind.

"Mom, we'd better get going. You promised me a late breakfast."

If Sarah was a victim of the cult, she isn't any longer.

Melissa opened the door. "Shannon, I'm really sorry for the way I left. When Marie told me about Vincent, I panicked." Melissa lowered her head. "All I thought about was getting to Sarah. I should have told you about my past. I didn't think any of this had anything to do with him—the body I saw, the creatures—I had no idea."

"Yes, you should have kept me advised and been more honest," Shannon said. "But I'm glad you're both okay."

"It was nice meeting you all," Sarah said. But Lorelei noticed she eyed Ian when she said the words. "I appreciate you helping my mother through this horror."

Lorelei didn't miss the girl's fake shudder.

Melissa waved goodbye and went out the door with Sarah.

"Lore," Ian said. "Did you get the same impression I did?"

"Uh, yeah. Shannon, I don't know if Melissa knows this, but that girl is a chip off the old block. In every sense of the word." Lorelei continued to stare at the door.

Shannon smacked her hand against her forehead. "Can I pretend I didn't hear that? Listen, Melissa mentioned she had been marked from birth."

"It's not just the symbol," Ian said. "It's the feeling I got. If Melissa is aware of it, she's not admitting it. I've seen that particular sign before. If that's the cult Vincent was involved in, they never let a marked person stray. If she was an innocent victim before this, she's not now. And Vincent did make that call from Sarah's land line."

"That symbol is associated with the Church of Satan," Joe said.

"Devil worshippers?" Shannon asked.

"Contrary to belief, there are no elements of Devil worship in the Church of Satan," Joe said. "Satanists don't believe in the supernatural, in neither God nor the Devil. To the Satanist, he is his own god. Satan is not a conscious entity to be worshipped, rather a reservoir of power inside each human to be tapped at will."

Joe handed Shannon another cup of coffee. "Vincent's cult created their own version of what it meant to be Satanists, practicing super-normal techniques for influencing the outcome of human events. They practiced rituals, sending forth visions of what they wanted to occur and controlling individual subconscious. Not too many were, or are, capable of such talent. But if your levels of adrenaline are high enough, you can infiltrate the subconscious minds of those you wish to influence, causing them to behave as you want, when you want. It takes a great deal of energy, but achieving such a feat was the ultimate payoff."

Lorelei wondered about Joe's abilities. He had managed to overpower Vincent while Ian destroyed the monsters. Could Joe be even more powerful than Vincent or Tony?

"That aligns with what Melissa told me last night at the hospital," Shannon said. "At first he practiced with small things like persuading her to have sex or letting him stay out with the coven for the whole night. Then she mentioned he moved on to convincing her to include other women during sex, then he got Sarah involved. She thought her daughter was safe because she had been out of the country for awhile. But being a master at astral projection means there are no hiding places. That's probably how he kept Sarah under his control."

"Well guys, I've got to go." Dale closed his laptop and placed it in his carrying case. "It is Thanksgiving after all, and we're going to our in-laws when I get back home. I'll be in touch with you all about whatever evidence I come across. Brandon wants to help as well. When we get finished, I'll write up a complete report."

"Thanks for all your help, Dale," Shannon said.

"You bet. Wait, Ian, don't you and Lorelei need a ride home?"

"No thanks. Shannon's splurging for a rental car for the two of us so that we can enjoy what's left of our first holiday together." He glanced over at Lorelei. "I'll be taking this amazing woman out to dinner somewhere."

"Cool." Dale dropped his briefcase and walked over, giving them both a big hug. "I'm so happy for both of you. It's fascinating to watch the romance of the century happen right in front of you."

CHAPTER TWENTY-SEVEN

This was the perfect day, Lorelei said to Ian as they pulled into his garage. "The scenic drive through the mountains in Tucson, the steak and lobster dinner with red wine, and your company. I can't believe we were in the restaurant for three hours. It felt like minutes."

Ian gazed into her eyes, then kissed her so lightly on her cheek. It felt as if a soft breeze had touched her. "You'll always have the best, Lore. You deserve it."

He got out of the rental car, opened her door for her, and held her hand as they walked into his house.

She stared into his amazing, smoky blue eyes. Ian could no longer read her mind. But he didn't have to.

He took her hand and led her into his bedroom. He threw back the covers, then slowly undressed her, picked her up, and laid her on the bed. She watched as he undressed and slid in next to her. He stroked her hair gently. Within minutes, she had fallen asleep.

Lorelei awoke around 1:00 a.m. with Ian's arms around her, her head against his bare chest. Though she hadn't moved, he seemed to know she were awake. He tipped up her head with his fingers and looked her in the eyes.

She softly ran her tongue along his lower lip. His sharp intake of breath followed by a moan made her want him so much more. At that moment, she felt as if she were on fire. Not merely a passionate spark, but a full blown heat that threatened to ignite her from the inside out. She imagined a large chunk of fuel smoldering slowly in a fire, glowing orange-red. The intense heat made the embers crackle and explode. And then she felt his desire against her.

"Ian, make love to me." She ran her hand lightly up and down his chest. "I want to be a part of you," she whispered, glancing up into his passion-filled eyes.

His hands caressed her breasts. "You are an absolute goddess."

Then he kissed her stomach repeatedly, working his way down. Every light touch, every kiss, every gentle bite brought her one step closer to a place she had never known. She lifted her hips and pulled him toward her.

"Lore, whatever you want from me, you'll get—now and forever." He teased her endlessly with his warm breath, licking her inner thighs. Then he worked his way down to drink.

She closed her eyes in passion, throwing her head back. And when she opened them again, they were on a lush, green hilltop, cool, damp grass refreshing against the fire inside her. A light mist surrounded them both and covered their bare skin. They both exploded inside each other. Bright pink magnolia blossoms rained down upon them from the tree above. He stroked her face and told her, "I hope you realize you're not going to get rid of me any time soon."

As she gasped in pleasure, he pulled her into a sitting position, still inside her. "Ian, can you see . . ."

"This is where Annie and Jeff made love. You're doing this, baby."

Even as they sat straddled together, Lorelei could feel him moving inside her, though his body was not moving. He teased her and did things she didn't think a man could physically do. She wrapped her legs tighter around him, grinding against him until she thought every muscle would explode.

As they came, she heard a waterfall in the background. Catching her breath, she said, "God, you are magic. You do things I never thought possible." She ran her fingers through his soft, wavy hair.

"We're both magic." He took both her hands in his. "There's something else you need to see. But don't be afraid."

"What?"

"Look down." His lips softly traced her face and shoulder.

The lush green hilltop faded. She looked below her. They both floated a foot off the bed.

She grasped him tighter. "Are you doing this?"

"I don't think so. Not on purpose at least." Ian gently guided both their bodies back onto the bed. They fell asleep wrapped in each others arms. And when she awoke, Ian was gazing into her eyes.

"Good morning, beautiful."

"It wasn't a dream?" she asked.

"I hope not." He kissed her passionately. "Feels pretty real to me." He smiled at her and she knew she wouldn't be able to live without him.

"Lore, Shannon called. She mentioned her and Joe took some archeologists back to the valley. Everything is gone—the pueblo and the monuments."

The ancients eliminated the source of the problem. But how could they make the site completely vanish? What other secrets does the astral race hold?

CHAPTER TWENTY-EIGHT

Two months later

An uprooted ponderosa pine lay on the reddish dirt; its darkened, stiffened limbs reaching out into its alien environment. A primal, jagged river of black rock spread out below the footbridge where Lorelei and Ian stood, only part of the lunar landscape north of Flagstaff, Arizona. To the west, the snowcapped San Francisco Peaks, the highest in Arizona, dominated the sky at over twelve thousand feet.

Walking along the trail in Sunset Crater National Monument, piles of black rock created unusual formations—reminders of cooling lava flows. A pale aspen, straight and tall, appeared to have been transplanted into the harsh and somber habitat.

Could Ian's healing abilities be the reason I'm still sane after everything that's happened? She glanced over to see him staring at her. Then his lips formed that sensuous smile that always drove her crazy.

"Dad look," Ian's son, Paul yelled, with so much enthusiasm that a few passers by glanced back in curiosity. "There's something sitting on that rock." The bright-eyed, brown-haired ten-year old pointed to a motionless lizard only a few feet away that blended in perfectly with its terrain.

"That's a horned toad," Ian said. "It's named that because of its squat, flattened shape and short, blunt snout. It looks sort of like a toad, huh?"

"Oh, yeah. Cool. Lore, can you see it?" Paul pointed at the rock.

Lorelei leaned over to see the reptile. "Yes, I do. And I think he knows we're watching."She gazed up at the slick, dark cinder slopes dotted with trees. Clumps of golden rabbit brush decorated the bottom of the hill.

Paul lost interest in the reptile and ran ahead on the trail. Ian put his hands on her waist, pulling her close. "I've wanted to do this all morning." He kissed her once softly, then with more passion.

Lorelei pulled away from Ian, breathless and trembling.

"Yuck," Paul said. "Are you guys coming?"

Lorelei laughed and chased Paul.

Paul ran ahead to a shady section of trail lined with ponderosa's.

"So we are finishing that bit of business tonight right?" Ian asked.

Lorelei stopped him for a brief second and whispered in his ear with her hand pressed against his chest. "Try and stop me." She gave him a flirtatious smile. "Where are we going tonight?"

"I believe it's your turn to decide," he said. "Not that I ever really notice where we are when we're intimate."

She had to turn away lest she get drawn into the intensity of his eyes. The first night they made love, Lorelei and Ian had found themselves in Ireland. The same spot where she had seen Annie and Jeff in her vision at the ranch. Every sexual encounter brought them to new places and new heights.

"Dad. Over here."

Ian and Lorelei followed Paul's voice, and found him climbing a rusted metal ladder—the top of which leaned against a section covered in lava rock.

Lorelei gasped in horror to see him already twenty feet above the ground with nothing but sharp rock below.

"Paul, get down now," Ian screamed, standing right by the ladder. "You're going to get hurt. This isn't for play. It's for the rangers to access that ledge above you."

Paul started to climb down, but slipped on the rung underneath and started to fall straight down.

"No!" Ian was ready to try and catch him, but he didn't need to. Something stopped Paul in mid-air, seconds before he hit the ground. Ian immediately pulled Paul into his arms, squeezing him tightly.

"Thank God," Ian said, choking back tears. "Are you all right?"

Paul began to cry from his frightening experience. "Yes," he sobbed. "Dad, I'm sorry."

"I'm glad you're okay."

Lorelei rubbed Paul's back as Ian held him tightly. Ian mouthed the words, "Did you do that?"

She wasn't entirely sure. She only remembered thinking the word "stop" right after Paul fell. Considering her special ability for instantaneous, controlled astral projection, Lorelei wasn't sure what else waited; especially since Ian had been teaching her meditation. *Could that be opening up other talents?*

Ian set his son back on the black, sandy soil with sprouting ponderosa's. Paul glanced at his father, then at Lorelei. "What happened?" Paul asked. But for some reason, he stared at Lorelei.

The maturity in Paul's big brown eyes stunned her for a second. Then he turned and faced her as if he already knew the answer.

A tear rolled down her face. "Honey, I don't know." She hugged him, whispering into his ear. "I think you have a guardian angel."

"I have two." He kissed her on her cheek then looked up at his father as if he were a hero. "Can we go see the ruins now?"

"Are you sure you still want to after that?" Ian stared at Paul in shock.

"Heck yes."

Ian placed his arm around Paul's shoulder and Lorelei walked on the other side of Paul. She pulled out the necklace that had been discovered on the Texas Canyon Ranch in Dragoon—the pewter pendant with the stunning emerald that helped stop Vincent Joiner from destroying the community, and possibly the world.

Did my mother have all these abilities? Or was it just my past life as Annie O'Shea? Paul stopped to look at a formation as they neared the parking lot.

Ian grabbed Lorelei's hand. "I think he's convinced both of us saved him."

"Maybe it was. Ian, I'm not sure of anything right now."

"That's okay. You're still learning. And I think the meditation techniques you've been practicing are revealing other aspects. Maybe I'm somehow feeding off of your energy. I don't know either." He hesitated, gazing into her eyes. "I just know I love you so much." Ian kissed her lightly on the lips. Lorelei counted the minutes until she could be alone with him.

"Are we ready?" Paul's question brought her out of her reverie.

Ian grinned at her as her face flushed in embarrassment.

"Let's go see what else we can find," she said. They walked back to the parking lot.

They descended in Ian's car down from the pinyon pine and juniper forest. "That's where we're headed after the ruins." Ian pointed to the distant, time-weathered mesas of light pink, blue, green and gray.

Dread and apprehension abruptly overcame Lorelei. She started to wring her hands together. Her breathing becoming shallower. The closer they got to the wide open valley below, the worse it became. She was so immersed in the sensation that she jumped when Ian reached over and stroked her face.

"Are you okay?" he asked.

Lorelei glanced back at Paul and smiled. "Sorry guys. Guess I got lost in my thoughts." She could tell Ian was worried. Slipping her hand in his, she glanced over at him and smiled.

The shine returned to his eyes. He squeezed her hand and then kissed it.

The largest of the Indian ruins loomed off to the left side of the loop road on the edge of the black sand country. The rich reds of the prehistoric structure matched the surrounding terrain covered in snakeweed, four-wing saltbush and juniper.

They pulled into the parking lot and walked through the visitor center.

"Dad, can I go ahead of you guys?"

"Sure, but stay within eyeshot."

Lorelei smiled as Paul ran ahead to investigate the pueblos. "Does your ex-wife take him on trips like this?"

"No. She doesn't have the patience to teach him anything herself. Emily gets very jealous when he spends time with me because he's so excited about our time together." Ian paused. "And I know Emily is jealous of you as well. Paul talks about you all the time."

"That's flattering," Lorelei said. "I really enjoy spending time with both of you. I've never had kids." Lorelei glanced away for a second, then looked back at Ian. "What with Patrick dying so soon after our marriage. But thanks to you, thoughts of his suicide aren't quite so painful anymore."

"No, because you now know it wasn't your fault, honey. Everyone has issues, some more serious than others. You mentioned he had bipolar disorder."

"He never bothered to tell me until after we were married. It didn't matter so much at first because the disorder was so well controlled with the medicine. Then he just stopped taking it without me even knowing about it. The autopsy showed only minute traces of it in his system. That's the only way any of us found out. I didn't even see a decrease in mood before it happened."

"Lore, back there in the car you became distant. Are you getting visions?"

"No, strong sensations. It became worse the closer we drove to these ruins. I hope it goes away."

"So you're still dealing with it?" Ian asked.

She nodded her head. "I didn't want to mention it with Paul around considering what he went through with that fall."

"I understand." Ian kissed her forehead. "I worry about you. Though with everything you've made it through, I probably shouldn't."

"It's great you care. That's what makes you so special," Lorelei said. "Plus the fact you're so damn hot." She placed her arms around his shoulders and pulled her toward him.

They stood in front of a pueblo with its partially collapsed stone walls, sandstone outcropping, and wooden support beams. Ian removed a blue jewelry box from his jacket. Lorelei's heart stopped when he lifted the lid.

"Lorelei Lanier, I know we've only been dating two months. But the way you handled yourself on that investigation made me realize how astounding you really are. Our time together has been the best of my life. I want you to know how much I care."

Her hands trembled and quaked. Tears rolled down her cheeks as he placed the extraordinary ring on her finger.

"Ian, this must have cost a fortune," she whispered. A striking one carat emerald had the center setting with five .20 carat star-shaped diamonds set into the five points of a pentagram. The ring itself was antique-like to match the style of the pendant.

"This isn't a proposal. I know it's too soon for that. I wanted you to know how I feel. And considering what the necklace represents, I couldn't resist."

She looked into his eyes.

"Do you like the ring?" Ian asked.

"It's gorgeous. The most beautiful ring I've ever seen." Lorelei kissed him gently on the lips.

Her eyes swept the wide expanse of ochre landscape dotted with brush and colorful mesas. "I'm so happy." She looked up at the strikingly handsome man standing before her—lean, six feet tall with light, wavy brown hair and smoky mountain eyes that drew her in the second she looked into them.

They continued walking on a gradual descent toward the circular community room. A searing pain made her collapse on her knees. She grabbed her side and gasped for air.

"Lore. Should I get help?" Ian asked.

"No. It's not me. Something's trying to communicate. Ian, get me out of here, please. Oh God!" she screamed. He scooped her up and ran with her to the parking lot.

She squirmed in his arms, still holding onto her side.

"Paul! Paul, we've got to go." Ian yelled so loud everyone turned to look.

"Coming dad," he replied.

Ian threw his keys to Paul. "Unlock the car."

"Ian, it hurts. What's going on?" She writhed in his arms as Ian ran up the stairs toward the visitor center.

"Baby, I don't know. You're going to be fine."

"Do you need some help?" a stranger yelled. Ian didn't seem to hear.

The closer they got to the parking lot, the more the pain subsided. She relaxed in his arms, her hands around his neck.

Paul had reclined the front seat, so Ian placed her inside. "I'm going to call an ambulance."

"Honey no," she replied, trying to reposition the seat forward. "I'm fine now. It's something, or someone, here. Maybe that was why I had the feeling of dread as we drove down."

"You scared me." Ian's hands shook as he knelt beside her and pulled her to him. "Are you sure?"

"Yes." Lorelei started to cry. "I'm so sorry. You just gave me an amazing gift. I ruined this whole day."

"Lore, stop. You've already made it special. I'm glad you're all right. You didn't sign up for all this."

Lorelei threw her arms around his neck. "I don't know what I'd do if I lost you."

"You won't." His intense gaze and tone of voice told her he meant it.

Paul climbed in the back seat and then leaned forward to talk to Lorelei. "It's okay," he said. "We can come back another time."

Lorelei turned to look at Paul. He sounded as mature as most men his father's age. It was almost as if the young boy had changed personalities.

"Paul sweetie, I'm fine. My episode had something to do with the history of the place. Let's go to the next ruin. I really want to explore this place."

"Was something communicating with you?" Paul asked.

"Yeah, only I wish they would have found a better way." She forced a weak laugh.

"Paul, why don't give us a few minutes? You can head down the trail, but not too far. Lore and I are going to have a talk." Ian stroked her face gently.

Lorelei watched Paul walk away from the car. "What really happened back there?"

He stared at her, waiting for a response.

She sighed, leaning her head back against the car seat. "I've enjoyed spending time with you lately. Why does this have to happen now?"

"Lore, what did you see?"

"A murder."

"Was this a crime from long ago when the Native Americans still lived here?"

"No. A few minutes after you placed the ring on my finger, I got this abrupt, horrible pain like someone forced a hot knife into my side. It was excruciating. But the farther away you carried me, the better I became. My vision showed a full moon shining down on the ruins. Then the scene went underground to the unexcavated sections."

"Well, there are many more rooms that haven't been uncovered yet," Ian said.

"Honey, I can't explain it. There's a blowhole here, a few actually. They are said to be associated with caves and passages. I saw a large, open area with more pueblos. Somehow, at least three people managed to get down there—the woman that was killed, the murderer and a child. The only person I could see was the woman, but I heard a child crying. The woman yelled at the child to run right before she was killed. As you picked me up, there was an overwhelming sense of confusion and terror. Though I'm not sure from who."

"Sounds like your visions have been getting much clearer

lately." He pulled her close.

"Definitely, since I've been practicing meditation and yoga. But it's not any less disturbing. A piercing scream echoed throughout my mind right before I felt the torment began. I'm terrified to go back down there. I've never felt anything that extreme." Tears rolled down her face. "Ian, I also had a very brief image of the victim and her child being taken. She's no longer alive, but I think there's an innocent little boy about Paul's age still down there."

"Oh God, Lore, I'm going to find Paul. I shouldn't have sent him off alone," Ian said.

After Ian left the car to find his son, Lorelei called Shannon Flynn.

"Hi, Shannon."

"Lore. Aren't you and Ian on a trip up north?"

"Yeah, we're at the Wupatki Ruins now. Listen, I think you need to find out about a possible crime here."

"At the ruins?"

"Yes, a very recent crime. And we're talking another underground mystery. I had a very clear vision. A mother and her son were abducted and brought here. And somehow, they were taken to the unexcavated section—I saw a wide open area which included more rooms. Ian had to carry me back to his car because of what I relived. The woman was murdered and the child ran away. And he's still down there."

Lorelei saw Ian and Paul gazing upon the expanse of ruins.

"The murder happened on Tuesday—four days ago. They could have been abducted that same day, or earlier. I got the impression that she was somewhat of a loner, so I don't think anyone knows they're missing yet. I'm not sure where they disappeared from, but I did see ponderosa pines everywhere."

"Were you able to get any names?"

Ian approached the car with his arm around Paul's shoulder.

"Her last name is Atwell. I got an "A" as the beginning of the first name. I couldn't pick up anything on the child. But the mother is from Arizona."

"Okay," Shannon sighed. "I'll look into missing person's reports in the state within the past week. Ponderosa pines don't narrow it down too much. Could mean Flagstaff or the surrounding area, or Payson, Pine, Strawberry."

"Sorry, that's all I have right now." Lorelei leaned her head back against the seat and closed her eyes. She was very tired and one of her fierce headaches had begun to stir.

"That's fine. I'll let you know what I find out. Try to enjoy the rest of your day with Ian."

"All I can think of is that poor child down there. I hope I'm wrong on this." Then Lorelei hung up the phone.

"Did you tell her the news?" Ian asked, getting into the car. He glanced at the ring on her finger.

Her eyes widened. "Oh Ian, I'm sorry. My mind is whirling with what happened back there."

Ian gave her a gentle smile. "That's all right. This new case is more important."

She glanced down at the brilliant emerald diamond. She held it up to the necklace and realized how perfect of a match it was.

"I have to work on some earrings next," Ian said.

"Ian, stop. Are we ready to head to the Wukoki ruin?"

"Are you sure? You look so tired, Lore."

"Yes, I'm sure. That's what we're here for right?" She didn't want to tell him—but she still had a feeling of trepidation.

He leaned over and kissed her cheek. "By the way, I did stop inside the visitor center. They weren't aware of any access points to the unexcavated portion. They looked at me like I was nuts for asking."

"Shannon's checking into missing person's cases. Tuesday is standing out for the murder, though I don't know when they were taken." Lorelei popped open a bottle of aspirin and downed a few with a bottle of water.

Ian kept glancing over at her in concern as they continued to the next pueblo.

The Wukoki ruin loomed like an ancient castle. Built on an island of red Moenkopi sandstone surrounded by a wash of black cinders, the structure seemed to have burst from the earth itself.

Lorelei, Ian and Paul walked down the dirt pathway to the structure. A large raven watched them from its perch on the highest wall. They climbed a circular stairway and stood in a ten by ten room open to the elements.

Ian held her face in his hands.

"You don't have to," Lorelei said.

But he continued to stare into her eyes. As he had done so many times before, Ian concentrated intently while the violet specks in his eyes danced and collided. A few minutes later, the headache had drastically subsided.

"Thanks, honey, I'm much better." Lorelei placed her arms around his neck, holding him tight. He responded by pulling her to him.

"You're staying with me tonight, right?" she asked.

"Of course." He turned away to find Paul investigating a standalone wall that extended across the pueblo. The sandstone floor contained bits of pottery and fallen stone.

Ian went over to Paul and they explored the two-story building.

Lorelei sat cross-legged on the edge of the roof looking down upon the valley below, her blonde hair blowing gently in the breeze. Closing her eyes, she imagined what it would be like to take flight. Then she did—her instantaneous astral abilities taking her well above ponderosa forests, pinyon pine and juniper, volcanic remains, Interstate forty, and views of the painted desert further north.

Her trip was brief, for she didn't want to scare Ian's son. Unlike his father, Paul hadn't learned about astral travel or the Wiccan religion. Paul's stepfather would have nothing to do with any of it.

The second she merged back into her body, it hit again. The feeling of dread. But this time she had a face with the sensation. It was someone very close to Ian and Paul.

Lorelei heard someone come up behind her, then felt Ian's firm hands on her shoulders. "You did it again, didn't you?" He leaned on his knees and hugged her from behind.

"Sorry, sweetie," she said. "I tried to make it short."

"It's okay. I really want to be with you when you make those journeys."

She stood up and wiped her jeans off. "You will next time, I promise."

"Lore!" Paul ran up excitedly. "Look what I found." Ian's son held up a quarter-sized piece of black and white pottery.

She leaned down to get a closer look. "What a great find. But you know you have to put that back where you found it, right? We have to respect the land and what's out here. If everyone were to take pieces of history, there wouldn't be anything left to learn about."

"Yeah, I know," Paul mumbled. "Dad already told me."

"I also told you to not pick anything up," Ian said. "Take it back where you found it."

While his son ran behind the ruin, Lorelei worried about the intensity of her recent angst. She didn't know how she would break the news to Ian.

"Ian, you should call Emily's husband." She watched to make sure Paul was far enough away to not hear what she said next. "I think something's happened to her."

Ian stopped abruptly and stared at her. "Lore, you're still jumpy about what happened."

"Honey, no." She took both his hands in hers. "You know how those out-of-body experiences clarify things. That's part of why I did it. I still had the trepidation, even after we left the other ruins."

"I know, I know," he said. "I hope you're wrong on this." He dialed Emily and Peter's home phone. "Peter, hey it's Ian."

That was all Ian could get out of his mouth before Lorelei heard Emily's husband yelling on the other end. And though she couldn't hear what he was saying, Ian's shocked stare told her everything.

"Okay, Peter. We're on our way back. Try and stay calm. We'll be there within an hour."

Ian grabbed her hand. "You're right. Unfortunately. Peter was about to call me. She left to get a few things from the store—that was four hours ago. He's been trying to call her on her cell, but there's no answer. The last time he dialed Emily's phone, a man picked up. Apparently they turned it on speaker by accident. Peter heard two men arguing. The one in the background was angry with the guy that picked the phone up."

"I hope she's okay."

"Hey, buddy." Ian approached his son, who waited at the car. "Listen, we need to get you home right away." He sighed deeply, pulling Paul to him. "We don't know what's happened, but your mother went to the store for a few things and hasn't come back yet. We need to go back and see Peter."

Paul's brown eyes welled up with tears. It was all Lorelei could do to not breakdown. But that wouldn't help any of them.

Lorelei helped Paul into the backseat and slid in next to him. She saw Ian's worried face and started to get back out of the car.

"No, Lore. Stay back there with Paul. I'll be fine."

As they drove in silence, she sat close to Ian's son, who stared out the window. Lorelei attempted to console him with her arm around his shoulder, but his stiff body language told her he didn't want the comfort. At least not from her.

CHAPTER TWENTY-NINE

Ian pulled into his ex-wife's driveway at 4:40 p.m. The dark red curtains inside the house brushed aside and a distinguished looking gentleman with white hair peeked at them and opened the door.

Lorelei, Ian and Paul walked up to the door.

Peter's eyes, red from tears, looked into Paul's. "We're going to find mom okay?"

Paul broke down, his body wracked with sobs. But instead of turning to his stepfather, he turned to Ian, placing his arms around his father's waist.

Lorelei wondered how strict Peter really was.

Ian placed a firm, but shaky hand on Peter's shoulder. "How are you holding up?"

Peter's slumped shoulders and exhausted demeanor revealed the toll the incident had taken. "The police have issued a statewide endangered person alert."

"That's good," Ian said. "They should be able to find her faster." Ian knelt down and hugged Paul. "Why don't you go to your room for a few minutes?"

With his head down, Paul walked down the hallway.

"Did you recognize the voices of either of the men that you heard over her phone?" Ian asked.

"No. Sounded sort of young though," Peter said. He started to sway in the doorway and had to grab the doorframe.

Lorelei wanted to feel sorry for Emily's husband, but something wasn't sitting right with her.

"Sit down." Ian guided him toward the black leather sofa a few feet away.

"I don't even know if she made it to the grocery store," Peter said. "At first, I thought maybe Emily decided to do more shopping. Until I called and heard the two men. I demanded to know where she was, but they hung up."

"The police must have been here questioning you," Lorelei said.

"Yes, they're at the store now to see if anyone spotted her—maybe check out the surveillance cameras in the parking lot to see if that's where she disappeared, or if something happened on her way home." Peter sat up, placed his elbows on his lap and his head in his hands, rocking back and forth slightly.

There was a knock at the door, and Lorelei opened it to two uniformed officers.

"Hello Ms....?"

"Lanier. Lorelei Lanier. I'm the girlfriend of Emily's ex-husband."

"I'm Officer Ralston. This is my partner Todd Denton."

Officer Ralston looked as if he trained for five hours a night in the gym. Biceps almost the diameter of a dinner plate, and a shiny bald head to match his shimmering skin.

The way he eyed Lorelei made her extremely uncomfortable. His eyes traveled from her legs and up to her breasts, where they rested for a few seconds. Ian placed his arm around her shoulder, glaring at the policeman.

She noticed Officer Denton appeared rather embarrassed. "We need to talk to Mr. Taylor and his son-in-law. Is that you?" He looked at Paul and smiled.

"Yes." Paul had come to the door and stood behind Ian and Lorelei.

Officer Ralston pulled Paul aside and Denton talked with Peter.

Ian guided Lorelei into the dining room.

"Honey, how are you holding up?" Lorelei asked.

He responded by throwing his arms around her, holding her so tight she couldn't breathe.

"I can't believe this is happening." Ian pulled away from her, looking in Paul's direction. "I wanted to see if you could see or sense anything."

"Nothing specific. It's just—I don't think the kidnapping is about money, if that's what this is. And something feels off about this whole thing."

"I'm not surprised," Ian said.

"What?" Lorelei asked. "Are you telling me you know

something?"

"No. I've heard Peter can be rather controlling," he whispered. "You already know that he doesn't like her practicing Wicca. And that was something she loved. Lore, I can't even imagine her giving that up."

"Don't tell me you think she planned this on purpose. Who would put their family through that? Why wouldn't Emily just make an excuse?"

"You mean like going to the store?" Ian said. "Her best friend called me saying this man had Emily on anti-depressants. Peter doesn't like to let her out of his sight. He apparently calls the neighbor across the street to spy on her while he's at work."

"Oh my God," Lorelei said. "For someone who is so spiritual, that must be really horrible. But Ian, you need to be telling the cops this."

"How can I tell Paul that his mother might be trying to get away from her own home?"

"You don't have to say it in front of Paul. Let one of the policemen know. They're going to question us anyways."

"Yeah, and I can guess which one wants to question you," Ian said. He glared at the beefed up officer that was talking to Peter. "That's definitely not a very professional way to act considering the circumstances."

Placing her arms around his neck, she kissed him gently on the lips. "Let's go back in there."

"Wait, honey," Ian said. "Are you sure you weren't seeing Emily's abduction at the ruins? Maybe you were just getting the setting or the incident confused."

"I'm positive. The woman at the ruins is dead. And she didn't look like your ex."

They walked back into the living room. "We might have to stay here," he told her. "I can't leave Paul right now."

Lorelei squeezed Ian's hand. "I wouldn't expect it any other way."

Peter stared at his cell, as if that would entice his wife to call. "They said the security cameras showed her leaving the grocery store. Nothing beyond that."

"The next step is to talk with friends and neighbors," Ralston said. "We still need to question both of you." He glanced at Ian and Lorelei. "Let's step into the other room."

Lorelei and Ian followed Ralston into the great room. "Mr. Taylor mentioned you and Emily were both involved in witchcraft." The policeman looked at Ian as if he had just run up the walls, over the ceiling and back down again.

"Yes, when we were married. But we were solitary—no covens," Ian said. "My religion is pagan and Wiccan."

"Interesting." Ralston jotted notes. "Do you think that this incident might have anything to do with her," he cleared his throat, "interests?"

Ian sighed heavily and rolled his eyes. "I guess it's possible since Peter didn't want her involved in that stuff. Maybe Emily decided to break away from him. But it's hard to imagine her putting Paul through all this."

"Do you know any of her," Ralston used his fingers as quotes, "pagan or Wiccan friends?"

"No. She mentioned being involved in a Celtic coven soon after we divorced, but I never met any of them. And I doubt she still is." Ian sighed. "Emily knew that Peter was having one of the neighbors watch her while he was at work. Her best friend told me how unhappy she's been lately because he's constantly trying to control her life."

"Which neighbor is this?" the office asked.

"Tiffany mentioned someone across the street—shouldn't be too hard to figure out." Ian stared sternly at Ralston.

For a split second, Lorelei thought that the Ian and the cocky policeman were going to get into a fight. Then she placed her hand around Ian's waist and he relaxed.

"Is this Tiffany Hamilton?" Ralston asked. "An artist in Sedona?"

"Yes. I have her cell phone if you need it."

"That won't be necessary. Mr. Taylor gave us her information. Do the two of you talk often? You and Tiffany that is?" Ralston glanced at Lorelei as if she were dating a total loser.

"No." Ian replied firmly. "She called me a few months ago because Emily sounded very depressed. Peter doesn't give her much freedom, and she can't practice her passion. Tiffany invited Emily up to Sedona for the weekend, but Peter didn't want her to go."

"Have *you* noticed the change in her behavior?" Ralston asked. The younger officer had walked up and was listening to the conversation.

"Not really. But Emily and I don't really talk that much."

Ralston turned to his partner. "Question the neighbors, particularly the ones across the street. Could be our missing person was being tracked by her own husband." He nodded toward Peter, who was sitting forlornly on the couch. "Find out if anyone's heard from her or seen her."

"Has your son said anything to you about his mother?" Ralston asked Ian. "Did Emily mention going away to him, or to you?"

"Emily didn't say anything to me. Mostly small talk when I come pick Paul up for the weekend."

"So what's next?" Ian asked. "Isn't there a way to track Emily through her cell?"

"Law enforcement routinely requests carriers, in this case Verizon, to continuously ping wireless devices to locate them when a call isn't being made. This pinpoints the location of the cell and those communicating with them. We'll also contact a list of friends, family, neighbors as well as businesses around the grocery store where she was last seen."

"She had a brand new car," Lorelei said. "It might have GPS tracking."

"It did," the officer said. "But the manufacturer said it had been disconnected."

Lorelei glanced out the window to see Ralston's partner talking with one of the neighbors. "I'll need your contact information," he said to Lorelei and Ian. "Right now, you're all suspects, so I need everyone to stay fairly close."

Peter remained dazed. Even though his demeanor seemed genuine, Lorelei knew something was off. And it wasn't just because of his history with his wife. *Am I picking up on his guilt? Perhaps he realizes that his actions might have driven her away.*

After the officers left, Peter got up from the couch. "I think I want to be alone." He looked at Lorelei and Ian. "Would you mind taking Paul back home with you?"

"Are you sure you don't want us to stay?" Ian asked. "Or at least stay at a hotel near here?"

"No," Peter said in an abrupt manner. "No, I'll be fine. Give me a call in the morning."

Lorelei couldn't tell if Ian eyed Peter with suspicion, concern, or both. She turned around to find Paul, but he already stood next to Ian—waiting to leave.

"If you insist." Ian hesitantly glanced at Paul. "Go ahead and pack a few things. We're going to stay at Lore's place tonight."

"Can I at least get you anything before we leave?" Lorelei's phone rang, but she disconnected. The caller ID revealed Shannon's number.

Peter shook his head no and walked down the hall toward Paul's room.

Whispers and sniffles emanated from the hallway. A few minutes later, Paul came back into the room, escorted by Peter.

"Take good care of him." Then Peter opened the front door and let them out. "I'll call if I hear anything."

"Was that Shannon trying to call you?"

Lorelei nodded and whispered, "I'll call her when we get home." She didn't want to talk murder in front of a child whose mother had possibly been abducted. Or worse.

She looked back at Paul. "Are you hungry? We can stop and get something to eat. How about McDonalds?"

There was no response.

"We can stop somewhere for you, Lore," Ian said. "You need to eat."

"No. I'll wait until we get home." Laying her head back on the seat, she watched ranch style homes pass by, surrounded by tall pines.

"Dad, why would mom go somewhere without her keys?" Paul asked. "I saw her car keys on the dresser in their bedroom."

"She couldn't," Ian said.

She glanced over at Ian. *What kind of act are they staging?*

CHAPTER THIRTY

A natural outcrop of stone extended from the wall of the pueblo. A foot wide crack ran down the center of the rock, and Lorelei could see through to the long flat mesas, red sandstone piles of rock, and brush-covered cinder hills beyond. The brilliant pink and orange hues of sunset burst through the opening, illuminating both sides of the nook and creating a radiance that spotlighted two s-shaped drawings.

Urgent voices echoed from under the earth. Whimpers and cries accompanied an argument between a man and a woman. The thin fracture on the ground wouldn't allow a peek into its depths. But something was wrong. Lorelei slid back out of the crevice. How did the people get underground?

She ran downhill toward the blowhole, a possible underground access point. She tugged on the rusty grate. It didn't budge. No one could have gotten underground through there. The hole was too small and the cover fastened too securely.

Bending her head down until sections of her long blonde hair dropped through the small square openings in the grate, Lorelei listened intently for any signs of movement or voices. It's way too quiet, she thought. She glanced up and noticed a much smaller ruin in the distance. Suddenly, she felt drawn toward it. But Lorelei didn't get far. Something, or someone grabbed on her silver cord connecting her astral and physical form. The unknown assailant yanked her so forcefully that she heard a ripping sound.

Lorelei awoke with a start, gasping for air and leaning forward to grab onto the dashboard. She glanced over at Ian, then let go of the dash and relaxed in her seat. "Thank God," she said.

"Bad dream?" Ian asked.

She just nodded as he stroked her arm.

Ian glanced into the rearview mirror at Paul, sleeping in the backseat. "What happened in your dream?"

Her astral abilities had improved through meditation. And it seemed her visions had been clarified through sleep. *Was this latest nightmare a sign of things to come?*

"I'll tell you later." She stretched and yawned. "How are you doing?"

"Ah, I see. Changing the subject."

Lorelei smiled tiredly. "Details for Shannon. Nothing you need to worry about. Not now anyway." She turned her head to look out the window. "Do you want me to drive?"

"No thanks, honey. We're almost there."

She watched the headlights of his Lexus cut through the darkness of Interstate seventeen heading south. And unlike the sparsely populated freeway, she knew their road was not going to be so clear.

An hour later they arrived at Lorelei's house. Paul got out of the car on the same side she did.

She placed her arm around his shoulder.

"Lore, do you know if my mom is okay?" His brown eyes looked imploringly into hers. She knew he wanted to hear that Emily was all right, but for some reason, she couldn't see any details pertaining to Ian's ex-wife. Lorelei's senses were telling her there was a reason for that.

Ian had come around to their side of the car and stood next to Paul. A single tear rolled down his face as he pulled his son close. "She can't see everything," Ian said. "But I have a strong feeling your mom is fine."

And while Ian didn't have psychic powers like she did, Lorelei knew him well enough to know his intuition was spot on ninety-nine percent of the time. She hoped that this wasn't the other one percent.

"Hey," Ian said. "How about we order some pizza?"

"I am getting kind of hungry." Paul followed his father and Lorelei into the Mediterranean style home with hanging tapestries of cottages by the sea, paintings of stately homes overlooking vineyards, beige walls, and a large rug with warm tones of maroon, brown and green.

While Ian helped Paul settle into his bedroom, Lorelei called for pizza delivery. Then she removed a glass from the cupboard and poured ice water from the dispenser.

Faint breathing came from right beside her.

"Who's there?" Startled, Lorelei dropped the glass. There was more breathing from her other side.

She jumped when Ian approached her from behind.

"Baby, I'm sorry," he said. "What happened?" Ian looked at

the mess on her slate floor.

She listened, but couldn't hear anything and didn't sense a presence.

"Ian, something, or someone was here."

His face paled, and he glanced back down the hallway to make sure Paul was still in his room. "What?"

Lorelei placed her hands on either side of his face. "I heard breathing from either side of me—like something was teasing me. And no, my house isn't haunted."

"Maybe whatever you connected with at the ruins followed you here." Ian glanced around the room nervously.

Lorelei didn't respond. She didn't want to give him anything else to worry about.

Ian pulled her so close she could feel his heart beating. She desperately wanted to make everything okay, but didn't know how.

"I love you," she said. "Paul can stay here as long as he needs to."

Ian bent over to kiss her, but stopped at her lips, his warm breath igniting a spark. Then he placed his own lips lightly onto hers, brushing them back and forth ever so gently.

"This isn't fair—you know what this does to me." Lorelei's breathing became shallow, her face flushed. "And I don't feel right doing this right now."

"I know," he moaned. "Everything about you drives me insane." He pulled away from her, taking a deep breath. "Let me clean this mess up."

As Ian swept the glass up from the kitchen floor, Lorelei decided to return Shannon's call. Pulling a windbreaker on, she stepped out onto her patio, sitting at the tiled mosaic table with designs of roses in full bloom. The waning crescent moon and millions of stars were her only company in the fall air. It was the reason she had moved to Cottonwood, Arizona—peace, quiet and extraordinary views.

"It's about damn time." Shannon said. "I called almost two hours ago."

"Sorry. Turns out Wupatki isn't the only abduction case. Ian's wife disappeared today while we were up north. We just got back from visiting with her husband. Paul's spending the night with us."

"What? Oh my God. What's their last name?" Shannon asked. "I might be able to find something out for you."

"Emily and Peter Taylor. Her husband is supposedly a real

control freak. Ian thinks she might have staged her own disappearance to be able to practice with her coven."

"That's not a very thoughtful thing considering she has a ten year old son. How are you all doing?"

"Okay, I guess. You know Ian's intuition. He has a strong sense that she's fine."

"You've had a rather busy day then."

"Did you find anything pertaining to the mystery north of Flagstaff?" Lorelei watched the lights from Sedona sparkle in the distance.

"There have been two missing persons cases within the past week, both up north. And one of them is Alicia Atwell," Shannon said. "The last name matches with what you picked up at the ruins, and you also mentioned her first name started with an 'A.'"

"That's right."

"Lore, did you get a description of her?"

"Long brown hair, feathered bangs, average height."

She heard Shannon typing on her computer.

"I'm looking at a picture of her now and she fits that description. Her boyfriend reported he hadn't seen or heard from her since Monday, the day before you mentioned the murder occurred. Alicia is thirty-six and lived in Strawberry off of Fossil Creek Road, which explains the pine trees."

"What about the child?"

"That brings up another question," Shannon said. "Alicia's single."

"What? I assumed they were mother and child because of the sense of protection I got from her."

"Did you get a good look at the kid?"

"No, damn it. I heard her yelling for the child to run. I only saw her and the shadow of the person lunging at her. I briefly saw the little boy's profile during the abduction flashback."

"I did come across three missing children's cases, though one is a girl," Shannon said. "I guess that narrows it down to two. Of the other two, one case is in Prescott and the other in Pine."

Lorelei heard the doorbell ring. Ian and Paul answered the door, greeting the pizza delivery guy.

"Shannon, Pine is only five miles from Strawberry. Maybe Alicia was babysitting a friend's child at her place. Or was it her boyfriend's kid?"

"No. He does have a child but she's fourteen." Shannon sighed. "Both of these cases are in Gila County, so the Phoenix FBI Division has authority. They're looking into any possible connection between Alicia and either of these children. Agents are talking to her neighbors, friends, and anyone else in the community."

"The murder occurred in Coconino County," Lorelei said. "Are you going to be involved at all? I don't think I can go back out there without your support."

"The national park service has jurisdiction. But I would like to go out there and talk to the rangers and staff. Were you able to narrow down where it might have happened, other than underground?"

"On the way home from Emily and Peter's place, I had a vision of a crevice in one particular section of the ruins. I would know it immediately if I saw it. There was light coming from below. I must have projected astrally in the dream, because something yanked on my silver cord so hard it stared to tear."

"Wow. That's a heck of a nightmare."

Lorelei didn't respond. Whatever, or whoever was involved in the murder might know who she was. She shuddered, remembering the most recent dream. She feared the vision had been manipulated to throw her off, scare her to prevent further investigation, or both.

What is it with me and subterranean investigations?

"Shannon, I need to get going. Ian's waiting for me inside. Let me know when you plan on heading out to Sunset Wupatki."

"I'll give them a call. It needs to be before or after hours. And I have to ensure we can get escorted out to that other structure you mentioned you were drawn to in your dream." She paused. "Don't hesitate to call me if necessary. If I get a heads up about Emily, I'll let you know."

"Thanks Shannon. Talk with you soon."

Lorelei slid the patio door open and entered the living room. Ian had heated up a few slices of pizza and handed her a plate."

"Thanks," she said.

After she took the plate, Ian placed his fingers under her chin, gently lifting it up so that her eyes met his. "I expect you to tell me more about that nightmare later. And the conversation with Shannon."

"Of course. She's going to contact someone at Wupatki to arrange a date and time so that all of us can go out there."

He stared at her.

"Ian, I promise I'll tell you about the dream I had in the car. I didn't want to go into it at the time. You have enough to worry about with Emily's disappearance."

"Let me decide what I can handle."

Lorelei couldn't explain it. But she knew the incident with Ian's ex-wife wasn't as it seemed.

CHAPTER THIRTY-ONE

Lorelei sat up abruptly in bed. The smell of bacon and eggs permeated the house. But she wasn't thinking about eating. Her vision from the night before reappeared. This time she was under the massive pueblo—able to see who the whispers emanated from in her previous dream—Emily Taylor.

How can I tell Ian his ex-wife is somehow involved in the mystery at Wupatki?

She noticed the comforter on his side was smooth and not folded back.

As she got out of bed, Ian came into the room and stood in the doorway. "You look so sexy." He climbed over his side and put his arms around her. "I'm sorry I didn't sleep in here last night. Paul was a little afraid to be alone."

"I understand, what with his mother disappearing. I didn't even notice. I must have zonked right out." She couldn't look him in the eye.

"I hope you had a peaceful sleep," he said.

"Sort of."

"Lore, I know you too well in our few months of dating. What are you hiding?"

She sighed. "I had a continuation of that nightmare. I saw Emily in that cave with Alicia and the little boy. Emily isn't the killer, but I did see her walk through a passage and into the cave with both of them. And Emily had her hands on their arms, dragging them in."

"So you're telling me my ex-wife is involved in a possible murder case?"

"I think so. Maybe it has something to do with her coven."

"Every time I think the pagan and Wiccan religions are taking a stride forward...," Ian said in frustration. "She's never been involved in human sacrifice."

"I didn't say it was cult related. Ian, I don't know. I'm getting bits and pieces."

"I'm going to finish fixing breakfast." Ian started to turn and leave.

"I'm sorry. I didn't mean to insult you or Emily. I know your religion is important to you."

"I know you didn't mean it. Guess I'm a little emotional worrying about Emily and Paul." He kissed her on the cheek, and whispered in her ear. "And you. Now come and get some breakfast."

"I'll be right there." While Lorelei got dressed, she noticed a silver object on the carpet. A black, triangular amulet with Latin wording around the edges was attached to a cord. In the middle of the charm was a circle.

She walked into the kitchen and showed it to Ian. He almost dropped the carafe of orange juice he held, then placed it on the counter.

"Where did you get that?" Ian asked.

"I was about to ask if this was yours. I found it on the floor in my bedroom."

He took the necklace from her. "No, it's not mine. This is a magic triangle amulet from the Key of Solomon. It's used to control evil spirits." He gazed up at her, worry and panic in his eyes. "That presence that you detected last night—was it negative?"

"Not that I could tell." She poured a glass of juice. "Have you talked with Peter?"

"I tried calling an hour ago, but got his voice mail. It's hard to believe Emily could be involved in such a thing—especially considering that child you saw Alicia with is about Paul's age. I wonder if Peter's controlling nature pushed her into this whole thing. I want to tell you you're wrong." Ian slammed a plate onto the counter in frustration. "But you've never been wrong before."

"Ian, do you believe in manipulation of dreams?" Then she turned the bacon.

"Absolutely. I've known people who have done such a thing. Is that what you think happened?"

"In last night's vision during the drive home. I can't prove it. I was at the main Wupatki ruin, and there's another smaller pueblo in the distance. In the dream I was out-of-body because something, or someone, yanked on my cord and I heard it tear. I don't know. Maybe it was my subconscious fear of not being able to find my physical form that caused it. I've never experienced anything like that in my other visions. It was as if someone knew that I was close to something."

She glanced over at him as he finished piling a batch of pancakes on a plate. Lorelei saw worry lines and he was suddenly very quiet.

"Ian, what are you thinking about?"

He turned and gave her a hug. "Honey, I'm sorry. It seems that the more you develop these talents, the more you open yourself up to further danger." He kissed her on the lips. "It scares the hell out of me to think of anything happening to you. I hope it was a bad dream and nothing more. But maybe we should take precautions."

"Like what?" she asked.

"There are many alternatives, such as a protection spell and the use of gems – opal provides protection and harmony and lapis can help with vitality and strength."

Lorelei wondered about the nightmare and if someone, possibly Peter, had really attempted to control her dream. Then Paul came through the front door.

"Hey." She gave Paul a hug as he stood staring at all the food. "I hope you're hungry."

He nodded his head up and down. "How did you get Peter's necklace? Paul asked, staring at the pewter triangle.

Ian stopped placing food on the table. He took the necklace from Lorelei and brought the charm closer to Paul. "Are you sure this is his?"

Paul stuffed a huge bite of pancake in his mouth and nodded.

Ian's fists clenched as he took a deep breath.

"Son, go ahead and eat. Lore and I will be right back." She followed Ian to her patio.

He held her hand so hard, it turned bright red. "Ouch, Ian, that hurts."

"Sorry. What the hell is that man up to? I thought he didn't want Emily to have anything to do with Wicca, and now it looks as if he's practicing the dark arts." He pulled away from her and placed his hands on either side of her face. "It was probably Peter that you sensed in the kitchen and…"

"And he visited me while I was alone last night." She shuddered, looking up at Ian. "I think Peter's practicing astral travel – that's how I heard his breathing and how he managed to leave that charm behind."

"Do you think he's the one manipulating your dreams?"

"Either him or Emily," Lorelei said. "I think I got too close to something."

"I don't get this," Ian said. "Does Emily even know about Peter's abilities?"

Ian heard his phone ring and ran in to answer it.

"No Officer. Paul's here. Yes, he did find Emily's car keys in their bedroom.

Ian paced back and forth through the kitchen. "No, he didn't," he whispered. "All right. Thanks."

A minute later, Ian sat down next to Paul at the table.

"What's going on?"

"Officer Trenton has been trying to contact Peter as well. They've attempted to call and have stopped by the house. He's not returning calls or answering the door. I told them I haven't heard from him either." Ian glanced at the amulet on the table. "But if I do..."

"Peter's not innocent," she whispered as Paul grabbed another pancake. "I don't know how he ties into all this, but if he can perform out-of-body, then I wonder what else he can do."

"That son of a bitch," Ian said, trying to control his voice. "To think he visited you while I slept with Paul."

Lorelei took his face in her hands. "You had no idea he would do something like that."

"I wonder if Emily is practicing the dark arts with Peter. Or maybe she left because she knows he's into that dangerous stuff. But then there's the vision you had with my ex-wife under the ruins."

"Why did you two divorce?" Lorelei asked.

"The problems started when Emily decided to spend too much time with her coven, neglecting her own family. Paul would cry his little eyes out at times when she left. She never admitted it, but the trouble began when a new member joined. Tall, dark and handsome, he was a high priest attracted to married women. Though Emily denied the affair, another couple we hung out with occasionally told me they had seen her with him at a romantic restaurant—a few weeks before her our anniversary."

"That must have been rough," Lorelei said. "She could be doing the same thing to Peter. Maybe he forced her into another man's arms." She looked over at Paul. "I wonder if Peter's taking matters into his own hands with all of this since the police can't find him."

Ian sighed. "I don't know. He may act emotional on the

outside. But my intuition's telling me there's something much deeper going on—especially since you found his pendant. Maybe he realizes you know something about her disappearance."

Lorelei took both his hands in hers. "We still have to make it back out to Wupatki for this case. Or at least I can. You should stay with Paul."

"I'm not letting you go there without me. I can't bear to think of you suffering like that again." He kissed her on the forehead. "Don't worry, I can handle it." Ian looked her straight in the eyes. A simple gesture, but one that made her heart stop every time.

How could Emily have ever let this guy go?

Ten minutes later, the doorbell rang and she answered the door to the spritely five foot six blonde woman that lived two houses down.

"Hi, Lore," Jodi said. "I came over to see if Paul wanted to hang out with us for a few hours. My son doesn't get to play with others his own age very often."

Lorelei glanced at Ian.

"Dad, can I?" Paul stood next to him, gazing up at him imploringly.

"Absolutely. I know where you'll be if I need you. Just behave yourself okay?"

But Paul was already out the door.

"Take care," Jodi said. "And let me know if you need anything." She glanced at Lorelei and Ian with empathy. Lorelei realized Paul mentioned what happened.

She had barely closed the door when Ian started kissing her neck. "Baby, I need to be close to you. I want to take your visions away, if only for a little while."

Every time he touched her or kissed her, it ignited something that was almost impossible to stop. Ian's desire became more obvious with every button she undid on his jeans. He attempted to pick her up, but she pushed him back against the wall with a force that surprised both of them. The small clump of hair revealing itself below his neck made her pull the long sleeved top up over his wavy locks. As Ian grabbed it from her and threw it off his head, she gently licked and nibbled every inch of his chest, working downwards. His hands tangled in her hair. She looked up to see his head thrown back in ecstasy. Her mouth stopped within inches of his desire, her warm breath teasing him repeatedly.

Grabbing his firm buttocks, Lorelei tauntingly licked his manhood slowly from the tip upwards. Hearing something hit the door, she glanced up to see that Ian had slammed his head back against the wall. Hard. He didn't seem to feel it.

His own passion drove her insane as she took him inside her mouth. A few minutes later, she stood up to face him. His grayish-blue specks had transformed into purple.

"You never did tell me where you wanted to go." He reached down to place his hand gently between her legs. He traced and tickled her inner thighs until she dripped with pure desire. "Oh God, Ian." Lorelei felt his firmness against her stomach. "Take me anywhere."

He moved his hand up inside her. "God baby, you feel like silk." Then he did what she had been waiting for. Lifting her leg to his waist, he lifted her up and guided his desire into her, placing her against the wall. Suddenly, she couldn't breathe as he gently, methodically entered her, then pulled back a little and stopped. Grabbing her hands and raising them above her head, Ian took his breasts in her mouth, nibbling, licking and kissing.

She didn't know how, but even though he stood still, his manhood throbbed and took on a life of its own. They fell down on the carpet and Ian buried himself so deep she didn't think it was physically possible. That's when it happened.

He had taken her back to Ireland. Tall, craggy brown cliffs were interspersed with green grass. And a castle prominently stood at the top. Waves crashed onto the small section of beach within ten feet of where they made love and the sand beneath her felt gritty, yet erotic as Ian's weight pressed her further into the dry, white grainy surface.

They exploded inside each other while sprays of water splashed upon their bodies, the damp sand intensifying her satisfaction.

Afterward, he held her close, the sweat on their bodies mingling. "God, the things you do to me," Ian whispered. "I can't stop wanting you."

She fell asleep, entwined in his embrace.

When she awoke an hour later, Ian lay next to her, stroking her hair. "Hey beautiful. Please tell me you didn't have anymore nightmares or dream invasions."

She leaned up on her elbow to gaze into his eyes. "Actually no, after that performance, just peaceful slumber."

Lorelei sat up in bed. She realized Ian must have carried her there while she slept.

Ian gave her a wink and a sexy grin. "I performed a much less erotic ritual while you slept—a simple, yet highly effective protection spell."

Lorelei appreciated Ian's love and concern, but she also wondered if his magic would result in a lack of evidence.

"Thanks, honey." She kissed him on the lips.

"Officer Trenton called a few minutes ago," Ian said. "Peter left town.

"What? The police told him to stay close."

"Peter used his charge card at a restaurant in Wickenburg."

"That could be taken as an admission of guilt since he's left town." Lorelei yawned. "Do you know of any connection Emily had there?"

"No. I've heard there's a coven in the area that's into astral projection and mind control. Perhaps that's why Peter went there. I mean, look at the physical evidence he accidentally left behind when he visited you."

"Ian, what the heck is happening? Emily's possibly involved in a murder/abduction scenario, Peter's traveling around Arizona and spying on me at all hours. If he's able to see where Emily is, she could be in danger."

Ian walked over to the dresser and picked up Peter's charm. "Or are they working together in some sort of underground mystery?"

CHAPTER THIRTY-TWO

Searing pain, shock, terror, and unbelievable screams of pain pushed their way into Lorelei's memory.

His hand clenched hers. "Sure you're ready for this?" he asked.

She clasped the emerald pentagram necklace. "I think so."

Shannon waited for Lorelei and Ian at the back of the visitor center. Her wavy auburn hair matched her sweater perfectly, making her complexion glow. And it didn't go unnoticed by Joe Luna, ex-FBI agent and shaman. Though they weren't as far along as Ian and her in their relationship, Lorelei saw the adoring way he looked at her. She knew Shannon felt the same way, but didn't want to admit it.

Lorelei gave Shannon, then Joe a hug.

Shannon lifted Lorelei's right hand up to get a closer look at her ring. "It's a perfect match to that necklace. It's beautiful."

"Not nearly as beautiful as the woman wearing it." Ian gazed into Lorelei's eyes.

"I don't know my friend." Joe slapped Ian on the back. "How is the engagement ring going to top that?"

Lorelei glanced at Joe. "Do you know something I don't?"

Joe winked at her and smiled. "I see Dale and Brandon coming. Let me head over and help them with their equipment."

Shannon watched him walk away with a slight grin.

Lorelei waved her hand in front of Shannon's face to get her attention.

"Sorry." Shannon cleared her throat, her cheeks turning red. "Let's spend the first few hours investigating at the main tower. Then we can move over to the structure north of here, where you attempted to travel in your dream until you were stopped by an unseen force."

"Have you heard anything else about Alicia or the child Lorelei saw?" Ian asked. "Or details about the connection between them?"

"You could say that." Shannon watched as Joe, Dale and Brandon approached with the ghost hunting equipment. "It turns out the little boy, ten years old as Lorelei pegged him, had been abducted by Alicia Atwell."

"What? Shannon, she was the one protecting him. Are you sure?"

"Yes. The child's name is Eric Ackart—lives in Pine. His parents reported him missing three days prior to Alicia's disappearance. We can't seem to find a connection between Alicia and the child. Her boyfriend saw a picture of Eric, and said he'd never seen him before. And Alicia never mentioned that she was babysitting or was close to any kids."

"How bizarre," Ian said. "Alicia kidnaps Eric, then they both get abducted? Lorelei had a vision of them getting taken at the same time, so that's why we thought she might be the mother."

Lorelei gazed north toward the smaller ruin, the location of her most recent dream. "But I had such a strong maternal sense."

"Maybe there was on Alicia's part," Shannon said. "Motherly, though she wasn't the child's mother. She might have been watching the child and took a particular liking to Eric. Or could be she met him and his parents somewhere. Pine and Strawberry are only five miles apart and both are very small communities."

"Speaking of abductions," Shannon yawned and stretched. "Have either of you found out anything else about Emily's disappearance?"

"We think so." Ian said. Then he glanced at Lorelei.

"Shannon, I had a vision of Emily here," Lorelei said. "She's not the killer. But I saw her with Alicia and Eric—she escorted them underground through a passage of some sort."

Shannon ran her hand through her hair in frustration.

"The police contacted me two days ago," Ian said. "Peter took off after we left his place. He ended up in Wickenburg the next day. And there is a very secretive coven in the area that practices mind control and out-of-body. We don't know if he's chasing Emily, or if he's headed to his coven."

"What do you mean?" Shannon asked. "I thought her husband was against all that."

"That's what we thought. Until he left a reminder of his abilities." He showed Shannon the pendant Lorelei had found. "Paul verified this was Peter's."

"Why do I have a feeling you're about to tell me this little triangle has something to do with the dark arts?"

"It's used for controlling spirits," Ian said. "Like Vincent Joiner tried to do, though in a totally different way."

"Caves, passages, ruins and the dark arts." Joe had snuck up behind Lorelei and Ian. "This mystery has all of the same elements as the one in southeast Arizona. And Lorelei is smack in the middle again." The Native American shaman stared at her in the same mysterious way he always did when he tried to make a point.

"This case is much more personal," Shannon said. "I'll contact the state police to follow up about Peter and Emily. They're obviously putting up a front. Especially if we find out Emily really is involved with whatever's going on at Wupatki."

Lorelei put her arm around Ian's waist, pulling him close.

"Excuse me," Joe said. "I need to talk to the park ranger over there about access to the site north of here."

Shannon watched as Joe walked over to an attractive park ranger with long black hair in a ponytail. Even though she was in uniform, Lorelei could tell the woman was shapely.

Lorelei wondered if Shannon was being honest with herself about her feelings for Joe. She knew Shannon still held insecurities from previous relationships, and it reflected in the way she kept glancing over during Joe's conversation with the other woman.

"So, boss," Dale said to Shannon. "Where do you want me and Brandon to setup?"

"Lore had a rather intense experience over there." She nodded her head toward the tallest prehistoric ruin. "We think there might have been a murder here within the past week or so. We have a name, but I want to see if the victim will try and communicate with us."

Ian looked over Dale's shoulder to check out the most recent addition to the team's ghost hunting equipment. "So this is the FBI's version of the ghost box, huh?"

"Yep," Brandon said. "This will create white noise, which is believed to attract spirits." "We can ask questions and hopefully receive answers immediately. Based on the original Franks box, this version was made by altering an AM/FM radio by cutting the mute pin, so it continuously scans the radio frequencies. Dale and I have been testing this at various locations, including Vulture Mine. We've gotten some amazing results."

Shannon looked at Ian and Lorelei. "Brandon and Dale

actually helped the bureau develop and refine the box for clarity of voice and tone. And this version has built-in EMF and temperature."

Lorelei's eyes widened. "That's awesome. I wonder if you'll be able to backup what I've experienced out here."

"That's what we're hoping for." Dale punched Ian lightly on the arm. "Oh, and if this guy doesn't treat you well, let me know."

"Will do." Lorelei nudged Ian flirtatiously. "But that's never been a problem."

Ian kissed her on the top of her head. "And it never will be."

"Oh, puke," Dale said. "You're going to make the rest of us look bad."

"I don't know what you're worried about," Ian said. "I've seen the way you look at Cindy. You give your wife everything she wants."

Brandon stared out at the smaller ruins north of Wupatki. "Aren't we supposed to be investigating out there as well?"

"Yes. Joe's talking to the ranger about that now."

Shannon smiled and waved at Joe. "Hey guys. Joe and the ranger gave us the thumbs up."

Shannon placed her hands on Lorelei's shoulders. "Are you ready to give this another try?"

"Sure. Let's get this over with."

"Ian, go ahead with Brandon and Dale," Lorelei said. "I have a feeling I'll be just fine."

Ian stood there staring at her, then sighed. "All right." He kissed her on the lips. "I love you. And I hope you're right."

She watched Ian, Brandon and Dale head down the pathway.

But as her and Shannon walked down the cement stairs to where she experienced the woman's murder, Ian had stopped and looked back.

"How are you doing?" Shannon asked.

"Fine. And we've already passed the spot where it happened."

"Maybe Alicia just wanted you to know about her murder. She might have sensed who and what you were."

Lorelei smiled and waved to Ian to let him know she was all right.

Lorelei and Shannon spent forty five minutes roaming the open pueblos, community room and ceremonial ballcourt.

"Are you picking up on anything?" Shannon asked.

"Only imprints from the Native American ancestors who inhabited this area."

Lorelei walked past a room labeled 16 surrounded by rock outcropping. "I'm trying to find that crevasse featured in my follow up vision of this place.

She quickened her pace as she recognized the foot wide opening.

Sliding into the spot from her dream, she glimpsed down to see a very thin fracture in the foundation. With her back against the rock wall, she slowly knelt down, trying to reach the crack where she had heard the voices. Air emanated from underneath.

"I take it this was in your dream?" Shannon slid in next to her.

"Yes. I heard whispers from underground—from here." Her fingers ran along a collapsed section of stone.

Something made Lorelei stop and look up. The rock wall she faced had the exact same solar system/astral travel map as the passages in Dragoon. They were on the opposite wall, directly across from the snakelike symbols.

"Hey, Shannon look at this."

Joe's voice over the radio interrupted Lorelei. She took a few pictures of the petroglyph map and snakes as Shannon responded to him.

"You and Lore better get over here."

CHAPTER THIRTY-THREE

Ian partially lay under a protrusion of red rock in the corner of the pueblo half mile north of Wupatki. He gazed into a massive chamber with additional rooms—an unexcavated level of ruins.

He heard footsteps running toward him.

"Ian," Lorelei said breathlessly. "What are you doing?"

"Get down here and see for yourself. Be careful not to hit your head."

"Nice meeting you here," he teased, as she scooted in on her stomach. "We believe this might be where the action took place." Ian directed his light downward. The beam reflected off reddish stones and tree timbers. A wooden ladder led to the roof of a small pueblo.

"There's another community room down there, though it's not nearly as large." Ian's flashlight indicated a large, circular section surrounded by stones.

She became very quiet and still. He couldn't hear her breathe. Her lips were slightly parted as they normally are during her psychic trances. God, this woman looks so beautiful—even with dirt smudges and little makeup. It all seemed so surreal sometimes. He had dreamed of being with her ever since they met six months ago. And now he was.

"Lore, I haven't heard anyone down there. But if Eric's been here that long, he might not be conscious."

She looked over at him. "Eric shouldn't be here. Emily was only supposed to take Alicia, but he was with her at the time."

"Joe and Shannon are looking for a way in," Dale said from behind them. "They might have to repel down."

"Thanks," Ian said. "Lore, are you sensing anything else from Alicia?"

Lorelei suddenly grabbed her stomach, screaming in agony. She rolled to her side, hitting her head on the rock above.

Shit! Not again. He held her face in his hands and tried to look into her eyes to alleviate the misery from her spiritual attachment, but he didn't have the space, and she couldn't stay still.

"Pull her out," Ian screamed. "Now!"

Dale and Brandon pulled Lorelei's feet to get her out from under the protruded rock, while Ian slid out to see if she was all right.

Ian, Dale and Brandon stared in horror as she writhed in torment on the ground. Reddish dirt and rocks stuck to her clothing as she rolled from her back to her side.

Joe and Shannon came running over when they heard her.

"This just happened when I asked about Alicia. She was fine before." Ian attempted to place his hand on her forehead. "I have to get her away from here."

Damn it, Peter. If you're doing this to her…

All of a sudden, Lorelei screamed, "No! Please don't. He said I could." Then she let out a piercing scream that caught the attention of the park rangers almost a mile away.

A tear rolled down Ian's face as she suddenly ceased moving, becoming limp. He pushed Shannon to the side and picked her up, holding her tightly against his chest. Within a few seconds, he felt her breath on his neck.

"Ian." She whispered softly. "Someone doesn't want me here."

"Lore, you scared us to death." Shannon rubbed her arm gently.

Ian saw that a male ranger was headed their way in a pickup truck. "I need to get her out of here. That wasn't Alicia. Something, or someone, is desperately trying to keep her away from here."

Lorelei groaned, holding weakly onto Ian. "You don't belong here."

"What?" Ian watched impatiently as the ranger approached.

"A voice came from right next to me before this happened. That's what it said."

"Do you know who it was?" Joe asked.

She looked up at all of them. "It sounded like Peter, Emily's husband. I think they're both involved in something under these ruins."

"Is everything okay?" The twenty something dark haired man squinted in the sun.

"Can you take us back to the parking lot?" Ian asked.

"Of course."

Ian carried her to the truck and got in next to her.

"Take care of her." Joe shut the passenger door. "Her talents are being detected by much more than just the spiritual realm. And I'm not sure a protection spell is going to do the job."

Joe, Shannon, Dale and Brandon waved goodbye as they drove away.

Tears rolled down Lorelei's cheeks as they pulled in front of Ian's Lexus. *If I ever see Peter again, I'll kill him for what he's putting her through.*

"Lore, we're back at the car." But she continued to stare out the rolled down window of the vehicle.

"Honey." Ian kissed her lightly on the cheek.

Lorelei slowly turned toward him, smiled weakly, then got out of the truck.

"Thanks for the ride," Ian said.

"No problem," Dave said. "I hope everything's okay."

"Hey." Dave stopped Ian as he followed Lorelei.

"She's the psychic right?"

"Yes."

"Does she do private readings?"

Ian turned his head toward the ranger in disbelief. Ian glared at the man who then pulled away from Ian's car.

How can I protect someone who seems to be attracting the worst type of element? And this time, it's my ex-wife's husband.

When Ian pulled into her driveway, he watched her leave the car, unlock her door and walk into the house—all without a word.

Ian followed her inside and heard the patio doors open. Her backyard was her retreat with the breathtaking city and mountain views, the cedar porch swing and rock waterfall.

As he stood at the threshold of the outdoors, she said something he didn't expect.

"I have to go back."

Ian sat next to her on the cushioned bench swing, placing his arm around her. "Lore, no. I don't want to see you get hurt."

She tightly held him in return. Then she pulled away from him slightly. Her beautiful hazel eyes looked so deeply into his, he thought he would never escape.

Lorelei held his hand. "I don't mean physically."

"An astral journey?"

Lorelei nodded in agreement. "It's my only option."

"Lore, it's obvious Peter means business. He might have been the one that killed Alicia. You have to let Shannon and Joe handle this."

"I can't abandon this case. After all, I'm the one that started the investigation."

"I don't think anyone would consider it abandonment. It's your health at stake. We know Peter has the same astral abilities you do. That's how he's been getting to you. He's also using telepathy."

"I'm going back. He can't make me suffer without my physical form." Ian knew she would whether he wanted her to or not.

"You had a vision of your silver cord being destroyed—probably because that's what's going to happen if you go back. He's going to be waiting."

"I'll make sure I project back right away if I sense anything. Ian, I have to. There's an innocent child down there. He's frightened and in a spot where he won't be found without my help."

He sighed deeply. "Then I'll stay here with your physical form. If something happens, I can tell by your vital signs and get you back to me. But Lore, I'm just as nervous about this as when we visited the ruins in person. We don't know what Peter's planning, or what else we're dealing with. And we know the protection spell doesn't work."

She placed her hand gently on his face.

Ian lowered his head. "When did you want to go back?"

"Soon." She lifted his chin and kissed him gently. "But first, I want you to help me relax." She straddled him on the swing, caressing his lips with hers.

With her body so close to his, he forgot about the potential danger and responded to her desire.

***

"White light." Ian's hands were wrapped around Lorelei's. "Remember to imagine a bright, protective aura around you." She gazed into his eyes. The dark blue specks had all ready started to swim and merge in an effort to calm her.

A single tear rolled down her face. The moisture tickled her right cheek, eventually breaking away from her skin, falling onto the carpet. The scent of passion still lingered in the air. And his naked body leaned over hers. She didn't want to leave him. She only wanted to be enfolded in his arms. But it had to wait.

Ian wiped her tear away with his thumb, while his fingers rested on her face, "You'll be fine. I'll watch you every second." Ian lay down next to her and pulled her close. "I love you."

"I love you too," she whispered in his ear, her hand against his chest. Then she disconnected. Her silver cord stretched and conformed as she traveled further away from her home. Minutes later, Lorelei's soul descended into the very room where Alicia Atwell had been killed.

CHAPTER THIRTY-FOUR

Butterflies began in the pit of Shannon's stomach. Or were they caterpillars that felt as if they were transforming into butterflies?

That has to be at least fifty feet. Shannon studied the distance between the entrance Ian had discovered and the floor of the cave. The protrusion of rock had been destroyed so they could gain access.

She jumped as Joe touched her arm.

"I'll climb down before you," he said.

"Thanks. That way I can just fall on top of you instead of hitting the ground first. Then we'll both be killed."

"Such a positive outlook." Joe shook his head and grinned. But it was one of those sideways grins that made him look so sexy. "If that happened, we could come back and communicate with Lorelei and tell her how it really is on the other side."

She watched him get connected to the harness, then climb down into the unexcavated ruins while the two rangers held the rope. *He's done this before,* she thought, as he scrambled stealthily down the solid rock wall.

As the harness and rope were pulled back up, Shannon took a deep breath.

The dark-haired ranger that had talked with Joe earlier helped Shannon into the harness. She imagined the woman messing with the device with a devious look on her face so that Shannon would plunge to her death. Then the woman could have Joe all to herself.

"You'll be fine," the female ranger said. Shannon could tell she was part Native American with her long dark hair and dark skin.

You'd better hope so. Because if I die, I'll haunt you forever.

Joe waited below as she threw her legs over the edge.

"Come on, babe," he said. "You can do this. You'll be rappelling down mountains next."

Her hands trembled slightly while she grabbed tightly onto the rope. Then Shannon was lowered slowly down. Joe's deep voice encouraged her on, though she was too busy concentrating on getting to the bottom. Every foot she descended felt like twenty, but ten minutes later, her feet landed safely on the ground.

Joe gave her a big hug after he released her from the harness. "Great job."

Shannon held him close, enjoying the warmth.

A familiar woman's voice echoed throughout the cavern. "I knew you could do it."

Shannon glanced up, but the ranger that helped her down was gone. Her and Joe stared at each other in shock.

"You did hear that?" she asked.

Joe nodded his head vigorously. "You know who that was, don't you?"

"Sounded like Lore," Shannon said. "It can't be. She's not here."

He smiled. "Think about it."

"Okay, Lore," she yelled aloud. "You could have warned us you were coming back through astral travel."

"I hope she's safe," Shannon whispered. "Do you think she can get hurt this way?"

"She can't feel physical pain. But there are still ways to harm her."

"Thanks for being here, Lore." Shannon looked around, not knowing where her to focus her attention. "Are you sure the boy is still here somewhere?"

"Yes." She jumped as a distinct response came from right next to her.

"For God's sake." Shannon glanced to her right where Lorelei's voice had come from.

"I'll see if I can find Eric," Lorelei said. "I envisioned him in a tight crevasse."

While Lorelei looked for the boy, Shannon and Joe closely inspected the ancient stone walls and pueblos with their flashlights.

"Over here." Joe knelt down, spotlighting a section of dirt by the first room. "I'm seeing smudges of what looks like blood."

Shannon removed a sample kit from her backpack. Swiping the ground with a q-tip, she carefully slid it into a small evidence bag. "I wonder if Alicia's body is here?"

Shannon and Joe walked through the subterranean maze of stone-walled rooms.

Her flashlight revealed a storage-like section in between two pueblos, full of black-on-white striped jars and bowls. Other artifacts she didn't recognize were scattered throughout the closet-like niche.

"Someone's been rather busy down here." Shannon nodded her head toward the pile. "How the hell are they getting these things out of here?" She glanced up at the opening where she had descended. "There has to be another way in. How did Emily get Alicia and Eric in here?"

"Good timing," Lorelei said. "Guys, head over to the large Swiss cheese rock. They followed her voice to a five foot tall boulder with smooth round holes covering the sides.

"Get on top of the rock," Lorelei said. "And peer inside that window."

Joe helped Shannon onto the boulder. She carefully stood up and glanced inside a five by two window created by stone and mortar. "Good find, Lore," Shannon said, while Joe stood up next to her.

A five foot tall aperture waited on the opposite side of the room they were looking into.

"There's no door in," Joe said. "We'll have to climb through this."

While Shannon gauged the distance to the ground from the window, her phone rang.

"Shannon, here."

"Shannon, it's Ian. I assume Lore's there with you."

"Sort of. Yeah, she's helping me and Joe."

"Tell her to get back to her physical form now. Her vitals are getting weaker."

"Lore," Joe yelled. "You need to get back into your body."

There was no answer.

"Maybe she's headed back." Shannon jumped off the boulder.

"What's going on?" Ian asked.

"She's not responding," Shannon said hurriedly. "She's probably headed back."

A piercing scream cut through the underground silence. "Iaaaannnnn!"

"Lore," Joe screamed.

"Something's got my cord. I can't return! Stop! What are you doing?" Lorelei yelled in desperation.

Shannon heard Ian's frantic cries on the other end of the

phone.

Shannon pulled her gun out and ran toward Lorelei's voice. She knew there wouldn't be anything to shoot at, but she felt she had to do something.

"In the name of God, let the woman go." Joe honed in on something in the far corner of the underground structure.

Shannon had never remembered feeling so helpless. "Lore," she shouted. "Lore."

"They're gone," Joe said. "I saw the outline of Lorelei and a tall male. He had her from behind."

CHAPTER THIRTY-FIVE

There was nothing Shannon or Joe could do. They couldn't see her. And even though she couldn't see what was behind her, she knew it was Peter. Her silver cord repeatedly yanked back forcefully, and a strange vibration emanated between her shoulder blades where the cord was.

He's trying to damage the tie to my physical form so that I can't return.

Lorelei and Peter ended up outside as she attempted to travel back to her body. She could sense his anger and determination. He wanted to kill her in a way he knew there would be no proof, just as Annie's brother had done with Jeff. Without thinking, she found herself spilling forth a series of unrecognizable sentences—the same language she had spoken in Dragoon right before they discovered the pueblo.

He suddenly let go of her. She could detect his fear and uncertainty. Then Peter was gone. Lorelei immediately returned to her body.

Within minutes, she was safe within her physical form and in sight of Ian. She gasped for air when she sat up.

"Lore," Ian grabbed her off of the carpet and into his strong arms. "Shannon and Joe couldn't tell me what happened. I'm so glad you're okay."

"Peter tried to kill me," she said, holding him tightly. "Ian, he yanked my cord over and over. I think he wanted to sever it."

Ian was so angry, he couldn't seem to speak. His strong arms trembled as he held her, but she couldn't tell if it was from fear, anger or both.

"I know you didn't want me to go for this reason." Lorelei looked into his eyes, tears rolling down her face. "Please don't be upset with me."

She tried not to cry, but it all came flooding out. "Everything was going so well. I found the tunnel that leads away from the ruins. It's how Emily accessed the cavern, and how a theft ring is getting the artifacts out."

Her tears spilled over his fingers as he held her face.

"I couldn't see Peter at first, but I could sense him."

Ian's blue-grey eyes were horrified. "Lore, how did you get away?"

"The ancient ones," she said. "I spoke in their language, and in a threatening tone. "I think they took over my form. He let go and vanished. Ian, he's a master at astral travel himself. How does he know where I am at all times?"

"It's like Peter's able to access your mind whenever he wants," Ian said. "He seems to have a permanent connection with you. It probably started when we visited their house."

Ian's phone rang. "Hi Shannon. She's okay. Looks like the race she connected with at the ranch helped out with her escape. Lore found herself speaking their dialect. And whatever she said made him run for cover."

Ian listened for a few seconds. Lorelei thought the phone would explode in his hands, he held it so tightly.

"Definitely sounds like Peter," Ian said. "Joe saw his outline."

Ian thanked Shannon and hung up the phone. "Lore, does this mean these ancient ones are following you around as your guardian angels?"

"I don't think so." She got up from the floor and went over to the couch. "I saw that same solar system/astral travel map that we found in the passages under the ranch. The drawing was hidden in a crevice. And there was a snake petroglyph directly across from the planetary depiction."

"A second site," Ian said. "Snakes are often viewed as messengers between humans and the underworld. Though it's strange those depictions weren't out in the open."

"Maybe the petroglyphs weren't supposed to be seen by just anybody," Lorelei whispered.

CHAPTER THIRTY-SIX

Shannon gazed down upon Alicia's lifeless body in the tunnel Lorelei had found. The head had rolled to the right, her long brown hair splayed slightly to either side with her arms positioned like a ragdoll's. Two stab wounds, one in the middle of her chest and the other on her right side, soaked her sleeveless peach top. There was no trail of blood, but Shannon could see spots on the ground where the victim had bled out.

Shannon could hear Joe yelling for Eric. Joe was scouring the different rooms and looking for any hiding places.

Bending down to examine the fatal gashes, Shannon noticed that it didn't seem to be a typical knife injury. Rather than a clean, straight line, there was a slight curvature with traces of an ochre powder substance.

"Hey, babe," Joe yelled, entering the passage.

"Over here." She lifted her flashlight to indicate where she was. "Come take a look at this."

"I don't believe it," Joe said. "I wonder if Lorelei knew the body was in here."

"Not sure. I'm thinking Alicia was killed in the community room and moved here. Notice that she's been placed off to the side—probably so that it didn't disturb them being able to take the artifacts in and out." Shannon bent down, showing Joe the trauma. "This isn't a typical stab wound."

Joe examined the woman's wounds for a few seconds. "A pottery shard," he said. "There's still a small piece buried inside the wound." He used his light to indicate the placement of the object. "Had to have been a pretty large piece—her wounds are four inches in diameter."

She circled the beam of her flashlight along the cracked stone walls and crevices, then on the ground ahead of her to see if she could find the murder weapon. Shannon didn't see the object in the tunnel, so she climbed through the window and walked back out into the open area where the pueblos where.

No way. Her flashlight divulged a piece of pottery, four inches long, which had been tossed into a pile of similar pieces. The potsherd was curved and reddish in color to match the substance on the entrance wound. *Sloppy, very sloppy. You didn't think it would matter in this underground hiding place, did you?*

She placed a call to the evidence response team supervisor as she closely inspected the edges of the shard. Blood stained the sharpest point of the makeshift knife.

Joe approached her from behind. "Whoever's involved in this theft ring must have been pretty confident no one would discover their riches or hideout," he said. "To abandon the weapon and the corpse this way is pretty careless."

Shannon gasped as she inspected the ceramic piece that killed Alicia. "Take a closer look at the weapon."

Joe bent over close, using his light to examine it. "That's the travel rune symbol. The same one etched into those monuments at the ranch. I guess the ancient ones did branch out after all. Only this shard shows a prone figure above the travel rune." Joe looked up toward the opposite end of the structure. "There's also a huge pile of pottery in the farthest pueblo. I wonder how much of it could be related to this unusual race of people Lorelei has connected with."

"I don't know," Shannon said. "It's rather ironic that this makeshift knife happens to be proof around the history of Annie and the race she was so close to—the very people that Lorelei, as Annie's reincarnation, is so bonded to." She pointed to the other end of the shard. "There's blood on the other end of this. "Whoever the suspect is should have a nice wound of their own on one of their hands. And hopefully they left prints for us."

She dropped the potsherd into a plastic evidence bag.

"We still need to follow the passage to see where it leads," Joe said. "There has to be an access point somewhere for Emily to bring Alicia and Eric here."

"I can't imagine an exit would be that far." Shannon headed back toward the tunnel. "They would want to get in and out of here in a hurry. Not hike for miles. I'll take a walk to see if there's an exit that leads above ground, and for additional proof of a theft ring or kidnapping. The crime scene investigators won't be here for another hour."

"Be careful. I'll keep looking for Eric. I've spotted at least three different sets of footprints down here. I'll have a member of the ERT use a trace evidence vacuum in the nook where the artifacts are stacked—maybe there's something we can't see."

Shannon hoped the little boy was okay and that they could find him very soon.

Why were Eric and Alicia kidnapped? Was her murder some sort of retribution for Eric's abduction? Or was she involved in this whole theft operation?

She hoped the body or the murder weapon would reveal a solid lead.

Five minutes later, Shannon noticed a sliver of brightness in the distance. Excited that it might be the entrance/exit for the possible artifact theft ring, she picked up her pace.

A ladder leaned up against the passage wall. Shannon carefully climbed up into the late afternoon sun. She squinted, her eyes tearing after being in the darkness for so long.

Once her eyes adjusted to the light, Shannon could see there was a long, flat mesa consisting of a layer of red Moenkopi and tan Kaibab limestone. The plateau was within twenty feet of the underground access point where she now stood.

Shannon climbed a few feet out of the tunnel, and saw a pile of red brick and sandstone rubble within ten feet.

"A smaller ruin," she whispered.

She stepped off the last two rungs and out into a field of penstemon and other wildflowers. Brittle sandstone and desert grasses crunched under her feet. She spotted a set of vehicle tracks imprinted into the soft soil. And they looked familiar.

The tracks would need to be photographed, measured and cast in plaster of Paris to determine the type of automobile.

As she started back down on the ladder, a brief, but strong breeze whooshed by Shannon as she descended into the tunnel. She had to grab onto the ladder to keep from falling. There had been no wind above ground.

She leapt onto the floor and glanced in the direction where the strange wind seemed to be headed. Turning her flashlight back on, she pierced the black void to catch an opaque mist floating in mid-air. She could see the outline of a woman—wisps of her long hair blew gently across her face. The apparition hung there, staring at her.

"Alicia?" Shannon asked. "Is that you?"

The female apparition turned and headed toward the pueblos where Joe was investigating.

When Shannon approached the area where the ghost had appeared, a baby picture lay face up. A sky blue background framed the wrinkled face of a newborn baby. And on the back were two words written in slightly smeared blue ink: ERIC ATWELL.

CHAPTER THIRTY-SEVEN

Lorelei touched Paul's hand, and brief flashes of a sandy-haired boy tiled themselves in a haphazard collage. His thin frame had managed to wedge itself into a dark, tight corner of the unexcavated ruins at Wupatki. Joe hadn't been able to find Eric because his hiding spot was a hidden hole. Eric was alone, terrified and on the precipice of death.

The vision abruptly ceased as Ian's intense gaze brought her back—his warm breath on her cheek and the scent of his musk sending her senses reeling. For a split second, she forgot about Eric.

"Ian, the little boy Alicia kidnapped, he's still down there. They haven't found him because he's in an almost invisible section of the ruins. He's barely conscious."

He immediately grabbed his cell phone and called Shannon.

Lorelei hugged Paul close, not wanting to think about him suffering the same fate. She wondered why she had gotten the vision of Eric while touching Paul.

She saw Ian's hand shaking. "Darn it, she's not answering."

"Try Joe," Lorelei said. "They're probably together." She glanced at her watch. It was 9:34 p.m. She cringed, realizing what Eric must be going through."

"Joe, it's me," Ian said. "Is Shannon with you?"

Ian hesitated, waiting for Joe's response.

Lorelei snatched the phone from Ian. "Joe, Eric's shoved himself into an almost invisible corner. He might be stuck in there. I couldn't tell if he was breathing, it was so dark in the vision."

"Okay," Joe said. "Lore calm down. The national park service has their own law enforcement division. I can get them back out there. Are you sure Eric's still underground? I looked everywhere and couldn't find anyone. I didn't find any footprints either."

"He's there! It's the far corner, opposite of where the passage is. Head straight back and to your left. There's a boulder on top of a hole."

"All right. I'll talk with you soon."

Ian held out his hand and pulled her onto the couch next to him and Paul. Placing his face next to hers, she noticed a single tear gather slowly, then release its moisture down Ian's right cheek. It stopped for a split second as if deciding the path to take.

"Lore," Paul said. "Is this kid the one that was with the woman that was murdered?"

"Yes," she whispered. " For some reason, I saw a vision of him when I touched your hand."

Paul cocked his head to the side. "I wonder why?"

"Maybe," Ian pulled him closer, his arm around Paul's shoulder. "It's because you're both the same age. And I'm sure he misses his mother as well."

Lorelei again saw a flash of maturity in Paul's brown eyes.

"How did the little boy know her?" Paul asked.

She took Paul's hand in her. "We're not sure how she knew him."

Lorelei and Ian's cell phones suddenly buzzed at the same time, indicating an incoming text message. She recognized Shannon's number and read the words:

FOUND A BABY PICTURE—THINK ERIC IS ALICIA'S SON.

She and Ian stared at each other.

"Talk about timing," Lorelei said, glancing at Paul.

"If he is," Ian said. "She must not have confided that fact to her boyfriend. She could have had him at a young age and put him up for adoption."

"We'll know when they find him. I hope he's still alive."

Lorelei leaned forward, startled. An abrupt message drilled itself into her thoughts, along with a distinct image of Texas Canyon Ranch.

I have to go back to Dragoon. They're waiting.

CHAPTER THIRTY-EIGHT

"I found him," echoed a male sheriff's deputy from the darkest recesses of the cavern underneath the Wupatki house. "Over here." Shannon and Joe raced over to see a barely conscious little boy squeezed into a hole, trembling with fright.

Joe tried to help the deputy lift Eric out of his prison. As soon as Eric felt someone pulling on him, he pulled back in terror. "No," he screamed. Then started to cry. "Please don't hurt me."

"Honey, it's okay," Shannon bent down to take his hand. "We're going to get you out of here." She glanced at her boyfriend. "This is Joe. And the man next to him is from the park service. Using her flashlight, she showed the boy the badge and uniform the officer wore. But the boy's eyes widened in terror. He became hysterical as he attempted to scrunch himself further down.

Reaching for his hand, she pleaded, "Please Eric. Your parents really miss you. We know you've been down here for a while. We need to make sure you're all right."

But he shook his head vehemently, staring with wide eyes at the red-headed officer.

Shannon pushed Joe and the deputy behind her, thinking Eric might be afraid of the men. "I promise no harm will come to you."

The sandy-haired boy lost consciousness."

"He's coming out now," Shannon yelled. She grabbed Eric gently by his arms and Joe helped her pull him up.

Joe felt for a pulse. "He's still alive, but we need to get him medical attention now."Joe carried him over to a paramedic who strapped him into a gurney. Two firefighters hoisted him to the top.

"Thanks for your help," the deputy said. "How did you know he was here?"

Shannon and Joe glanced at each other. "Let's say that the FBI has access to some rather unorthodox, but highly reliable resources."

"I don't suppose you'd be willing to divulge this resource?

There are occasions when we can use that sort of help."

"Maybe," Shannon replied, handing him her card. "Give me a call and I can setup a meeting."

"We've worked with a few psychics, but it didn't pan out. Found a guy that seemed to be able to provide us with the level of detail we expected, but turns out he knew a psychic in another state who was giving him the information."

"Unfortunately," Shannon said, "many professional psychics and mediums aren't very professional at all. And many don't have the capabilities they claim to, making it harder for the ones that do." She handed Deputy Ryan her card. "I can talk to Lorelei and see if she would be up for branching out."

"Sounds good," Ryan said. "How are the thieves accessing this place? The officer glanced up at the opening fifty feet above. "They can't be getting artifacts in and out through there—wouldn't be able to hold that many items at a time, and would take them forever to get them out."

"Follow us," Shannon said. As Shannon, Joe and the deputy headed north toward the exit, she wondered why Eric had been so terrified of the uniform. *Is a policeman or sheriff involved in the trafficking of these artifacts and possibly the murder of Alicia?*

They climbed through the primitive window to gain access to the tunnel. The deputy shook his head in disbelief. "I knew these ruins held a lot of secrets, but this..."

They continued into the passage until they arrived at the opening.

"Ladies first," Joe said.

Shannon stepped off of the ladder and into some brush. The distant howling of coyotes sent a chill down her spine as Joe and the deputy came up after her.

She suddenly remembered why the tire tracks she found earlier that day looked familiar. They were the same prints as the park ranger vehicles.

"This might explain the fear of your uniform," Shannon bent down her knees and pointed to the ground. "These tracks match the ones left at the site of the unexcavated pueblo when one of your rangers drove up to help Lorelei."

"ERT did get some plaster prints earlier today," Joe said. "So we can determine if they match the vehicles the rangers are issued."

"There are a number of them driving around out here, though

they wouldn't need to go this far north of the Wupatki pueblo," the deputy said. "We might have to start patrolling out here more often now." His cell phone rang. "I need to head out. I'll check with all of the park rangers to see if they've spotted anything unusual. Be back with you soon."

"Thanks officer," Shannon said. "For everything."

Shannon gazed back at the shadow of the towering Wupatki ruin. "I'll have to get a statement from Eric to find out if he can identify anyone. I also need to find out if he's really adopted." She gazed intently at the tracks. "I would freak out down there alone in the dark. I can't imagine what Eric went through. Hearing what happened to Alicia, and wondering if they would come back for him."

"He must have ran for his life, and been too terrified to move. Considering how afraid he was of the officer's uniform, I'm guessing park service staff is involved."

Shannon shook her head. "Thanks to Emily, that poor child is going to be having nightmares for quite a while. Why would she leave him here? Especially when she has a son the same age."

"She might not have been here when it all happened," Joe said. "I guess Alicia had second thoughts about being a mother to Eric. Ultimately, that's the reason he ended up down here. And I have a feeling she was involved in the smuggling ring. Maybe she was getting too greedy."

"Yeah, well that greed could permanently impact Eric." Shannon put her arm around Joe's waist as they walked back to her car. "Alicia never had any previous charges. She might have been so desperate to get her child back that she didn't see any other option."

"I don't think they planned on killing her," Joe said. "Whoever did the deed grabbed a pottery shard. They must not have been armed. The killer probably wanted to question her about something. Alicia could have been involved, stole some inventory. Then she confesses and it pisses someone off. Or maybe she wasn't cooperating. So they grab a nearby pottery shard and stab her to death."

"I think they got cocky when it came to Eric," Shannon said. "Probably figured they didn't have to chase him down. He wouldn't be able to find his way out since it's so dark down there, even during the day." Shannon stopped and turned to face Joe. "I wonder if Peter's the ring leader since he's obviously so protective of this place."

"Not sure. But Lorelei discovering his master scheme isn't the only reason Peter has issues with her. He's threatened by her abilities," Joe said. "He's somehow keeping track of her at all times. That charm is associated with the dark arts, so he could be trying to maintain control of her."

"It doesn't seem to be working," Shannon said.

"That's why he's after her with such vengeance. He's obviously highly telepathic to have picked up on her relationship with the ancient ones. Yet another reason to be jealous. Maybe he wants to gain that special connection."

They got to Shannon's Jeep and pulled out onto the highway.

A black SUV passed them heading the opposite direction. The vehicle slowed down. Shannon saw an arm holding a pistol reach out the driver's side.

Shannon quickly veered her car off to the side of the road. A single gunshot exploded through the driver's side window. She slammed on the brakes and grabbed her Glock, but Joe was already out the passenger side. He stood in the middle of the road, legs splayed out to either side, both hands tightly holding his pistol, arms extended to aim at the vehicle.

The perpetrators were already gone.

"Are you all right?" he asked, running over to her.

"I think so. We must have really pissed someone off."

Shannon noticed glass shards embedded in his left cheek. "Joe, you're hurt."

He brought his hand up to the wound. "A surface scratch. This happened because we're hanging out in their territory. The warnings are going beyond the astral plane."

Joe winced in pain at a one-inch piece of glass that moved when he talked. "How come you managed to escape such injury?"

"Just lucky, I guess." She quickly jumped into the car. "Don't worry. I'll get you to the hospital in Flag." Her hands were trembling as she gripped the steering wheel. "What are you smiling at?"

"You," he said. "You do care."

Shannon didn't reply. She merely gave him a sly grin.

CHAPTER THIRTY-NINE

Lorelei couldn't believe what she was seeing. She glanced at the LED screen on her camera. The earthly hues of the pueblo and monuments representing the ancient ones were in stark contrast to the brilliance of the yellow and orange sunset. But when she snapped a photo, the LED only revealed the valley and surrounding box canyon.

The tunnels leading to the ruin had also vanished, probably hidden from view—like the other reminders of the astral race. But Shannon and Joe managed to find a shallower, less steep section of the chasm, which allowed Lorelei to carefully climb down into the arroyo and up on the other side to reach the sacred spot.

Shannon and Joe made a trip back to Dragoon with a few archeologists right after the mystery ended. There was nothing there. According to the final case study files, the Indian ruins and the five stone pillars had all vanished.

Have the formations been here all along? Merely invisible to the naked eye? Lorelei suddenly realized she might be the only one capable of seeing the history before her. She texted the image to Ian in Phoenix. CAN YOU SEE ANYTHING IN THIS PIC?

While she awaited his response, the air became oppressive and charged with energy. The colorful clouds were painted over with a rapidly encroaching darkness that quickly turned the environment from alluring to ominous.

Large, dense raindrops pounded against her bare arms, stinging her repeatedly. Glimpsing up at where the ruins should be, she knew it was her only retreat from the intense storm.

She started to use the camera's LED to find the ruin, but the storm became too intense. Female whispers echoed around her in the voice of the ancients. They wanted her to follow them.

She gasped as she quickly ran up the hill toward safety. The ruin appeared out of nowhere—just as it had looked when she saw it last during her journey to the heavens.

By the time she had made it to the small pueblo, she was completely soaked and chilled to the bone. "Darn it." She shivered from the dampness. "Figures, the one time I don't come prepared, something like this happens."

A familiar, somehow comforting presence whispered softly to her. As during the investigation in the tunnels and her recent astral experience, Lorelei understood its almost inaudible language. And its intent.

Though the ruin overlooking the valley had been empty when she first looked through the camera, there were now a few blankets lying on the ground, perfectly folded. She placed one on the damp surface to sit on, and wrapped the other around her shoulders.

The incessant drumming of the rain against the stones lulled Lorelei into a calm, meditative state. Warmth flooded through her veins while a crackling sound and the smell of smoke came from somewhere nearby. She felt completely safe and secure. Yet she had come here for a purpose.

Sitting near an unseen fire and welcomed by her prehistoric friends, Lorelei closed her eyes and projected to a place where she had no intention of traveling. At first she was frightened, remembering the last incident where her silver cord had been tampered with. But this time seemed different.

She didn't know how she had arrived at her destination so quickly. Hovering over a run down trailer in the middle of nowhere, Lorelei descended inside. A smoke-infested environment gradually subsided to reveal wood-paneled walls, dirt-covered carpet and a group of three men; one of them with Peter Taylor. He sat with three other men. They were all handling pottery and artifacts—the same black-on-white zigzag patterns as those at Sunset Wupatki.

Peter sighed, leaning toward a chunky, sweaty man with a cigar hanging from his mouth. "I told you Jarred. She's been taken care of. You won't have to worry about her stealing any of the inventory or revealing our secrets."

Trying to hear more of the conversation, she lowered herself just below the ceiling. The cigar smoker was talking, but Peter didn't seem to hear. He slowly stood up, staring right where Lorelei's soul awaited.

How can he know?

Mr. Fat and Sweaty became impatient. "Hey Peter," he said.

"How many more shipments can we expect?"

Emily's husband abruptly placed his hand up in the air to tell the man to be quiet. He stared directly at Lorelei.

"Do we have company?" Another man pulled out his pistol and started out the front door.

"Not that kind of company," Peter said. He reached up. She wasn't aware that she could be frozen with fear without her physical form, but she was. Or was Peter's intense stare binding her to the spot?

Lorelei realized how dangerous this man was. But even as his hand went through her astral self, there was no reaction.

What happened? Peter acted like he knew I was here. Or is he waiting for the perfect moment to pounce?

Broken boarded up windows, chipped off-white linoleum floors, and bark scorpions on the smoke stained yellow walls told her this place had been abandoned for a while.

As the men continued to discuss details of the theft, she looked around for Emily but didn't see her. Nor did she find a stash of artifacts as she expected. Hearing movement in the living room, she decided not to risk any further exposure.

She rose above the trailer and saw a red truck pull next to it. A young woman with shoulder length light brown hair got out of the automobile. She stopped right before the stairs to the trailer and looked up.

Sarah! Melissa's daughter!

Sarah also gazed directly up at Lorelei, who floated fifty feet above.

Lorelei's eyes opened wide after she arrived back in her body. The downpour had stopped and she desperately wanted to be home with Ian. During her time away, he had sent three text messages. "Lore, please call me. I know something's going on—I can feel it. I hope you're okay."

Wanting to hear his voice, she dialed his home phone number.

"Thank God." he said.

"Ian, I'm coming home now. I need to see you. And there's so much I have to tell you."

"Sure. Just be careful. It's dark and it's a long drive to the valley. Get on your Bluetooth when you get to your car. I'll talk to you on the way home. Let me know if you need to pull off and stay anywhere."

"Did you get my text message?"

"Yes. But baby, nothing showed up in the picture."

"I wanted to make sure because everything's visible to me. I'm in the ruins and staring at the five pillars now."

CHAPTER FORTY

"I can't believe this," Shannon said. "So you were able to see the ruins and the monuments? Then you journeyed to a trailer where you found Peter Taylor, Emily's husband?"

"Yes," Lorelei sat next to Ian on her couch. The patio doors were open with the sound of the rock waterfall. The scent of lavender permeated her living room.

"There's a reason I felt so compelled to drive to Dragoon on such short notice. The ancient ones wanted me to know what was going on. I saw Peter with three other men." She started to tremble recalling the event. "Guys, he knew I was there. He stared right up at me and put his hand through the air where I levitated. But that isn't all." Lorelei played with the ring Ian had given her. "Sarah was there."

Shannon leaned forward in her chair. "You mean Melissa's daughter?"

"Yes. She was heading into the trailer. I think she also sensed my presence because she stared up at me. I have no idea how she's connected with Emily and Peter."

"Damn." Shannon placed her drink on the coffee table. "These dark arts people sure have a way of finding each other, don't they? Vincent Joiner takes over Jeff O'Shea's malevolent form, then Emily and Peter manage to have a tie to Vincent's daughter Sarah, who lives in New Mexico. Or at least she did."

Shannon realized Lorelei and Ian were right. Sarah is taking over where her father left off. And she's going to be out for revenge.

Ian's jaw tensed and his fists clenched. "Just thinking what Emily and Peter are up to infuriates the hell out of me. How can she be so selfish, putting Paul through this? And that bastard is trying to kill Lorelei."

"Emily knew you and Lore had Paul for the weekend. So Paul could stay with the two of you. They must have planned their escape after Alicia's murder. Or maybe in spite of it."

"I have to wait and see what fingerprint or DNA evidence we obtained from the crime scene," Shannon said. "He had Emily kidnap Alicia. Maybe he didn't plan on having her killed—only wanted to frighten her. He didn't have any priors or history with the police or the feds. However, he is a professor at NAU and guess what he teaches."

"Archeology or anthropology." Lorelei glanced at an oil painting of an elaborate porch overlooking the Aegean Sea.

"Actually, both," Shannon said. "Peter could have found out about the access to that site from a fellow archeologist or a professional contact."

"Or Peter could have found out through more unconventional methods," Ian said. "Telepathy or projection."

Shannon started texting on her BlackBerry. "I need to get a list of his students, colleagues and other professors he works with, so we can determine if any of those men Lorelei saw during her out-of-body travel might match up. And find out if anyone was aware of what he was up to. Hopefully, we can get a name from prints on Alicia's body or the murder weapon."

Joe walked over and sat next to Lorelei. "I've heard of such talents like Peter has. "He can detect not only spiritual presences, but astral souls as well. He probably did know it was you. Think about it. All of your terrifying visions and encounters occurred after you and Ian visited Emily and Peter's home."

"Wait," Shannon said. "You're saying that he somehow picked up on her abilities?"

"Yes." Joe gazed at her intently. "He knew Lore and Ian had been at Wupatki with Paul. He must also have sensed she knew what was going on. Peter locked in on Lorelei in an almost permanent, telepathic way. That's how he's been keeping track of her."

"What do I tell Paul?" Ian asked. "I'm not sure he's ever going to see his mother again."

"This had to be an act," Shannon said. "Emily's friend could have been in on it as well, making people think the couple were having problems. They must have tried to use that as a guise for the theft operation."

"How do Emily and Peter know Alicia?" Lorelei asked.

"She's a student at NAU," Joe said. "One of Peter's students. We don't know if there was anything going on between them."

"One of Alicia's neighbors did identify Emily as the one Alicia left her house with," Shannon said. "And he noticed Eric as well."

"Did Eric's parents verify his adoption?" Ian asked.

Shannon nodded. "They've had him since he was two months old and confirmed the baby picture I showed them."

"I can assure you Lore. Your dreams are not safe. Even if he gets placed in jail, he is still strong enough to get to you—from one soul to another."

Ian stood up and started to pace. "He won't be able to harm her if I concoct a harmful ritual."

"You know it would come back on you three-fold," Joe said. He turned to face Lorelei. "I think that's why the ancient ones lured you back there. And why only you can still have access to the ruins. There's much more to the purpose of that dimension than we originally thought. To enhance astral abilities and other spiritual talents, yes. But I also think their dimension was, or still is, used to destroy those with negative intentions."

Ian stared at Joe in shock. "Wait, so you think Lore is attracting these individuals? So that she could destroy them?"

Joe placed the question back on Lorelei. "You should ask your girlfriend."

"Like I said, I think they wanted me to know about Peter. But I'm not sure it's to destroy him. Vincent Joiner caused total chaos by transforming the magical pillars into something malevolent for deliberate harm to a whole community. Peter's intentions aren't quite that destructive."

"How do we know Peter, Emily and their cult don't have something more sinister planned?" Joe stood by the patio doors, staring out into the yard. "If they're willing to murder a woman and abduct a child and leave him lost and alone . . ."

Shannon smacked Joe on the arm. "Just tell Lorelei what you saw in your dream. Stop being so damn dramatic."

"It begins with the tunnels, ruins and the pillars," Joe said. "That's where all of the energy is. But in my vision, I saw you drawing off that very energy—without being in Dragoon."

"How do you know that's what I was doing?"

"Because Lore," Joe kneeled down in front of her. "The triangle which formed prior to Vincent's demise—I sensed a stronger version of that surrounding you. All of the most positive colors have attached themselves to you—especially pale yellow, turquoise, and silver—those relate to spirituality and awakening of the cosmic mind.

And with every encounter with the ancients, I've noticed these levels get more powerful."

Lorelei leaned down, elbows on her knees and palms on her forehead. The exact position indicating a migraine was coming on. Shannon had no idea how much more her friend could handle.

I'd be in a fricking loony bin by now.

When Joe first started telling Shannon about the clear mental images he had, she didn't believe him. Until all of the ones he had pertaining to Shannon came true. He didn't always reveal information regarding the bad visions, but she knew when he was holding back, so she would make Joe tell her. The most interesting thing about his visions was that they had a tendency to appear after their most unabated sexual encounters.

Ian brought Lorelei a few Tylenol.

"No," she moaned. "I need stronger medicine than that."

"Excuse us," Ian said. "Time for a healing session. We'll be right back."

"Okay," Shannon said. "But if I hear any gasping or moaning, you're in for one hell of a contest."

Ian and Lorelei walked into her bedroom.

"Joe, when do you think this is all supposed to happen? I mean, I assume that your vision involved Peter."

"No. But he had to know Lorelei invaded his privacy. Trust me, he's coming after her. She'll know how to stop it when it happens."

"Do you think she's going to be ready for him?" Shannon asked, glancing back at the hallway. "Look what happened to her during the last investigation. Vincent tried to kill her. Can she really protect herself?"

"Shannon, she's had this amazing gift all along. She saved herself from an agonizing death by projecting out of that mine shaft, managing to communicate with a camper miles away, telling him where she was. The ancient ones didn't show Lore what Peter was up to in order to potentially solve this case. We're talking about individuals who think at a much higher level. Travel to them is the solar system, other planets, other dimensions. They didn't think in terms of material possessions. Their main objective was to be one with the universe."

"Well, considering how much she had to deal with on the Dragoon investigation, I'm hoping Lore can handle this battle with Peter, and her future as an astral queen."

"It's not going to be that dramatic. She's an amazing woman," Joe said. "I know she's up for it." He took her face in his hands. "But I prefer someone much more down to earth to keep me in balance."

"God, you make me so hot," she whispered into his ear. "I could throw you down on this floor and. . . "

"Uh um," Ian said, clearing his throat. "I can't take you two anywhere."

"Excuse me." Shannon got up and went to the patio door. "I need some fresh air."

Lorelei walked out right behind her. "Mind some company?"

"Of course not." Shannon sat down on Lorelei's swing and patted the spot next to her. "Are you feeling better?"

"Much," Lorelei said. "It's funny. Most women say they have headaches to avoid sex. But my other half can actually cure headaches, so I guess I can't use that as an excuse."

"Oh please, Lore. I've seen the effect you have on each other. You wouldn't come up with an excuse not to have sex with him." Shannon caught Lorelei staring at bruises on her arms. "And yes, I realize the irony since Joe and I have almost killed each other a few times."

"Speaking of Joe. Why haven't you told him how you really feel?"

Shannon turned and looked at her quizzically. "What? Where did that come from?"

"Don't act like you don't know. And don't get mad at Joe—he hasn't said anything to Ian. This is just vibrations and images I'm picking up from you. He's attempted to get you to admit it, hasn't he?"

"Maybe."

Lorelei sighed heavily.

"Every time I make that type of commitment, that's when things start to go wrong. I guess I'm afraid that if I tell him I care about him, he'll lose interest or become a total jerk. I can't bear to think about that."

Lorelei sniffed a vanilla votive candle inside a green glass holder. Shannon knew her friend wanted to make a point without making her angry.

"Who was the one giving me the lecture about Ian during the investigation in southeast Arizona?"

"I know. But it's a lot less complicated when relationships don't involve you."

Shannon and Lorelei enjoyed the shimmering city lights and cool February night air in silence for a few minutes.

"I'm sorry if Joe scared you," Shannon said. "He really cares for both of you."

"Of course. And I'm sure he really did envision it. It's so overwhelming to consider that I have all that power. I mean, little ole Lore. Why did I get picked for all this? Having psychic and medium skills is one thing, but finding out that I'm a reincarnation of an influential witch, being in unison with an extinct race of people, and having the ability to stop those with talents in the dark arts?"

"Sounds like fodder for a great novel."

As Shannon followed Lorelei back inside her house, she wondered exactly what the race they were all calling the ancient ones had in store for her friend. And how many times Lorelei would risk her own life for those who didn't deserve to live.

CHAPTER FORTY-ONE

Shannon slammed both her hands on the table. Her green eyes glared down fiercely upon the beefed up bald man. The intense heat from the lights created tiny sweat droplets that threatened to spill into his eyes. In frustration, he wiped them at the last second with the back of his meaty hand.

"Damn it, Ray, we have your fingerprints all over the body and the murder weapon. And an eye witness. Who's in this with you? Are you stealing artifacts, or are you just a hired hand?"

"What weapon?" Ray asked. Alicia's suspected killer attempted to intimidate Shannon by leaning forward in the uncomfortable metal chair, staring back at her.

"This one." She held up an evidence bag with the shard of pottery—smudges of blood on either end.

"A two in one deal Ray. Your blood on one end and Alicia Atwell's on the other." Shannon placed the bag in front of his face.

Ray immediately tried to hide his right hand by placing it low in his lap. He wouldn't look her in the eyes after she produced the ochre colored ceramic object. Shannon nodded at the other agent.

"Let's see your hand, Ray."

He wouldn't budge. Shannon sighed. "We can do this the easy way or the hard way." She eyed her male counterpart who stood next to Ray.

Her partner started to lift Ray's arm, but the burly man jumped up quickly and caught the agent under his chin with his elbow, knocking him backwards. Then he started toward Shannon. She whipped out her Glock, shooting him in the shoulder.

"Fucking bitch," Ray yelled, staggering back a few feet.

"First degree murder and now busting up a federal agent." Shannon turned over his shackled wrists to reveal a slice in the middle of his right palm.

As two other agents escorted him to the hospital, Shannon

received a call from a forensic scientist who was searching through Ray's voice mails and computer.

She took a deep breath before answering the phone. "Hey, David," she said. "Since there wasn't any physical evidence in Ray's house, did you discover anything through technology that would tell us who else is involved in this Native American artifact theft ring?"

"You could say that. Found a record of a text message on his cell from a woman. It read, I'M COMING AND I HAVE ALICIA WITH ME. SHE WASN'T ALONE. We're working with the phone company to verify that the person that made the call to Ray is Emily Taylor."

"Great," Shannon said. "What else?"

"E-mails," David said. "From and to an address named HISTORYBUFF50@YAHOO.COM. This person didn't sign any of the communications, but we're tracing the IP address to find out what computer it is. I'll send a soft copy of the correspondence, but one stated, 'She'll be brought to you. Get her to tell you where the inventory is—use force if you have to."

"Those last six words are pretty potent. Thanks for your help." As she hung up, she hoped the evidence would trace back to Peter Taylor.

Shannon smiled when she saw Joe's cell number on her BlackBerry. "Hey, babe, how's your day?"

"Rather exciting," she said. "Ray attacked my partner and came after me, so I had to put some shrapnel in him. We've confiscated his phones and computer and they've come across some interesting evidence. David also found a text message to Ray. A woman called Ray's phone and said she was on the way with Alicia. He's going to confirm if it's Emily." Shannon opened the e-mail from David with the phone record attachments. "Where are you?"

"I'm at the hospital with Eric."

"How's he doing?"

"Much better. They've kept him under close observation for malnutrition and dehydration. I showed him a picture of Emily, and he verified she was the one that took him and Alicia. Eric also identified Ray pretty quickly. But there's more emotional turmoil for the child than Alicia's murder."

"Did Alicia tell him she was his mother?"

"Yeah. Poor kid's all confused. His adopted parents didn't know who she was. And they never thought it would come to this.

The amazing thing is that he's been sleeping very well, not having any nightmares. He told me he had company underground."

"Did he mean another person?"

"No. He described a human form that was short. I believe Eric thought they were real."

"What do you mean, 'they?'"

"The individuals he witnessed under the Wupatki ruin had tattoos of a travel rune symbol with a prone body above. I believe Eric saw the ancient ones."

CHAPTER FORTY-TWO

Dale froze. Whispers emanated from all around him. He and Brandon had returned to Wupatki after hours to see what evidence they could find pertaining to Alicia or the ancient ones.

He slowly lifted the thermal imaging camera and scanned the surrounding rooms. There was nothing there. Dale could feel the temperature drop. And the EMF read twenty-five degrees—ten degrees cooler than the baseline.

Trembling from the cold, he picked up the ghost box.

Could I be experiencing the energy from the race of people Lorelei is so entwined with? Why haven't they showed themselves to her like they did with Eric?

Dale couldn't imagine *himself* being down here alone for over a week—let alone a child.

"Are you the ones that lived here, and in the passages and ruins in Dragoon?"

Brief static cut through the silence. Then a single voice emanated from the device.

Dale recognized the unidentifiable language from the investigation in southeast Arizona.

"I know who you are," Dale said. "You're the people my friend Lorelei is somehow connected to. Or do you know her as Annie O'Shea?"

The ghost box blasted static for a few seconds, displaying an EMF of 6.2. Then it went dead. A humming began to echo throughout the underground chamber. The noise reverberated so loudly that Dale had to place the thermal imager in his jacket pocket and put his hands over his ears. He ran over to the window near the tunnels where Brandon was investigating. "Brandon, can you hear this? Brandon!"

Invisible threads entwined themselves around his arms, hands, face and legs. He swiped and slapped his face, arms and legs repeatedly. He couldn't see anything, but still the anomaly continued to torture him.

This is what Shannon, Lore and Ian experienced in the passages under the ranch.

"Is this your way of communicating?"

A minute later, the incessant noise and uncomfortable sensations ceased.

Brandon shot out of the tunnel and jumped through the open window leading to the pueblos. To Dale, it looked as if he were competing in a pummel horse competition.

"Did you experience what I did?" Brandon asked. "I felt like I was being attacked by a giant spider web."

"Yeah, and that weird humming noise. That's what happened in Dragoon. It must have something to do with that prehistoric astral race. I mean, it occurs underground and near ruins where there's proof of them inhabiting."

"I wonder if that energy was used to help them with astral travel." Brandon used his flashlight to check for movement.

"Could be," Dale said. "That would make sense, especially if you consider the energy needed for a ghost to reveal itself or manipulate an object."

"Hey, didn't the evidence from the ranch show a blanket-like mist coming down over Lore, Ian and Shannon?" Brandon asked. "There was also audio with an unknown language."

"Yeah. It was the same dialect Lorelei spoke in. And I heard that same language briefly through the ghost box a minute ago. I was recording at the same time, so hopefully she can decipher what was said."

"I don't know, Dale. Lore isn't able to decipher their language—yet somehow she finds herself speaking the dialect."

"Did you come across Alicia's apparition?"

"No," Brandon said. "I think she revealed herself to Shannon to explain why she took Eric." He replaced the batteries in his recorder. "I wonder if Shannon knew the tunnel extending from this ruin continued."

"What? She didn't mention it to me," Dale said. "Only that she had found the one access point above ground—where we came in."

"Come with me."

Ten minutes later, they arrived at the end of the passage.

Dale stared at the ceiling. "Aren't we close to where the

sandstone mesas are?"

"They should be almost above us." Brandon shined his light into the corner.

Dale gasped. A pile of stones leaned up against the rock wall.

No. They've been mortared there. Part of the top stack had fallen to expose darkness. His gaze followed Brandon's light to the emptiness of another tunnel heading west.

CHAPTER FORTY-THREE

The trickling of the copper wall fountain in the entryway tried to lure Ian into a false sense of security. The warmth of the stone fireplace did nothing to help the fear he felt inside—for himself, for Paul, and for his ex-wife. He had spent two years decorating his home as the ultimate retreat with its warm tones, hardwood floors and rustic southwest flair. But tonight, sitting with Joe, Shannon and Lorelei to uncover the mystery Emily was involved in, the material meant nothing.

Shannon sat on the arm of the couch next to Ian, her arm on his shoulder. "The phone company confirmed it was Emily that communicated with Ray, Peter's hired man. Eric validated Emily abducted him and Alicia, though he also mentioned Emily seemed surprised he was there."

Ian still couldn't believe what he was hearing in relation to his ex-wife. He kept trying to tell his son what was going on, but he couldn't go through with it. How do you tell someone you love so much, that their own mother decided to abandon them and pursue a life as a criminal?

"Did she," Ian cleared his throat, "take them at gunpoint?"

Shannon hesitated and then closed her eyes. She couldn't look at him.

Ian shook his head in disbelief.

"Emily knew how to use a gun, but she always had it with her for protection. To think she's using it to threaten people, including an innocent little boy her own son's age."

Lorelei held Ian's hand. "How was Alicia involved? I know she was a student of Peter's, but was she really stealing some of the inventory like I overheard during my out-of-body?"

"Yes. She said she didn't think anyone would notice," Shannon said. "But someone did. And I think we all know who."

"Peter," Joe said. "That man monitored the tunnels and

underground pueblos with his astral abilities. He must have witnessed Alicia stealing."

"But why would I have yelled out 'he said I could' during the beginning of the investigation?" Lorelei asked.

Shannon checked her phone. "Because that's what Alicia told Ray right before he murdered her. I guess one of the other people involved told her she could take a few things—that no one would notice. What Alicia didn't know is that person was a cult member who had it in for her. Ray admitted to the artifact theft and murder. But he's terrified to fess up about the remainder of the people involved in the ring, including Sarah."

"What about Peter?" Ian asked tiredly rubbing his eyes. "Did you get any evidence against him? I'm worried about what he's got in store for Lorelei." He placed his arm around her.

"We retrieved three e-mails that specifically mentioned the Wupatki site. And there are a couple others that mention site two where they've discovered pottery and artifacts. The IP address of the incoming e-mail on Ray's computer was traced back to a library computer. Unfortunately, none of the staff remember anyone of Peter's description coming in. Not a surprise considering those communications were sent on Saturday afternoons, their busiest times."

Ian stood up. "The hardest part is that she, they both, betrayed Paul. Hell, I have no feelings left for Emily, but I always thought she was a great mother." He shook his head as he paced back and forth. "God, I can't believe it was all a lie." Ian glanced at Shannon. "Do you know when this all began?"

"According to Ray, Wupatki was their latest discovery. Two rangers were bribed, which explains why the tracks by the tunnel entrance matched those of the park vehicles. And why Eric was so afraid of the uniform."

"Last night I dreamed Emily took off rather quickly," Lorelei said. "I saw her leave in the middle of the night with luggage."

"Flagstaff Police and FBI are patrolling their place in case they return," Shannon said.

"They're gone for good. You won't be able to find them," Paul said. Ian was shocked to see Paul standing in the hallway, his large brown eyes red from crying. Ian walked over and gave him a big hug.

Ian did his best not to let his emotions go, but a few sobs

wracked their way from the deepest recesses of his body.

"Mom talked to me just now when I slept," Paul continued. "She said she was sorry and she had to go away."

Ian stared into his son's eyes. Tears rolled down both their faces. "Did she tell you where?"

"No," he mumbled.

Ian sighed and stood up. "Listen guys, I need some time alone with my son."

"Sure." Shannon and Joe got up and started toward the door.

Joe placed his hand on Ian's shoulder. "Let us know if you need anything."

"Lore." Ian approached her, putting his hands on her face. "I care about you so much."

"It's okay," she said. "I'll go. I need to get some work done anyways." He watched her walk into his bedroom to get her things. The last thing he wanted to do was send her away, but he wanted to give Paul the opportunity to open up.

He met her in the hallway as she was coming out. "Do you have any idea how beautiful you are?"

"God, Ian. I'm so sorry for what you're going through, for Paul." Her voice cracked.

He placed his arms around her waist and pulled her close. "I love you. But Paul and I have some things to figure out."

"I told you honey, it's all right." She placed her arms around his shoulders. "Take as much time as you need."

"It won't be that long. I couldn't handle being away from you more than a few days." He kissed her gently on the lips. "I'll talk to you tonight, okay?"

"I'll be waiting."

She gave Paul a hug. "I'll see you soon sweetie. Everything will be fine, I promise."

"I know," he said. Within an instant, the mature Paul came out of hiding. His stature heightened, his voice deepened slightly, and his eyes took on a seriousness Ian had never seen.

"Because you and dad will always be together."

CHAPTER FORTY-FOUR

Lorelei knew what was going to be written in Brandon's recent report before she opened the file named, WUPATKI INVESTIGATION. Brandon and Dale had experienced the same phenomena that she, Shannon and Ian had in the passages under the ranch. The intense humming, whispering voices and unexplainable cobweb sensations that overtook their whole bodies—it had to mean the ancient ones were present. And it made her a little jealous.

She gasped when she read Brandon had discovered another tunnel leading west.

If I can communicate with this extinct race without even knowing the language, how come I don't know more about their underground realm?

After reviewing the evidence detail, Lorelei laid down on her bed. The scent of sage wafted throughout her bedroom, new age music emanated softly from her stereo, and the trickling of the waterfall in her yard created a tranquilizing environment that soon put her to sleep.

No bad dream awoke her. There were no external noises. Lorelei sat up with a sudden start three hours after her head hit the pillow.

She glanced nervously around the room. *He's here.*

"What do you want Peter?" she asked. "We all know what you and Emily are up to, what you're both guilty of. How long have you been using your astral abilities to spy on people?"

The atmosphere became ominous—like the air right before a thunderstorm.

She desperately wanted to call Ian or Joe for help, but had left her cell phone in the living room.

That's when it rang.

Could that be Ian?

She slid out of bed and ran for the phone. As she grabbed it, it was violently thrown from her hand.

***

Ian abruptly sat up on the couch, and saw the 8 1/2 x 11 picture of him and Lorelei taken in Santa Fe.

Something's wrong. Ian grabbed his cell phone and dialed her number. No answer. "Lore, if you're there, please call me. I love you."

Ian and Paul had talked for hours after everyone left. Ian didn't understand why, but Paul didn't seem to have a lot of anger and resentment toward his mother and stepfather. Or was it that he was holding it in?

"Paul, get dressed. We need to head over to Lore's place."

"Dad, why?"

He replied sternly. "Get ready to go. Now." He was panicking. He had let her go knowing Peter would be after her.

He quickly dialed Shannon's phone. When she picked up he didn't give her a chance to respond. "Shannon it's Ian. I think Lore might be in trouble. Meet me at her place if you can."

"You think this has something to do with Peter?" Shannon asked.

"Yes. He's coming after her." Ian continued to call Lorelei on redial. But there was still no answer. So he prayed.

***

Lorelei glanced at the counter where she had placed Peter's amulet. It was gone.

Every fiber in her being told her to run outside. Standing in the middle of her backyard with the stars above and the twinkling lights in the distance, tranquility overcame her—a peacefulness the highest trained meditative mind couldn't produce.

There's not going to be a battle. There doesn't need to be. Then she began to speak in the ancient ones dialect.

Lorelei imagined the five pillars and ruins in Dragoon. She focused on the force field that stretched between them, trapping Vincent. That's when she felt an energy extend itself—first on either side of her, then in front and behind. Until the humming began.

She couldn't see Peter's astral form. But she didn't have to. As soon as she started speaking their language, his anger quickly turned to confusion and fear. Yet it didn't stop him.

A single current of electricity ran through his out-of-body form as he passed into her highly charged domain. For a split second, she was able to see an outline of Peter's astral form—his hands grabbing for her, his cold gaze glaring at her in contempt. He knew he had lost the battle.

Lorelei stood still, listening and watching for Peter. Her phone rang, so she ran into the living room where Peter had tossed it on the carpet.

It continued to ring, but she couldn't see it.

Lorelei looked desperately around the couch where her cell had been carelessly tossed. "What the hell? It was right here."

"Need this?" Lorelei responded to a female voice in the kitchen. Sarah's astral form gazed at her coolly.

"Sarah. What are you. . . "

"Don't be so stupid. You know exactly what I'm doing here. I heard your thoughts at the ranch a few months ago. You and Ian realized who I was, what I represented. I wanted mom to believe I was happy for dad's death. But he made me the person I am today."

An electric current sizzled through Sarah as she hovered a foot above the granite tile. A massive spark overcame Lorelei's cell phone and it burst into flame.

Lorelei backed away as Sarah approached her. "How do you know Peter and Emily?"

Energy somehow continued to flow through Sarah's soul.

"Afraid yet?" Sarah leapt forward and touched Lorelei's arm briefly.

She screamed in agony and grabbed her lower arm as an electric shock tore through her body.

"Peter's not as strong as he thinks," Sarah said. "Dad kept telling him he just didn't have what it takes. However, I always did. And I'm going to make you suffer the same way you made my father suffer."

Pounding on Lorelei's front door startled Sarah.

"Lore!" Ian pounded frantically.

"Ian," she yelled. "Help me!"

The pounding stopped. She knew Ian would try and climb the fence to the back yard.

"He's going to be too late," Sarah said. She started to grab Lorelei's arm.

Disbelief and shock crossed Sarah's features. "Mom, no! Don't do this!"

Within seconds, Sarah vanished.

Melissa knew what was happening!

Ian threw open the patio door and came running toward her. "Are you all right?"

Lorelei held him tight. "Ian, Sarah was here. I took care of Peter, then she showed up. Her powers—she could have killed me."

"I shouldn't have sent you away."

She looked into Ian's eyes. "It's okay. Peter and Sarah have been taken care of. The ancients helped me handle Peter. There's no way he's going to be able to harm anyone again. At least not through his astral talents or the dark arts."

"You've done it," Ian said in a shocked tone. "What Joe mentioned. You've managed to summon the energy of the ancient ones."

"I'm not the only one. I believe Sarah achieved the same feat through Vincent. Ian, when he died, she somehow absorbed the energy used to destroy her father."

Ian glanced around nervously. "Where is she now?"

"I think she's dead."

***

Burnt bits of metal rested on the thick sage carpet—the only reminder of Sarah Harlowe's terrifying abilities. Shannon observed Lorelei, sitting on the porch swing with Ian and Paul.

"Talk about a narrow miss," Shannon whispered to herself. "Lorelei is an expert in that arena."

Shannon received Ian's phone call while she was visiting the Phoenix headquarters. Racing to Cottonwood at eighty miles per hour, she made it to Lorelei's house in an hour and fifteen minutes. By the time she arrived, Lorelei had single-handedly taken care of Peter.

But no one had expected Sarah's arrival. Melissa had killed her daughter to save Lorelei. Or at least that's the impression Lorelei received during Sarah's pleas to her mother. Shannon attempted to contact Melissa, but she only got her voice mail.

Would she really murder her own flesh and blood? Or did Melissa distract Sarah to get her back to her physical form?

Shannon picked up the remains of Lorelei's phone off the floor.

Ian walked into the room and glanced at the melted device in her hand. "I don't think you'll be able to find any fingerprints."

"I figured that based on the fact that her physical body wasn't involved."

Shannon noticed Lorelei and Paul playing kickball in the backyard.

"So, Lore and I need to know." Ian emptied his glass into the sink, observing the liquid wash into the drain. "What happened to Emily and Peter? Are they gone like Paul saw in his dream?"

Shannon sat down and patted the cushion next to her. Lorelei glanced up and watched through the patio door. For a second Shannon thought she would come in, but Lorelei looked away and kicked the volleyball back to Paul.

"Only time will tell. But many of their clothes are gone along with both the cars."

"What about Tiffany? Maybe she could tell you where they've gone."

"I haven't been able to contact her," Shannon said. "Her phone's been disconnected and we've attempted to stop by her place in Sedona. A neighbor of hers living in her condo saw her leaving around one this morning."

Ian sighed, smiling weakly at Lorelei as she waved from outside. "Tiffany's been in on it with them."

"She might not have been involved in the theft ring or abduction—an accomplice perhaps. If Emily and Peter are into mind control, they could have convinced Tiffany to help by lying for them. Ray still isn't talking about who else is in on this artifact theft operation, though he did admit to killing Alicia."

"Eric described Emily as the one that kidnapped him and Alicia," Ian said. "Emily delivered Alicia to Ray—to her death!"

Lorelei walked into the house.

"Damn it. Part of me wants you to hunt Paul's mother down. The other half hopes you don't find her and Peter so Paul doesn't have to live with what they've done."

He pulled Lorelei to him and held her tightly. "What am I saying? Of course you need to find them. I mean, Peter tried to . . ." Ian couldn't finish his words.

Lorelei grabbed Ian's hand and kissed it. "I'm fine. We all knew I would somehow survive whatever punishment he dished out. Maybe that's why I felt the need to go back to Dragoon and see the ruin and monuments. The ancients might have known what he would attempt and empowered me during my last astral travel to that trailer."

"What about Sarah?" Ian asked. "Do you know what happened to her? It's hard enough to bear the thought of Peter finding a way to get to Lorelei, but Vincent's daughter seeking revenge is twice the nightmare."

"Honey, I told you she's dead."

Ian turned to face Lorelei. "Are you sure? I don't want to think of someone that young dying, but I also don't want us to worry about another threat."

Shannon poured red wine for Lorelei and Ian, then handed the glasses to them. "Hard to believe Melissa would kill Sarah, especially considering she did everything she could to protect her from her own father. Joe found out Sarah did have another identity, lived out of the country, and was being watched by the FBI. But Vincent still managed to get to her."

Lorelei took a sip of wine. "Do you think things would have been different had Melissa stayed with Sarah?"

"Not necessarily. Maybe Vincent would have killed her and run away with Sarah. I'm surprised he didn't kill Melissa when he had the chance in Dragoon. We're not sure how Sarah's connected with Emily or Peter."

Shannon's cell phone rang.

"Hi Adam. Did you find out anything about Melissa and Sarah?"

"Unfortunately, yes."

Shannon plopped herself down on the couch. "So Lorelei's right. Sarah is dead."

"Yes. It appears Melissa murdered her daughter. She said Sarah was trying to kill someone through her astral abilities. This all occurred at the ranch where the labyrinth is."

Shannon couldn't believe what she heard. "She must have known just how powerful Sarah was."

"The time matches up to the visit Lore received from Sarah." Adam puffed on a cigarette. "So Melissa won't be indicted for murder."

Lorelei and Ian knelt in front of Shannon.

"Sarah is dead." Shannon whispered. "Melissa must have realized the damage Vincent did to her daughter."

"There is no turning back when it comes to cults," Ian said. "Sarah would have kept killing, like her father did. Melissa knew it."

CHAPTER FORTY-FIVE

"Ian, honey, come take a look at this," Lorelei said. She could hardly believe what she had found in a lost bit of video footage from the Vulture Mine investigation.

Ian walked over to her desk and peered closely at the laptop.

"Holy crap." Ian glanced at Lorelei, then back at the screen. "Is that what I think I'm seeing?"

"Yes. This is the same map from the passages at Dragoon, the pottery we found at Wupatki, and now there's evidence of them inhabiting, or at least visiting, the area where Vulture Mine is now. Only there's another panel next to it with a large cross.

Ian pointed at a rough etching in the lower right corner. "This looks sort of like Shiprock in New Mexico. See the wing-like protrusion extending from the main peak? But the other portions of the map have almost been worn away by the elements."

"Oh my God," Lorelei said. "What if this is a complete depiction of where they lived and practiced their religion?"

"Not only that." Ian turned her desk chair to face him. "This could be the reason there was such high energy underground at Melissa's ranch and at Wupatki. These passages must have been a significant part of what they were about. It could be that these sites are feeding off of each other. Or maybe they're a series of leylines not only impacting Arizona, but the four corners. I think Brandon is right. Lore, this phenomenon is what helped them achieve such astral feats. Based on your performance with Peter last night, you've now got the ability to draw on that energy."

Lorelei put her arms around his neck, pulling him to within an inch of her face. The scent of his musk, the wavy lock of hair that had fallen onto his forehead and those exotic eyes that turned to violet to help heal—she realized they were entwined in ways neither of them understood yet.

"We have to go back to Vulture Mine. To discover more about

the ancients. And about me."

- The end -

Made in the USA
Middletown, DE
20 June 2017